DUST
CITY

FOR MY FAMILY.

Dust City

RAZORBILL

Published by the Penguin Group
Penguin Young Readers Group
345 Hudson Street, New York, New York 10014, U.S.A.
Penguin Group (USA) Inc., 375 Hudson Street, New York, New York 10014, U.S.A.
Penguin Group (Canada), 90 Eglinton Avenue East, Suite 700, Toronto, Ontario,
Canada M4P 2Y3 (a division of Pearson Penguin Canada Inc.)
Penguin Books Ltd, 80 Strand, London WC2R 0RL, England
Penguin Ireland, 25 St Stephen's Green, Dublin 2, Ireland (a division of Penguin Books Ltd)
Penguin Group (Australia), 250 Camberwell Road, Camberwell, Victoria 3124,
Australia (a division of Pearson Australia Group Pty Ltd)
Penguin Books India Pvt Ltd, 11 Community Centre,
Panchsheel Park, New Delhi – 110 017, India
Penguin Group (NZ), 67 Apollo Drive, Mairangi Bay, Auckland 1311, New Zealand
(a division of Pearson New Zealand Ltd)
Penguin Books (South Africa) (Pty) Ltd, 24 Sturdee Avenue, Rosebank,
Johannesburg 2196, South Africa

Penguin Books Ltd, Registered Offices: 80 Strand, London WC2R 0RL, England

10 9 8 7 6 5 4 3 2 1

Library of Congress Cataloging-in-Publication Data is available

ISBN 978-1-59514-296-2

Printed in the United States of America

DUST
CITY

ROBERT PAUL WESTON

razOr
bill

AN IMPRINT OF PENGUIN GROUP (USA) INC

Animals, whom we have made our slaves,
we do not like to consider our equal.

—Charles Darwin, *The Descent of Man*

It is easier to get into the enemy's toils than out again.

—Aesop, "The Lion, the Fox, and the Beasts"

"Dear father," she replied. "Do what you will with me.
I am your child." Thereupon she held out her hands
and let him chop them off.

—The Brothers Grimm, "The Girl Without Hands"

ONCE UPON A TIME

ONCE UPON A TIME, FAIRYDUST CAME FROM WHERE YOU'D EXPECT. FROM fairies. I was only a cub, so I don't remember much of what the City was like back then. But I have a strong sense that things were different. Dreams could come true. You read about it in the paper. I've seen the clippings. Mrs. L has some of them pinned up in her office: PAUPER GIRL GETS A FAIRY VISIT, ELEVATED TO LIFE OF LUXURY!

PUMPKIN INTO PARLOR CAR OVERNIGHT!

Then one day, the miracles dried up. The fairies stopped drifting down to bless us with their charms. All at once, they were gone. It happened like magic.

It was months before anyone ventured up to Eden. Back then, there was no road that could take you there. City planners had yet to build it, which they did with private funding from the thaumaturgists. The Empyrean Skyway, they called it, a coiling ribbon of suspended asphalt.

When they finally arrived, there was nothing there. Eden was a ghost town. The streets were deserted, the houses locked and empty. The fairies, as far as anyone could tell, had abandoned us.

It wasn't long before the wealthier hominids moved up there. There had always been an unofficial division between us and them, but the boundary was never as clear as it became after the fairies vanished.

The big thaumaturgical companies took over. "Enchantment for all," they promised. They began mining dust runoff from quarries outside the City, magic that had seeped into the land from the fairy days. Thaumaturgical-grade dust was made from actual leftover miracles. They said it was as close to the old-time magic as you could get.

Maybe so, but fairydust from Nimbus or Luster Labs is nothing like the real thing. Or so I've been told. To be honest, I'm too young to remember. Apparently, fairydust didn't always come in vials. It wasn't used merely for getting rid of a headache. Once upon a time, it was all about dreams and destiny.

With the wave of a wand, old-time magic could look inside you, take stock of your deepest potential, and then make it happen. It was like pressing a fast-forward button on your life. The dull were made vibrant; the poor became rich; the dim-witted were transposed to genius. With *real* fairydust, whatever the magic saw in your heart was precisely what you became. It was life-changing stuff and better yet, it stuck. Even the big spells—provided the dust came direct from a fairy—could be permanent.

The only permanent effects you can count on from today's recycled brands are at about the level of basic first aid. You can sew up a gash or shrink a bruise, but not much more. That's all there is these days. Low-grade remedies, and there's a *ton* of them. Toothache fairydust, headache fairydust, strength-enhancing fairydust, fairydust tranquilizers, fairydust for numbing nerves, fairydust for knitting bones, fairydust to raise self-esteem, fairydust to lower cholesterol, and on and on. Red, blue, green, yellow, golden silvery fairydust. The stuff was *everywhere*, but it pales in comparison to the old-time magic. Or so I'm told.

Either way, it doesn't matter to me. I'm holding out for the real deal. I like to think one day the fairies will return to Eden. They'll hoof the thaumaturgists out of their fairy palaces and dreams will start coming true again. The way they did when I was a cub, once upon a time.

PART ONE
ST. REMUS

1
BUTTERFLY ON FIRE

ONCE, THIS WHOLE PLACE WAS NOTHING BUT TREES. BEFORE THAT, IT WAS a shadowy smudge at the bottom of the sea. Before that, it was packed in ice for a million years. But once, and pretty recently in the grand scheme of things, it was nothing but trees. At least that's what Mrs. Lupovitz teaches us in science class. But sometimes, it's hard to believe.

These days, the City's a clutch of steel, cut through with glass cliffs and canyon upon canyon of cement. The only trees are the deadwoods, sprouting from the endless plain that surrounds the City on all sides. If you look out through St. Remus's west wall, you can see them: thousands of branches, rising up like grasping hands.

The St. Remus Home for Wayward Youth is an arid compound built around an old cathedral (which is now the mess hall). The buildings here are either strangled with ivy or streaked with the remnants of polluted rain, and all of them— the courtyard, the dormitories, the old rectory—they're all hemmed in by a thirty-foot wall topped with razor wire.

Today is Visitors' Day.

Somehow, Jack convinced me to come down to the mess hall with him. He wants to introduce me to his girl. Apparently, she's anxious to meet me. Apart from the ones she passes on the street now and then, she's never met a wolf before.

"You're gonna like her, trust me," Jack says, stalking over the cobbles. He says it in that loose, offhand, Jack sort of way that sounds more like hucksterism than a method of eliciting trust. Nevertheless, I do: I trust him, the little thief.

"I *hate* Visitors' Day," I tell him, which makes perfect sense. No one's coming to visit me. Not unless Dad escaped from prison (and who's to say that if he did, I'd want to see him?).

"Come on." Jack tugs my sleeve and hastens us around the corner of the rectory. Then he stops dead.

There's a crowd of uniformed guards huddled around one corner of the mess hall. It looks like the building's grown an oily gray scab. Jack rushes forward. "Look," he says. "There's something going on."

We move closer and I can see Roy Sarlat standing in the middle of the crowd. Roy's the biggest wolf at St. Remus. He's been in and out of juvenile detention centers like this one all his life. He's down on all fours, padding back and forth. Every step scours the ground. He's angry. Never a good sign with Roy.

Jack wedges his face in between the hips of two guards, but one of them slaps him back. "I can't *see*," he complains.

"Lemme up on your shoulders." Before I can say no, Jack's scaling my back like a gecko.

Roy paces and growls inside the tightening corral of guards. For the moment, Jack's forgotten all about the girl waiting for him inside the rectory. He's perched on my shoulders like a sports fan in the cheap seats, winding his fingers into the hair on the back of my neck, pulling himself higher. Both of us know we're in for a show.

Roy opens his mouth, teeth glistening, and growls from deep in his gullet. "Anybody comes near me," he says, "and I swear I'll use these." His jaws open wide and he clamps them shut, snapping crooked fangs together and launching out fireworks of spit. It's a clear show of ferocity. *Teeth* are taboo, and not just here at St. Remus. Break out the choppers while robbing a market stall and it goes from petty larceny to felony in a snap (no pun intended). If Roy starts biting, it'll be an automatic week in lockup.

"I got family in there," he growls. "And I mean it, anybody comes near!" He claps his jaws again.

There's a phlegmy voice from within the thickening crowd of guards. "Did I hear you say *anybody*? Because I don't think that's what you meant." The guards shuffle and murmur. The crowd parts and Gunther lumbers into the open. "Sorry, Roy," he says. "You know the rules. Can't let you in until y'bin searched."

Roy growls again. More saliva squeezes out through his teeth. The muscles in his legs knit together and swell.

Gunther grins and starts rolling up his sleeves. His truncheon hangs heavily from his belt, but he doesn't need it. His arms are already thick as the trees we never see. All the guards at St. Remus are goblins (or "globs," as we inmates call them), and without a doubt, they're the nastiest breed of hominid. But Gunther? Gunther is in a class by himself. While every glob in the world is a huge, ugly, snaggletoothed, knuckle-dragging, short-tempered vulgarian with all the delicate charm of a city bus (just before it runs you over), in Gunther's case, all of that would be a compliment.

"Fair enough," he says. "Let's do this the hard way."

Roy, of course, is the kind of canid who's always prepared for the hard way. His long white body leaps up so fast it's a streak of light. Gunther, meanwhile—*stupid* Gunther—should've seen it coming, what with Roy down with his ribs to the dirt, ears slicked back. Three of Roy's claws catch Gunther's cheek and three matching spurts of pea-soup goblin blood spatter on the stuccoed wall. The splotches hang there for a second, then start a syrupy descent.

Up above me, Jack whistles. "Aw, man," he says. "Roy is *so* dead."

For a second Gunther stares. You can see that the sudden pain in his face startles him. He stands there dumbly, gaping at the blotches on the wall, stains of his own blood.

Meanwhile, Roy rears up for another pass. He lunges again, but Gunther's not as slow-witted the second time around. He claps his apelike arms together, catching the big wolf by the throat. Roy spits and gnashes. His eyes dart everywhere at once. He's a huge guy—over six feet when he stands up straight—but with his throat crushed in Gunther's huge mitt, Roy's a stuffed toy, limp and lifeless. He bats his arms weakly against Gunther's barrel chest, then against his drumlike paunch, and then not at all. Both his arms go limp as wet rags.

"There," says Gunther happily. "That's better. Nice and calm." He holds Roy aloft with one hand, teasing the wound on his face with his other one. "Wolves," he says with a sour expression. "Filthy animals. Oughta lock up the lot of you." He brings his hand away from his face and examines his blood. It's thick and gluey and slung between his fingernails like cobwebs. "Even still," he says, pausing in thought. "It was a nice shot." He grins like a connoisseur, licking his fingers clean.

He turns his attention back to Roy—the panting wolf draped over his arm like a flimsy coat. "How 'bout we clean up this mess you made." He presses Roy's head against the wall and starts wiping. The blood spatter morphs into the shape of a melting insect, a deformed fairy, a butterfly on fire.

Gunther grins at the mess he made. "Good," he says. "All clean." He looks over his meaty shoulder at the other guards. "Okay, he's ready now. Get in here and search him."

Two of the guards come forward and rifle through Roy's pockets. All they find is an envelope—sky-blue paper containing some sort of letter. They pass it to Gunther. Roy barely notices. He's lolling in and out of consciousness now, a silver thread of drool spilling over his lip.

Gunther is more amused than anything else. "Well, well, whadda we have here?" He drops Roy in the dirt, where two of the guards pin him down.

"Don't," Roy mutters.

Gunther opens the envelope and takes out a letter, handwritten on matching baby-blue paper. His lips move as he reads and he smirks, the gloating smile of a bad winner. Roy looks up from the ground, shaking his great white head.

On my shoulders, Jack clenches my hair and pulls. "I can't see what it says!" He's waiting for Gunther to read it aloud. But that's not what happens. "How sweet," says Gunther. He slides the letter back into the envelope. "Let him up. He can go in now."

Jack spits on the ground, narrowly misses my shoe.

"Hey!"

He shakes his head and comments simply, "That sucked." Then, ever the acrobat, he rolls off my shoulders and flips to the ground. "We didn't even get to find out what's in the letter."

"Maybe it's private."

Jack shrugs. "Whatever. Let's get inside. You can meet Siobhan."

2
GRAVEL AND HONEY

JACK WEAVES THROUGH THE MESS HALL, NEVER ONCE LOOKING BACK TO see if I'm keeping up. At the table in the corner, there's an elven girl. I recognize her from the gallery of clippings Jack keeps pinned over his bunk. She looks just like her pictures. Moon-pale skin and peaked ears, puffy lips and a pair of almond eyes that are a little too far apart. She's beautiful, in her own way.

Jack pecks her on the cheek and takes a seat, beside her instead of opposite, which isn't officially allowed. One of the guards glances over, but he lets it go (in a mess hall filled with delinquent wolves, the scrawny hominid with his elven girlfriend are the least of your worries). Besides, with haunches like mine on this side, there's not much room left, not even for Jack's skinny butt.

"Henry," he says, "meet Siobhan. Siobhan, this is my roomie, the guy I wrote you about."

"Hi." I flash her a grin that I'm hoping isn't too wolfish. She's barely five feet tall, so tiny and perfect you can't help but feel like a great, hairy beast next to her. She has the scent of an elf, too, all nutmeg and incense.

She stares at me, gazing into my snout like it's about to snap her head off.

Jack shrugs. "Big guy's harmless. Nicest wolf you'll ever meet." He pauses for a moment. Then he adds, "Almost to a fault."

Siobhan casts her eyes around the room. It's not official policy, but we all know St. Remus is pretty much exclusively for animalian youth. The room is bristling with the usual suspects—wolves, foxes, and ravens, with a few wayward mules and hedgehogs thrown in for good measure. Jack's the only hominid here.

"If you're so nice," Siobhan says to me, "what are you doing in this place?"

"Well," Jack whispers, taking the opportunity to slide closer to her. "Henry had a lapse of judgment, let's say. He was up on—"

"I broke a window," I tell her. I don't like to talk about it. Being a wolf is already enough to warrant a nasty first impression. Why make it worse?

Siobhan looks puzzled. "A window? And they sent you here? They really *do* come down hard on you guys, don't they?"

"Well," says Jack, "there *were* extenuating circumstances." He hugs Siobhan close, like they're planning a robbery. "See, Henry's father is a *killer*. Judge probably thought, y'know—like father, like son. It runs in the blood." Jack enjoys basking in the fact that his roommate is the son of an infamous murderer. He rarely misses a chance to bring it up. Probably because, in spite of outward appearances, he knows I'm harmless.

"As far as I'm concerned," I tell Siobhan, "I don't have a father. He doesn't exist."

Siobhan shakes her head. "Even still, just for breaking a window? That's harsh." She reaches over, almost as though she wants to pat my paw. But she stops halfway and pulls back. "Anyway," she says, "you don't look like a killer to me. And I'm an elf. I'm pretty good at reading folks."

Jack agrees. "That's why she hooked up with me."

Siobhan rolls her eyes at him, but he doesn't react. "Why don't we get down to business," he says, lowering his voice. "Did'ja find them?"

A look of worry passes over the elven girl's face. Reluctantly, she nods. "I did."

"Good." Jack puts his hand out below the table. "Have you got them with you?"

I'm beginning to feel a little uncomfortable. "Would you two prefer to be alone?" I start to rise, but Jack waves me down.

"Sit! You'll draw attention to us."

Siobhan stares at Jack's open hand. "If I give you these," she says slowly, "you're not gonna do anything stupid. Right?"

"Define stupid."

"Let me put it another way . . . " She lowers her voice further. "You only have to be in here another six months. It's not that long. You're not planning anything, right?"

"Trust me," he says. I can even smell the sincerity on his breath. "I'm not planning anything. I just feel—I dunno, sorta naked without them. And they *are* good to have around. Just in case." I can see his fingers, opening and closing below the table.

Siobhan looks to the guard standing by the door. Lucky for us he's ignoring our little confab. He's paying more attention to Roy, who's only just now stumbling in, coughing and wheezing. His woozy eyes search the unfamiliar faces. Ripples of apprehension churn the air. Roy Sarlat has that kind of effect on a room.

"Fine," says Siobhan. "Here ya go." Her hand comes out of her purse with a small leather pouch. It's stained with oil and tied shut with a rotten shoelace. I wonder what's inside of it. Judging from way Jack's eyes are sparkling, it must be something pretty precious.

"Great," he says. The moment the pouch is in his hand, it vanishes, spirited away into some secret pocket sewn into his uniform. It's an apt demonstration of his skill as a thief. It's the whole reason they sent him to St. Remus in the first place. "Thanks, babe," he says. "I think I could kiss you."

Siobhan smiles. "So go ahead already."

He pulls her forward and wholly in spite of myself, my

ears prick up. It's some old instinct, kicking in when I least want it to. I hear oceans of saliva, crashing together like tidal flows. Finally, their lips part. It's about all I can take. I wave a forepaw and rise up from the chair. "That's it. You guys do whatever you like, but I'm leaving."

Both of them look at me, apparently bewildered to find I'm not into Visitors' Day voyeurism.

Jack stretches across the table. "Sorry, big guy. We'll cut it out. You can stay."

But my mind is made up. "Nice meeting you, Siobhan."

She looks me up and down. "Jack's right," she says. "You seem like a nice guy."

"Thanks."

Jack stands up halfway off the bench. "C'mon, *stay*. You need to get outta the room sometimes—and I mean besides goin' to class or seeing Doc."

"No point to Visitors' Day when you don't have any visitors." I turn my back and lope off.

I'm only a few tables away, when my pace slows. There's one table left without an inmate. Over on the visitor's side sits a green-eyed she-wolf. She's chocolate brown all over except for her ears, which are tipped milky white. There's a hefty camera slung around her neck and she looks my age, sixteen, maybe a little older. She smells like cherry blossoms—subtle and sweet. I love that scent. She looks up at me and every hair on my back stands up all at once (I hope she doesn't notice).

"Hi," I say.

"Hello." She lifts the camera in front of her face and there's a flash. The whole world turns white and for a second I figure she's only a hallucination. When the spots fade, however, she's still here. "I hate the whole *say cheese* thing," she says. "Makes you look *completely* unnatural." Her voice is like gravel and honey. She leans forward, her eyebrows raised, and whispers to me. "But, uh, I think you might have the wrong table."

My thick canid brain sends a message to my feet—*Idiots! Keep walking, she just told you to scram*—but the wires get crossed and it's my forepaw that springs to life, reaching across the table. "My name's Henry."

"Fiona."

Our fingers are about to meet when somebody raps me on the shoulder. I turn around and there's Roy—with his sulfurous yellow eyes, his jigsaw puzzle grin, his dead white hair, slicked back from his brow and still smeared with goblin blood.

"That's my sister," he says.

Oh. "I was just—"

"You were trying to talk to my sister?"

"I was—uh . . . just . . . um . . . " In my peripheral vision, I see Jack and Siobhan on their feet.

Roy snarls. "Don't lie, Hank-man. I can smell it all over you." He balls up a fist, full of every bit of anger and humiliation he suffered outside at the hands of Gunther, and punches it deep into my unsuspecting gut.

I double over, coughing and gasping for air. Only Roy's not done with me. As my head falls forward, he comes up with a knee, smashing me full in the face.

There's another flash of light—decidedly more agonizing than the one from Fiona's camera. I see an explosion of stars that erupts like a fountain of fairydust.

After that, there's nothing to see at all.

3
NOTHING TO BE AFRAID OF

FAST CLOUDS AND A GHOSTLY MOON HAUNT THE SKY. TREES LOOM OVER ME like bridges. I drop to all fours, padding into them, letting them swallow me up. They're electrified with wind, so soon all I can hear is the rush of leaves . . .

Shadows and moonlight cling to the inside of my eyelids. Everything's heavy, smothered beneath too many blankets. My head's been replaced with something weightier. An anvil, maybe, a team of blacksmiths hammering away at it. So yeah, I don't feel so good.

A hot stream of fluorescence trickles through. I sniff with my snout, but the only thing I can smell is the nothingness of a room wiped clean, so I pry open my eyes. A ceiling sags above me, a water stain creeping out from the corner. The left side of my face is puffy and tender.

"Good," says a familiar voice. "You're awake. I was about to call an ambulance."

I turn my head and a swallow of breakfast bubbles up,

headed in the wrong direction, but I manage to keep it down. The kind face of Mrs. Lupovitz floats into view, a gray and motherly cloud.

"Lie still," she says. "Mr. Sarlat gave you a nasty concussion." She winces over me. "Look at that face!" She turns to a glass cabinet full of small brown bottles and plastic vials. "I've got just the thing."

She opens the door and takes out a plastic canister of fairydust, glistening and silent in its tube. The powder lurking within is a soothing, ocean-blue variety. Just looking at it dampens some of the throbbing in my skull. But I won't let her give me any. "Leave me alone," I say. "I'll be fine."

"You ought to take something."

Mrs. L finds an edge on the tiny cot, which is way too small for my beastly heap. Her soft, old-lady haunches press against the small of my back and for some stupid reason a photo of Fiona's face flashes into my head. Roy Sarlat's sister. Just my luck.

Mrs. L hooks her claws into my shoulder and turns me. Another batch of renegade bile surges up from my stomach. "I don't want anything," I tell her. Maybe it doesn't make sense, but when your mother was killed in an accident involving a truck full of fairydust, it leaves you with a generally poor view of the stuff.

Mrs. L waves the vial in front of my face. The label's printed with a bright, oblong halo, circling around two

stylized letters: an *N* and a *T.* Below the image are the words
Nimbus Thaumaturgical, Inc. It was a Nimbus truck that
crushed my mother.

"This is just about the mildest blend available," Mrs. L
tells me. "A basic analgesic. That means a painkiller that
works by—"

"I know what analgesic means." I turn back to the wall.
"Just let me sleep it off."

Mrs. L shakes her head. "Sleeping is absolutely *the worst*
thing you can do. Either you take this now or I'll be forced to
call the hospital, and believe me, they'll make sure you take
something ten times more potent than anything I've got here
at the Home."

I ignore her. I shut my eyes and watch the darkness swim
around inside my head like heat off a summer highway.
Sometimes I can be pretty mulish.

"Do you have any idea what you look like right now?"

"Why? What do I look like?" The vanity card. *Well played,
Mrs. L.*

"See for yourself."

I pop my eyes open to find I'm staring into a mirror. I'm
not pretty: a big, bad wolf, one half of his face busted open
like rotten fruit.

"I guess . . . I guess I can have a little."

"There's a good boy." She uncorks the vial and I get a
whiff of a stale, chemical tang. Like scorched plastic, long

cooled from the fire. She sprinkles a thimbleful into the chub of her old-lady palm. "Ready?"

"Okay," I say. "Go ahead."

Mrs. L puckers her lips and blows gently. The dust leaps up like a living thing. It swarms around my head like a flock of determined gnats, toying with me, swelling and teasing around my eyes and ears. Instinctively, I recoil, but the dust is buzzing and relentless. When I close my mouth to stop it wheedling in between my lips, it merely regroups, streaming up my nostrils and clogging my throat.

Mrs. L strokes my paw, soothing me. "Don't fight it," she says. Her voice is a cup of sugar. "Open up and take a breath. Otherwise, it can be rather unpleasant."

No kidding. A din fills my head like a screaming television tuned to a dead channel. The dust is in my brain, drumming up random thoughts. Colors, sounds, scents appear and fade at random—a siren; my father's face; the humid scent of hot soup in winter. Then it's all gone, and there's this alarming coolness in my chest. All at once, I'm reminded why fairydust is so popular, why it's such big business, why it's in every supermarket, pharmacy, and back alleyway in the city. Because *it works*.

The pain in my face evaporates, draining out of my head and retreating from behind my eyes. My swollen skin tightens like a fresh bedsheet, clinging to my skull, good as new. Mrs. L waves the vial again, tauntingly, with a hefty dollop of I-told-you-so.

"See?" she says. "Nothing to be afraid of."

Sure, Mrs. L, tell that to my mom. No matter how harmless it is, it won't change the fact that my mother was mashed to death under a truckload of the stuff.

When I come out into the hall, Gunther's waiting.

"Welcome back, Whelp," he says. "I was wondering how long you'd be out." He checks his watch. When he looks up again, a surprised grunt comes out through his nose. "Looks like you're all patched up." He thumps closer to examine me, looming over my face. He's huge. Apart from giants, who mostly keep to themselves up in Eden, goblins are the largest creatures in the City. Somehow, they're considered hominids (but just barely).

"What're you looking at?" I ask him, rather boldly.

He frowns, which is *not* pretty. His face is a shipwreck of bloodshot eyes, blubbery gray skin, and a mouthful of tusks, haphazardly dashed over a fat skull. Meanwhile, his torso protrudes with a gravity-defying paunch, hanging so far over his belt that when he comes round a corner, you see the squat pip of his belly button bursting through his uniform long before you see the glob himself. It's a belly so bloated that you expect him to topple over. But he never does. Gunther's legs are as unshakable as monuments.

The drum of his belly nudges against my chest. "You sure you wanna be talking to me like that?"

I look down. "Sorry, Gunther."

"Good boy." He grabs my chin and twists my head back and forth, examining my face. "Let Mrs. L patch you up, huh?" He chuckles. "Thought you were scared of the stuff."

I shrug. "I'm not scared."

Gunther laughs. "Whatever you say."

"Why are you here, anyway? I'm not in trouble, right? Roy started it."

"I know. I tossed him in lockup hours ago. I'm not here about that. I'm here cuz Doc sent me to fetcha. Your session started half an hour ago."

Instinctively, I look to my wrist, peeling back the woolly blossom of hair that bursts from the cuff. I've been out for hours. He grabs my shirt and hauls me after him. "Quit stalling. We don't wanna keep the good doctor waiting."

Every wall in Doc's office is lined with brimming bookcases. The air slumps around everything like an old tarp, musty and still. In the corner, half lost in gloom, is Doc himself. He's a charcoal-hued mountain wolf with thick, aging streaks of gray. It's as if his hide is wrapped in a dark river, running fast and shallow over long, wet stones. It gives him an impression of speed, like Doc's always moving a little quicker than the rest of us.

"I've been informed," he says, without looking at me, "you were caught in a bit of a bust-up this morning." In the stillness of his office, Doc's voice has a soothing quality, crumbly and sweet like a rich pastry—one that's slightly burnt around the edges.

"Yeah," I say. My tail dips shamefully between my legs. "With Roy."

"Mmm . . ." Doc nods but he doesn't turn around. His attention remains focused on the easel before him. Doc's always painting. Nature scenes: trees, meadows, valleys, rivers—all done in photographic detail. "He's a difficult case, that one, our young Mr. Sarlat. Yet I've found that if you dig deep enough, you'll find he always has some reason, albeit misguided at times, for his acting out."

"He thinks I was hitting on his sister."

"You see?" Doc's brush pecks the canvas one last time and he turns to me. His face is cadaverously thin, balding with age. "I knew there had to be something."

I lope to the plush green wingback Doc reserves for us inmates. "All I did was say hi," I explain. "That's all."

"Mmm . . ." Doc drops his brush into a murky jar and places his palette on the desk beside a fortress of paperwork. "Now," he says, taking a seat behind the desk, "where were we?" He flips open a file—*my* file—and plucks up a fountain pen. He skims the words for a moment and then jots something down. I wish I knew what he was writing.

"How have you been this week?" he asks.

"Okay, I guess."

"You look tired. Have you been sleeping? How're your dreams?"

"Nightmares. I can deal with them."

"I see." His pen scribbles something new.

I turn my attention to his painting. It's a single tree. The bark's peeling away from the trunk in strips. Halfway up, it doubles over, a bit like Doc himself. The uppermost branches kiss the earth, mistaking themselves for roots. The genuine roots twine and lollop over one another like a pile of worms before finally burrowing into the earth.

"The juniper tree," he tells me, following my gaze. "I'm quite proud of this one."

"Looks creepier than your usual stuff."

"It's a real tree, in fact, growing right here in the city. Fascinating root structure, don't you think? That's what attracted my interest. I always find I'm drawn to the roots of things. Foundations, underlying causes . . ." He trails off, lost in thought.

"Must be nice to get a break from this place once in a while." Doc comes in a couple times a week. I'm not sure what he does with the rest of his time.

"Mrs. Lupovitz tells me you took a fairydust remedy following your injury."

"She said I had to. I had a concussion."

"That's good. I'm proud of you, on account of your misgivings about dust in general."

I slump in my chair. "Why's that surprise everybody?"

"Well," says Doc, "after what happened to your mother—"

"What's she got to do with this? I took some dust, okay? No big deal."

He dashes something else into my file. "You know, Henry, fairydust is a perfectly natural remedy."

"Except that it's not. It's mostly chemicals, right? It's not like old magic."

"Perhaps." Slowly, he replaces his glasses, edging them up his snout. "Oh, dear," he says, looking at the clock. "You were a tad late getting to me today. We've had so little time, and here I've gone and done most of the talking."

"That's okay. I wasn't really in the mood."

Outside, I'm met with a cool rush of wind. It's an early foretaste of winter. The breeze is swift and fluid, streaming through the shag of my hair. The shadows, however—the ones cast by the walls and gates that hold us in—are dull and solid and lifeless.

Above them, higher than even the intricate peaks of the City's skyscrapers, is Eden. It hovers there, a huge, lazy insect, the spires of a thousand fairy palaces bristling like antennae. Sometimes, I wish I could see them up close. But I know I never will.

None of the animalia are allowed in Eden.

4
BETTER LIVING THROUGH ENCHANTMENT

THE THREE MAIN SPECIES AT ST. REMUS ARE WOLVES, FOXES, AND RAVENS. Each group has its own unofficial leader. The ravens have Eddie Aves; the foxes, Jim Vulpino; and for the wolves, it's Roy. These guys are chosen based on the only criteria that makes any sense in here: strength and speed. Not necessarily in that order. Every day during Open Hours, out in the yard or over in the sports field, you can pretty much count on a race.

They break out spontaneously. The newest birdbrain comes in and challenges Eddie to a low-soaring competition and of course, some of the other birds'll try their luck. Eddie always wins. Same goes for Jim and Roy. The three of them have their own private dynasties going. At least that's how it's been as long as I've been here.

Now and again, there's an interspecies race. A free-for-all. Once upon a time, that sort of direct competition wouldn't happen. But thanks to the zillion generations of evolution that brought animalia on par with the hominids, races between the species are possible.

In the ancient days, nobody would've thought to pit a raven against a wolf. The size difference alone would've made the thing ridiculous. But evolution is all about brain power, that's what Mrs. L teaches us. And to have the right kind of brain, large enough to be capable of speech and all the rest of it, you need a big fat head to house it. And to lug a brain and a head like that around, you need the body to keep up. So these days any raven is practically the same size as any hominid.

According to Mrs. L, because of certain aspects of the raven's wing structure, the birds were the first of the animalia to evolve the brains and thumbs and everything else. Wolves, foxes, mules—we were late to the table. Which is probably why we've kept up such a bad reputation. Even now.

In an interspecies race, each group brings its own particular forte to the table. The foxes are sly, of course. Tricky. Wolves are all about brute strength. Especially Roy. The ravens have the power of flight on their side (provided they don't fly too high, in which case you can count on the globs up in the tower shooting them down with tranquilizer guns loaded with sedative blends of fairydust).

Jack always urges me to join in. He has a theory: Although Roy's the bigger wolf—the biggest, in fact—his muscles get in the way. Jack tells me I'm sleeker, more aerodynamic. That's my edge. But I've never raced. I never will. I just watch.

Out the window I can see a drove of them, coming across the field toward the courtyard. The globs are up in the tower, eyeing them impassively, rifles at the ready. You'd think the ravens would take the win, air travel being what it is. But it's not as fast as you think. A fox or a wolf down on all fours, like in the ancient times, can give them a run for their money. And they do. Jim and Roy are neck and neck for the lead, with Eddie flapping behind, followed by the rest of the motley herd.

When they hit the courtyard, gravel kicks up in clouds around them, enveloping the pack, but Roy, Jim, and Eddie punch free, leaving the others to skirmish in the haze. Jim tries a fake, but Roy doesn't flinch. He's too determined. He wins these free-for-alls nine times out of ten. I have no idea why Jack thinks I could beat him.

Indeed, it's Roy who's first to reach the wall of the rec center. He slaps it so hard I can feel a tremor come through the floor. He rises up and pumps a victorious forefist in the air. Eddie alights and hunches over, panting and leaning heavily on his knees. Jim, meanwhile, claps Roy on his back, but we can all see it's a begrudging gesture. The others—the losers—fall in behind, sputtering like old engines.

"You could've won that," Jack comments to me from across the room. He's over by the TV that's bolted high in the corner. He has the remote in his hand and he's carefully pressing the buttons, but nothing's happening on the screen. The TV's stuck on the news.

I shake my head. "Not my thing," I tell him.

We're sitting around the rec center, a large L-shaped

room perpetually shedding its skin. The walls cast off paint in snowy flakes and the edges of the floor are feathered with hair balls and grit. Board games in sun-faded boxes populate the shelves near a pair of Ping-Pong tables. The pool table is piled with swollen paperbacks and garbage. It's been like that ever since some fight broke out in here, years before my time. Apparently, the cue ball was used as a blunt instrument.

Most of the time, we loll away our Open Hours on the moldy couches, watching TV in a vain attempt to keep up with the world outside. That's what we're doing now: me, Jack, a few of the other outsiders—meaning beasts with not enough of their species getting into trouble to throw together a gang.

Jack shakes the wrecked remote. Something rattles inside it. "Do you know how to get this working?"

I shake my head. "The batteries are running out."

"Can you reach up there and switch the channel? I'm not tall enough."

I ignore Jack's request. I'm watching a trio of mules play cards at the folding table. From an evolutionary point of view, mules were the last to get wise, so to speak. Their forehoofs aren't anything like those of hominids or wolves. Mules evolved differently, with hooves that became jointed, crablike claws—ebony pincers, offset by a stubby opposable thumb. They have never been reviled like wolves, or mistrusted like foxes and ravens. As always, they are largely ignored. I'm guilty of it myself. I don't even know these guys' names.

I watch their forehoofs struggling to clutch the smooth, delicate surface of the playing cards. Their game is a silent one, a sort of three-way solitaire with each of them placing a card down in turn.

The TV's on a commercial now. It's a scene from up in Eden, bursting with lush greenery. I've seen this commercial before. I can mouth the words to the soothing voice-over. *"For more than a generation Nimbus Thaumaturgical has been on the cutting edge of research and development into fairydust products for both hominids and animalia."* The camera pans over Nimbus Headquarters, a sprawling industrial estate built at the very heart of Eden. Then the camera magically penetrates one of the walls to reveal a bright laboratory. *"As the originators of fairydust processing, the Nimbus brothers were the first to harvest fairydust runoff from the city's surrounding land."* The perspective shifts to show the arid desert beyond the City walls. In the background, there's a picturesque ridge topped with a copse of deadwoods. Karl and Ludwig Nimbus, the company founders, stand proudly in the foreground on the edge of a quarry. *"With or without fairies, you can count on Nimbus to provide you with the closest available product to old-time magic."* The camera cuts to a pharmacy, the shelves brimming with colorful vials. Finally, there's a shift to the haloed Nimbus logo and its ubiquitous slogan: *Nimbus Thaumaturgical ~ Better Living Through Enchantment.*

Jack hammers the remote on his palm. "Damn! Seriously, Henry, you know how to work this thing?"

Before I can offer Jack any help, my ears instinctively prick up. I hear the doors at the end of the corridor slam open. A whole menagerie of sound is barreling toward the rec center. A moment later, Roy and the others roll in.

Roy's grinning a mouthful of fangs. "Nice try at the end there, Jim, but you oughta know you'll never outfox me. I'm too fast."

Jim shrugs. "We'll see."

Roy goes straight for Jack. "Gimme that!" He snatches the remote out of his hand and shoves the boy backward. It's enough to throw Jack into a somersault, but it's hard to truly shove him off balance. He wads himself into a ball and rolls with it, coming up beside the defunct pool table, hopping up on the edge and swinging his legs. He even whistles a tune, like it was all part of the show.

Roy mashes every button on the remote before he figures out it's broken. He growls angrily and throws it backward. It soars straight for Jack's head but he dodges left and brings his hand up to catch it. It slaps loudly into his palm. "Ow!" The mules look up from their game, blinking in silence.

Jack's faster than he looks.

Roy reaches up to the TV, raising the volume manually. It's a news story about a raid on a gang of water nixies from along the reservoir. There's a montage of seized refinery equipment and a gaggle of nixies being hauled off in saltwater tubs.

Roy settles into a nearby armchair. "We missed you in the race," he says. "Too chicken, I guess."

"It's not my thing."

"It oughta be. You're a *wolf*. Didn't anybody tell you?" He stabs a paw in Jack's direction. "Quit hanging with the baldies. *Run* with us. I'd have a lot of fun making you eat my dust."

"I try to avoid dust whenever I can."

"Whatever." Roy turns back to the TV. "Once I get out of here, I'm gonna get me some work with those guys, see? Nixies. There're the only ones who'll give a wolf a decent break." He points idly out the window. "And *that* is also why we race. It's practice, Hank-man. Like an investment in the future. Face it already: You gotta live up to your species one of these days." He looks at me sideways. "Don't you wanna make your father proud?"

"No," I tell him. "I don't."

Roy opens his mouth to say something, but he's interrupted when Eddie flaps in. *"Cheat!"* he squawks.

Roy chuckles. We can all see Eddie's feathers are badly ruffled. "You cut the corner by the rectory."

Roy picks something from his teeth, right from back in the molars. It comes out tied to a string of spit, and Roy flicks it down at Eddie's feet. "I'm trying to watch," he says. The screen's full of police tape and flashing lights.

Eddie takes a step forward. "Admit you cheated. We all saw it. Right, Jim?"

Jim says nothing. He's staring at the screen, too.

"Admit it, Roy! Tell everybody how you—"

Roy's paw lashes out. He catches Eddie by the neck and the poor bird comes right off his feet. Only this time it's not on his own power. I can easily imagine Roy crushing Eddie's larynx with a pop of his fist.

"Excuse me?" Roy rises from the chair and pulls the bird in close. Eddie's hard black eyes bug out like a frog's. "I think *you're* the one who's got something to confess."

Eddie's focus starts retreating to someplace inside his avian skull. His beak hangs loose and a wormy tongue lolls out. Roy puts his snout to the bird's cheek, almost like he's giving him a kiss. "*You* need to admit that you are lying," he whispers. "I won fair and square. Didn't I?"

But Eddie can't admit anything. He can't even speak. He twitches and his feathery arms hang limp.

"Put him down, Roy." It's Gunther, finally deigning to intervene.

"Whatever." Roy loosens his grip and Eddie—belying his species—drops like a stone. Roy giggles through his snout. "Not much of a flyer, I guess. Maybe *that's* why you lost." Roy settles back into the armchair. It creaks like a sinking ship under his weight.

The other ravens move to help Eddie up, but Roy glares at them. "Let him lie." They know better than to argue with Roy, so Eddie stays there for a while, splattered on the floor like spilled soup.

Gunther says nothing. He fades back into the corridor,

leaving the rest of us to watch Eddie floundering on the tiles. There's a certain tenseness in the room now, and since nobody knows how to alleviate it, we simply turn our attention to the television. We watch it in silence for a long time before Eddie finally scrapes himself up off the tiles. He stumbles away, wingtips dragging behind him.

5
BUBBLE OF MUD

JACK AND I ARE BACK IN THE YARD, SITTING IN OUR USUAL SPOT. IT RAINED all night and the field's nothing but mud. Through the damp haze, I'm keeping an eye on Gunther. He's propped against the wall of the dormitory, laughing with the other guards.

Jack's twisting his toe, digging a little trench in the mud. "Got a letter from Siobhan yesterday."

I nod, gazing through an open section of the exterior wall. It's been patched with triple panes of chain link. "How's she doing?"

"Says she'll come visit again. Real soon, probably." Jack untucks his shirt. Underneath, instead of the smooth pink skin of his belly, there's a manila folder. "Got something for you," he says. He slips the folder out of his pants and places it on the dull rock between us. The color blends in, almost to the point of invisibility. "Remember how you told me once you always wonder what Doc's writing about you?"

I suddenly realize what Jack's done. "You *stole* it?"

Jack smiles but it's only halfhearted. "It's what I'm good at."

"You probably read it, too. So now what—you know everything about me, right? About my mother and my nightmares and—"

"Naw!" He digs his foot deeper into the muck. "Which is not to say I didn't read it. Because I did. Well, sort of. I started to, but here's the thing: It's the wrong file."

"Then why'd you say it's for me?"

"I saw the one that said Whelp, so I took it. Except it's not yours."

"Whose is it?"

"Your dad's."

Acting on instinct, I grab for the file, flipping it open.

Dear Henry,
You must think—

"Hey!" Jack yanks my arm. I'm so gutted with shock I lose my grip. Jack lays the file back on the stone. "Someone's gonna see."

"That's my dad's handwriting."

Jack's eyeing the rectory. "You can read it later."

"He sent me a *letter?*" I can see the thickness of the file. There's more than one. "How come I never got them?"

Jack taps the folder. "I think your dad wants to see you."

"So you *did* read them?"

"A little. I think maybe Doc thought reading them would screw you up or something."

My eyes burn into the bland manila. If the guards find out I have this, they'll not only take it back but they'll figure I stole it. I need to find out what Dad wrote, but I'm staring so hard, it feels like someone will notice. So I tear my eyes away.

"Why would Doc keep them?" I wonder. Through the patch of chain-link I can see the ridge that runs along the edge of the City, out where the quarries start. There's a dirt road out there, bypassing the school as it cuts onto the overpass. There's a vehicle speeding down the ridge. It's probably a delivery truck, probably from Nimbus. They're always driving too fast. They never stop for anything. I turn back to Jack. "I need to read it," I tell him.

Jack nods. "Let me hold onto it for now." With one swift motion, he slips the file back under his shirt. "You're coming, right? They're gonna think you stole this."

"What? Coming where?"

He dips one hand into the folds of his uniform. It comes out with the battered leather pouch Siobhan gave him on Visitors' Day. He tips it and a big seed, about the size of a pea, dribbles into his palm. He holds the seed in his fist and pokes his foot into the ground, which leaks back at him, spongy with stale rain.

"What're you doing?" My head's swimming. "Let me see the file."

Jack doesn't answer. The truck coming down the ridge races through a puddle of sunlight and flashes suddenly, blinding me. Jack's looking up, contemplating the wall. He opens his palm, plucks up the seed, and with his thumbnail he peels away nothing more than a sliver. "Trust me," he says. "Your dad wants to see you."

The truck is down from the ridge now, coming toward the school along the lone highway—only now I see it's not a truck. It's a little convertible. A fast one. Jack drops the larger chunk of the seed back into his pouch, slipping it into the mysterious folds of his shirt.

I rub my forehead. I'm sweating. "Can I see the file?"

Jack ignores the question. "There's still some of the old magic left in this city, but it's rare. So you have to know when to use it." He works his tongue inside his mouth, stirring up spit and drooling a drop into his palm. With a fingertip he pushes the flake around to moisten it. Then he tosses the mixture into the pit he's been digging with his shoe. "As soon as you see a nice sturdy vine," he tells me, "grab hold. But don't wait too long. I only used a sliver, see? So it's not gonna last long." He refills the trench and tamps it down.

"Jack?"

He gets up and retreats a few paces back toward the school. "I'd get outta the way if I were you."

Good advice. In the spot where Jack tossed his sliver and his spit, the moist earth is swelling up in a bubble of mud. A fiddlehead of a sprout pops through the center, green and leafy and unfurling like a fist into an open hand.

Then, with the miraculous speed of magic, it whips against the wall and begins to climb. More green tendrils split from the stalk and twine around one another, until the main trunk is as thick as I am. It's some kind of plant—half grapevine, half oak tree.

I can hear them shouting from the admin buildings.

"Here!" Jack pulls a piece of paper out of a pocket and slaps it into my paw. "In case we get separated, this is where I'll be!" He steps up and latches a fist into one of the rising vines. The stalk grows higher and pulls him into the air, spiriting him all the way up the wall.

Meanwhile, here comes the little convertible. It's turned off the road now, skidding over the arid emptiness toward us. There's a girl behind the wheel. She's got a handkerchief tied across her nose and mouth, and a baseball cap yanked over her eyes. Her features are obscured, but anyone who's ever seen the pictures taped over Jack's bed would recognize those unmistakable eyes.

Jack's at the top of the stalk now, rising over the wall. He swings his weight and tips the whole thing sideways, bowing it over the cement. The plant seems to understand him, knowing just what he wants it to do. It grows higher and then, with all the gentleness of a new mother, slips Jack perfectly into the convertible.

"*Hurry up,*" he shouts at me through the fence. "Grab on!"

What else can I do? I step up, grasping a vine of my own. But the moment I've got it in my paw, it snaps off with a quick tear. As soon as it parts from the main trunk, the vine withers and crumbles to nothing. I hear Gunther pounding across the yard, the muddy ground splashing and quaking beneath him. I reach for another vine, but before I can, his truncheon comes down on my shoulders. I sink to my knees as more blows pin me into the mud.

"I'm sorry!" Jack yells through the fence. He slaps his belly, where the letters—*my* letters—are concealed. "I should've left them for you!" He points at me and I realize he's indicating the pocket where I put his address.

The tower guards start shooting and Siobhan slams the accelerator. Jack lurches over the seat as the car careens toward the road. Wet clumps of earth fountain up from the wheels and the car leaps back to the asphalt, rushing into the city.

Gunther's knee comes off my back and, dim-witted as ever, he tries climbing after Jack. With his feet wedged in the thickest tendrils, he strains to tug himself off the ground. But suddenly the plant's deep green drains away—summer turning instantly to autumn. Gunther yelps as the stalk withers and the huge glob sploshes down in a filthy puddle. Suddenly, I understand what Jack meant: with only a sliver, the magic doesn't last long.

I can't help but laugh out loud, first mockingly at Gunther's failure, then jealously at Jack's freedom, and finally bitterly at what I've just learned about Dad's letters. My laughter is rewarded with another deluge of blows from Gunther, culminating in one clean shot to the back of my skull. The whole sky sparkles with stars and all I can hear is the sound of a distant engine, roaring and free.

6
STICK OF GOLD

THE OFFICIAL TERM FOR LOCKUP IS "REHABILITATIVE SECLUSION." IT'S located in a building at the far corner of the grounds. It's a new one, thoroughly modern, no cobbled walls or ivy. It's merely a honeycombed strongbox of soundproof cells. Roy spends every other week in this place, but for me, thanks to Jack's escape, this is my maiden voyage.

I've been here all week, in an empty six-foot tomb with walls like sponges, padded and soft and perfumed with the staleness of age. It certainly gives you time to think. In my case, I've been thinking about my parents.

My mother's name was Emily. She died before I was old enough to remember her. All I have are the fabricated memories you make up from old photographs, which goes a long way to explaining why, inside my head, she's always smiling.

Growing up, it was just Dad and me. All that time, he had me convinced he was a carpenter, doing odd jobs around the neighborhood. The phone would ring, and after speaking to somebody in hushed tones, he'd announce that he was going out on a job. Then he'd vanish, sometimes until late in the night. I always stayed up to wait for him, even though he forbade it. He always came back looking exhausted.

I didn't find out what my father really did for a living until the day of the murders, the day the sirens came shrieking to the house to haul Dad away for good. I've also been thinking about Doc, about his files and the letters—*my* letters—that he'd been keeping from me (letters that Jack has now run off with, the little thief).

The first thing they make you do when they let you out of lockup is go see Doc. He has to make sure you haven't lost your marbles in here. When I see him again, I'm going to walk into his office with a whole lot of questions. How long has Dad been writing to me? How come you kept the letters to yourself? What gave you the right? And so on.

I'm cataloguing the questions in my mind when the door swings open. It's Gunther, yawning at me, his thick tongue wriggling between stalagmitic teeth.

"All right, Whelp," he mutters. "Let's go."

It's raining outside, hard and fast. I had no idea. In lockup, you can't hear a thing from the outside world. There's a pit of broken earth where Jack's plant burst up a week ago. Gunther doesn't look at it as we pass, jogging through the rain. We're both soaked by the time we arrive at the old rectory.

Inside, the corridor's a tomb—dim, silent, and empty. Outside, the daytime clouds are even darker than dusk. Rain mauls the windows. You can hardly see Doc's paintings on the walls. The shapes in the frames are indistinct. I'm about to knock when I see the office door's already open an inch or two, which is odd. He never leaves it open.

"Doc?"

No answer. The light in his study's even dimmer than out in the hall. A cold drop of rain rolls down my neck, icy as it weaves through my hair.

"Doc? It's Henry." Nothing. "I think—" Where is he? "I think we have some stuff to talk about." It's so dark in here I can hardly see.

"Doc?"

My eyes are adjusting now. I see something, something I can't explain. The air in front of me swims like shadows over glass. There's something floating in the middle of the room. *Floating*—dead center, in the middle of the musty air. It looks like—

"Dad?"

I blink. Something's wrong with me. My father is floating there, hovering in the air. I stare at him, hoping the vision will disappear. Hoping I'll wake up. But there he is—the hazy shape of a ghostly wolf. Then I realize: It's not a vision at all. And it's definitely not my father.

It's Doc.

My eyes are finally adjusting to the darkness. I can see more now. I can see it all: The rope around his neck. The cord rising into intricate knots strung over the rafters and pulled taut. Doc's jaw slack, his tongue flopping down like a thinly sliced steak.

He's dead. And it's fresh. He's still swaying.

"Doc?!"

My vision goes black again and my knees buckle forward, propping me against the desk. One foot slips into the gap below the paneling and something loose clicks against my toe. It feels like Doc's fancy pen, so I tease it into the open, rolling it out with the ball of my foot. It's not his pen, though. It's something else, something gleaming, something that catches all the light in the room.

A stick of gold.

I crouch down, one hand on the edge of the desk to steady myself. For whatever reason, I pick the thing up and slip it into the pocket of my uniform. I want to keep it.

I turn back toward the door. "Gunther?" He can't hear me, I know, but I say it anyway. I call out as loud as I can but it's no better than a rasp. "You need to come in here. Something awful has happened."

7
FRESH SCABS

AFTER THEY TOOK DAD AWAY, I WAS ON MY OWN. IN AND OUT OF FOSTER homes for years. Whenever I could, I'd go for long, meandering lopes around the city. Every time, I ended up on the crest of the Willow Street Bridge, right above the spot where it happened.

Along the bridge there are low barriers that look like they're made of cement, but that's only partly true. The cement was diluted with cheap limestone to cut costs, so over time, the limestone crumbles. If you run your hand along the top, you always come upon one or two loose bricks.

Last winter, I was standing up there on the Willow Street Bridge and sure enough, I dislodged a big chunk of rock. There was a transport truck swimming through traffic below me, just about to head under the bridge. I could see the Nimbus logo on the cab.

I don't know what I was thinking. Maybe I wanted to frighten the driver. Maybe I figured it would just bounce off. But when I dropped the hunk of stone, it didn't glance off the windshield like I'd hoped. Instead, it smashed clean through. It hit the driver on the back of his head. An inch to the left, they told me later, and it would've killed him.

That was the window I broke—the windshield of a Nimbus truck. That's how I ended up at the Home. It's also how I first met Detective Inspector White. She's the same one who arrested my father.

"You really did it this time, didn't you?"

I look up at Gunther. It's just me and him in the St. Remus staff room, a drab space haunted by ghost-scents of reheated food. Right now, however, it's an interrogation suite.

"What do you mean?" My voice croaks like a frog's. "I didn't *do* anything. He was just hanging there."

Gunther shakes his head.

There've been quite a few suicides here over the years, but rarely on the part of the staff. It's never before been the visiting psychiatrist who offs himself. And this is Doctor Rufus Grey, renowned animalian psychologist. That means they're taking it seriously. No messing around. They're sending in the real deal. They're sending Detective White.

Right on cue, I tune in the tick-tick-ticking of high heels. Gunther pushes himself out of his wall-slouch and wipes the scowl off his face. He grins at me. "Now you're gonna get it."

But when the door opens, it's not White. It's Cindy, the Chief Administrator at St. Remus. She clinks into the staff room on glassy, towering heels. They look as cozy as a pair of

47

icicles. Apparently, those stilettos are her one holdover from a previous life. (Once upon a time, Cindy was a low-class hominid, but one who married well. For years she lived up in Eden, chumming around with the aristocrats of the so-called inDustrial Revolution. At some point, however, she got bored with it all. She realized she was more comfortable down here with her own people, so to speak—the animalia and the working poor.)

"Hello, Henry," she says. "There's someone here who'd like a word with you."

Detective White's scent gives her away. She's got one of the oddest bouquets I've ever whiffed. Apple cider and old coal. Cindy steps aside and the famous detective enters the room.

"We meet again," she says.

I nod.

At first glance, Detective White doesn't appear all that tough. She's an ordinary woman, shorter than Cindy by half a head, although that's probably on account of Cindy's heels. White's legs, on the other hand, are buried up to the knee in a battered pair of trench boots. She comes over and leans on the table. "Must've been quite a shock, huh?"

"It was," I tell her. Up close, I recall how well she lives up to her name. Her face is pale as a bowl of milk, floating with stark features that match her scent: apple-red lips and eyes like blackened embers.

"Why don't you tell her what you found?"

I describe the scene as I remember it, though I'm careful to leave out the stick of gold. It doesn't seem related and besides, I want to keep it for myself.

White listens intently, her face calm. When I'm finished, she says, "You two were close, weren't you? You and the Doc?"

"I guess," I tell her. "It's hard not to be when they make you see him every week."

She turns her head in a broad circle and her back cracks up and down, a spineful of arthritic knuckles. "Losing friends left and right these days, that's what I hear."

"What do you mean?"

"Your friend Jack disappeared, too."

"So?"

White pulls out a chair and straddles it backward, folding her arms over the backrest. "Guess you're having a bad week." Her hands hang from her wrists like the branches of a dead tree, hard and rough, her fingers encrusted with fresh scabs. When she notices how I'm staring, she holds up a fist. "Admiring my manicure?" She picks off a scab and lets it flake to the floor. "That's what you get for spending half the day interrogating muscle for the mob." She points a thumb over her shoulder, over at Gunther. "You think *he's* big, you oughta see the guys Skinner's got working for him."

Gunther frowns. *"You?"* he says to White. "They had *you* interrogating one of Skinner's guys?"

"Two of them, actually."

Skinner. I know that name. I remember it from my father's trial.

"No way," says Gunther.

White smiles mischievously. "You wanna bet?"

Cindy wrings her hands. "Gunther, please."

White tightens a loose screw on the chair's headrest. "Not everybody knows this about me," she says, "but I never had a family. Not a real one anyway. I was raised by miners. Seven of them. When a girl grows up in a situation like that—well, let's just say she learns how to take care of herself."

Gunther laughs, but the volume's turned low. "So what? Doesn't mean you can take on a glob. And *never* one of Skinner's guys."

"You wanna bet?"

"What do I get if I win?"

White looks up at him and smiles. "Respect."

"You got a deal." Gunther stretches out his meaty hand. "But how you gonna prove it?"

"Like this." She grabs his thumb and jerks it back toward his wrist. Gunther's face flashes with shock and his knees buckle. White yanks on the pinioned digit, and the arm it's connected to noodles up behind the goblin's back. In a flash of leverage, she's got him curled on the floor, whimpering like a cub with a fatty jowl glued to the linoleum.

She clears her throat. "Convinced?"

Gunther yawps in anger, but it's about all he can do.

White tweaks the thumb a little harder. "I asked you a question."

"Okay, okay, you win! I'm convinced! You're gonna break my arm!"

"So pay up already."

Gunther's eyes go knuckle-white with fear. "But we didn't even bet anything!"

"Sure we did. All you gotta do is say it."

"Okayokayokay! I re*spect* you! I do, I really do!"

Fast as before, White releases Gunther and returns to the chair. She straddles it again and shrugs. "It's all math, really. Physics. Put the fulcrum in the right place and you can move the world. Or at least some big, dumb glob." She squints at me. "You study math?"

I shake my head. "Words are more my thing."

"You oughta do some math."

Cindy gives Gunther a look of concern. "Maybe you ought to wait outside."

"You sure, Ms. Rella?"

She nods and Gunther backs into the corridor, glowering at White the whole way. He's got his one sore arm cradled in the other like a newborn.

"Now then," says White. "Where were we? Ah, yes— Doctor Grey. He once gave a talk at the academy, all about rehabilitating the usual suspects. Harmony between the species and all that. Made it sound convincing. I nearly believed it could happen. Then I actually started doing the job. Hoofing the beat in Darkforest, or down in Dockside." She pauses. "Now, when I say 'hoofing,' please understand it's just an expression. No offense."

I squint at her. "I'm a wolf. Hooves are for mules and goats."

"Sure." She rises from the chair, rubbing her mouth. "I think I've heard enough. They only sent me out here to cool off. Think it worked, too." She glances at the door. "Apart from chicken-winging your head of security, that is."

"Gunther can handle it," Cindy tells her.

White turns back to me. "I know you didn't have anything to do with this, Henry. Any fool can see you're nothing like your father." She places her hands on the back of the chair, gripping it with her bloody knuckles. "Your shrink killed himself. End of story. It's not that uncommon. You'd be surprised by those guys. Not as stable as they make out to be, if you know what I mean." White turns for the door. "I'd say I'll see you around, kid, but it's probably best you stay outta my way."

She ambles for the door and throws a backhanded salute over her shoulder. Cindy and I listen to the echo of her boots fading down the corridor, heavy-soled footfalls that thump out a slow, unstoppable beat.

8
BLOOD MEMORY OF THE SPECIES

EARTHWOOD CEMETERY IS AN OASIS OF GREEN AT THE HEART OF THE CITY. It may be mashed in on all sides by asphalt and brick, but once you're inside, the grounds are lush with hedges and trees and tightly cropped grass. The cemetery lies under the base of the Empyrean Skyway, spiraling above us, all the way up to Eden.

Our buses rumble past the two gigantic guardhouses that cut the Skyway off from First Avenue. It's impossible to tell whether the guards standing inside notice us. They're like statues, towering and expressionless, which is typical of giants. To them, we must seem like insects. The guardhouses slide past the windows as we turn away, rolling in through the cemetery gates.

Near the entrance, there's a hominid funeral already underway. The mourners frown. Our old buses are too rusty, too loud, too brightly emblazoned with the St. Remus logo to belong in a noble and austere place like this. Nevertheless, here we are.

Then, in only a moment, we're gone. Maples and oaks and great shaggy willows swallow us up as we move through to the far side of the grounds. We park in a distant lot.

When the guards usher us out, we see the grave is right up front, a shadowy rectangle carved from the earth with perfect precision. The coffin lies beside it, on top of what looks to be a deep red picnic blanket. Without too much ado, we take our seats.

The priest is a slender raven. He sails above the treetops like a storm cloud. With one dignified flap, he alights between the coffin and the grave. His cassock grips tight to his body. The fabric is seamless against his tar-black feathers; you can't see where the vestment ends and the priest begins. The two are separated only at the throat, by the stark white square of his collar. His murky eyes scan across us all, hushing us one by one.

"Let us begin."

His voice crackles like an old record. "There are those who believe that when we take our own life, we do not deserve the respect of a proper burial. There are those who would stoop so low as to claim that any *wolf* who leaves us in this manner is performing a civic duty. But no, the death of Doctor Rufus Grey is a great loss for this city. Few citizens, no matter what their stripe, can claim to have contributed so selflessly to combating the City's urban unrest."

Cindy sits down in front. She's swaying minutely, but I can only see the barest profile of her face. She might be crying, but I can't tell. Mrs. Lupovitz, on the other hand, down at the end of my row, is shuddering like a train off its tracks, tears streaming down her face.

The priest recounts how thoughtful, kind, well-educated, generous, insightful Doc was. I can't help searching for a scrap of dubiousness in his avian eye; not too many folks would deem insightfulness and generosity wolfish traits. But there's no irony in the priest's voice. He's a bit monotonous, maybe, but he's nothing if not sincere. Once he's done, he turns to the forest that overshadows the grave.

"David?" he says.

Suddenly, the trees ripple like a mirage. They shake as if blown in a wind, but the air is perfectly still. Something shines through the branches. It's an ember, gleaming and orange. It floats high off the ground, lighthouse-height and half lost in the thickest leaves. Then come the hands. They reach out toward us, enormous and stiff and deeply tanned, parting the poplars like a garden hedgerow.

A giant.

He steps into the open as gently as he can, but the ground still trembles. He's dressed in soiled overalls and a canvas cap. He must be the gravedigger. The ember is the enormous stub of a cigarette, clinging to his pillow-sized lip.

The priest frowns. *"David,"* he says sternly.

The giant plucks the cinder from his mouth and lets it drop. It falls, big as a meteor, and when he stamps it out the ground shakes.

The priest spreads a wing toward the grave. "Go ahead, David."

Stooping forward, the giant gathers up the seat belt–like straps lying under the coffin, lifting it with hardly any effort at all. The polished box floats up and then down into the darkness of the earth. With the flat of his foot, David sweeps the nearby pile of soil into the hole, burying Doc forever. Finally, just as he did with the cigarette, the giant's enormous boot tamps everything down.

"Thank you," says the priest. The giant nods carefully and retreats into the trees.

At some point during the eulogy, I made up my mind. Here among the cleanness of the trees, the rareness of the air, the sadness of the day, I've realized there's nothing left for me back at St. Remus. Without Jack or Doc, I'm on my own. And without those letters, I'll go crazy thinking about them. Plus, I've got this slim reed of gold in my pocket, something I can pawn off once I run out of loose change. All I need now is the right exit strategy.

Pebbles and stones are scattered in the grass, maybe shards of crumbling gravestones or leftovers from what David dug up. They've given me an idea. It's probably a stupid one, misguided and half-formed, but it's all I've got.

As I stand with the others, I let my paw hang down and brush the grass, scooping up the largest rock I can find. When we're all up and marching back toward the parking lot, I hang back as far as I can, right in line with the rear guard. He's bumbling along, looking nervously into the trees. That gravedigger must've spooked him. It's rare to see a giant working down here in the City. Most of them live up in Eden.

Roy's big white head looms over the rest, but it looks oddly small after the proportion-skewing sight of the giant. I feign a yawn and a stretch, and when I drop my arm I do it quickly, releasing the rock, letting it lob through the air in a lazy arc. Nobody notices. Nobody but me. I'm watching it sail away, end over end, straight for Roy's head. Now, what exactly am I going to do if—

"OW!" Roy spins around and slaps one bewildered paw to the base of his skull. The other one jabs backward instinctively, back at the guy behind him—who just happens to be his chief rival, Jim Vulpino. Sly and quick, the fox dodges left.

But Roy's even faster. He catches Jimmy on the chin and a pair of his friends rush in to defend him. In a second, the fight snowballs into an all-out campaign of fists and growls.

The priest flaps up, hovering like a spirit. "Please," he squawks, "this is hallowed ground!"

The guard beside me snaps out of his stupor and lumbers into the fight. For a second I'm all alone. I drop to all fours between the chairs, and I stalk for the bushes. Behind me I can hear the snaps of teeth, the dull thuds of knuckles against hairy hides, the shouts of the guards. I can even hear the rising percussion of hearts—in time with the desperate thundering of my own. And miraculously, I make it. I'm into the brush, into the trees. Now it's merely a matter of time. Waiting to see if they miss me. Could it really be this easy?

I watch them reload the buses, drenched with sweat and blood, and it isn't long before everyone's aboard. The engines start up and the wheels start rolling. Shaking his head, the priest glides off, presumably to the next burial.

I lope deeper into the thicket, careful to keep low. My ears slick back. My chin skims along a bed of fallen leaves. It's good to feel how naturally my fingers grip the soil. It's a throwback to the primordial times, back when forepaws and hind legs were practically indistinguishable. That's what this is, this stalking through the bush—it's a blood memory of the species.

I push in, burying myself deeper and deeper in the leaves and shadows. The whole forest trembles and closes in around my body, welcoming me back.

9
APPEASE THE GIANT

BUT I DON'T GET FAR.

I'm suddenly pressed to the earth. Something heavy, like a pair of warm cushions, pounds into my back. They come together and pinch my spine. I'm lifted off the ground, suspended in the air like a cub in his mother's mouth—only this is one *hell* of a mother.

"YOU ARE NOT SUPPOSED TO BE HERE."

I'm above the trees, face-to-face with the oversized gravedigger. The veins on his tuberous nose are thick and ropy, like the roots of a tree in one of Doc's paintings. His beard reeks so strongly of tobacco I can feel the nicotine creeping down my throat. When I start choking it only makes him angry. He shakes me, and I flap like a hooked fish.

"YOU ARE SUPPOSED TO BE ON ONE OF THOSE BUSES."

Then I see it—the reason he's a gravedigger down here in the City instead of living like a prince up in Eden. There's something wrong with him. There's a wild, empty look in his eye. He's not all here. He's loopy.

This could be a problem.

"I HATE WOLVES. WOLVES BITE," he informs me. He opens his mouth (not a good thing). His teeth are boulders of coal, the cavernous valleys between them filled with the worst imaginable mash. The stench is—well, it's indescribable. He pulls me closer. "BUT I CAN BITE TOO."

"David, no!" Somebody yells up from below. "Put him down, please." I half-expect the priest, but no—it's a girl's voice. A voice like gravel and honey.

Slowly, both David and I peer down through the hanging branches of a larch tree. There she is, beautiful and improbable. Fiona, Roy Sarlat's sister. She's got her camera aimed up at us. "Say cheese!" she says.

"CHEESE!"

I feel David's grip loosen ever so slightly.

Fiona's camera clicks and she squints up at me. "David's not fond of strangers."

The giant nods his mountainous head in agreement. "I DON'T LIKE WOLVES." He turns to me with a passionate frown. "EXCEPT FIONA FRIEND. SHE BRINGS ME TREATS."

"*I do,* don't I?" she says, speaking as if to a child. "I'm a friend, just like Father Corviday is a friend." She points up at me. "And that's our friend, too."

"HE IS?"

"My friend is your friend, right, David?"

With some effort, David winks one eye shut. He brings me in close to ogle me with the other. "WHAT'S HIS NAME?"

"Um . . ."

Great. She doesn't even remember me. "Henry!" I shout down in a stage whisper.

"That's our friend, *Henry*. Now put him down."

David pouts out his lip until it's bigger than my bunk back at school. He nods thoughtfully. "HENRY FRIEND," he says. A moment later, I'm safely down with Fiona.

"Thanks," I tell her.

But she ignores me. "David? I brought you something. Look." She opens a large shoulder bag and retrieves a plastic container filled with a sharp, sweet-smelling chocolate cake. A couple slices are missing. She creaks open the plastic lid. "Ta-da!"

David's eyes glaze over and his jaw drops. "THANK YOU!" He stoops down to collect his prize, tossing the whole thing in his mouth like it's a bonbon. His rotten teeth grind it up, and muddied saliva streams into his beard. I can't help thinking that, were it not for Fiona's fortuitous arrival on the scene, that'd be *me* in there.

"MMMMM," says the giant. He turns and galumphs into the trees, vanishing all over again.

"Thanks."

Fiona ignores me. She's fiddling with the closure of her

shoulder bag. "Damn! This is a brand-new purse. It's what I get for lugging a cake around all day."

"I thought you never bothered with the whole 'say cheese' thing."

She looks at me, puzzled. "What would you have said?"

"Uh . . ."

Fiona gives up on the clasp of her purse, letting it flop loose. "Look at this. I totally stretched the leather."

"So . . . do you work here? You're a babysitter for giants? In a graveyard?"

She laughs. "No, I don't *work* here. Why does anybody go to a cemetery?" She points at a modest grave two plots over. It's a two-foot slab lying flush with the earth. It says:

Charles Ferdinand Sarlat
RIP

A plastic pot of flowers sprouts up in the corner.

"I'm sorry."

"Don't be," says Fiona. "He was a jerk. Prob'ly where my brother gets it from. When Mom remarried, she made me promise I'd still visit him once a week. A promise is a promise." She motions with her head into the woods. "Which is why I'm such good 'friends' with David. I learned early on that if you happen to be a wolf and you wanna lope around this place by yourself, you need to appease the giant." She shrugs. "It's not a problem. David has simple tastes. Candy or cigarettes. I don't approve of the latter—and I don't need to. I'm always able to steal the leftover cake from my work. It's a bakery." She looks into the trees and laughs. "Nobody understands why I never get fat."

The whole time, she's hardly looked at me. Me, on the other hand—*I'm staring*. She ties the closure of her purse into a makeshift clasp and finally pays me some attention. She studies my face, leaning her head sideways, all the way to her shoulder. "We've met, right? You look kind of familiar."

"Actually . . ." Only I trail off. I'm not terribly keen to remind her that I'm the guy her brother beat up about ten seconds after we (almost) shook hands.

Before I can make up a story, though, she leans in and reads the insignias sewed into my uniform. "Wait a sec," she says. "You're from *St. Remus*?" She looks around. "Didn't they just leave? I saw my brother, getting himself into trouble like always." She squints at me. "I don't get it. Why're you still here?"

"I didn't want to go back."

She raises her eyebrows. "I wasn't aware that was their policy."

"It's easier than you think," I say, feigning the confidence of a master escape artist. "Everybody's doing it."

Surprisingly, she nods in agreement. "I've lost count of how many time's Roy showed up at my window in the middle of the night." She shakes her head, inhaling fretfully through her snout. "Enjoy it while you can. They always catch you in the end. The police, I mean."

"Oh."

"So what's your plan?"

"My plan . . ."

"The reason you escaped?" She smiles. Her teeth are nothing like Roy's, which have probably been knocked out and rearranged more times than he can remember. Fiona's teeth, however, are smooth and pristine and gleaming white. "You got a girl on the outside, right?"

Sure, I think. *You're pretty much it.* But instead I say, "I need to find a friend of mine."

I can't help but wonder if she's scared of me, if she sees me as an escaped thug. While I'm wondering, she turns and starts off toward the gates. "Which way are you headed?"

I lope after her. "Toward Elvenburg, I think."

"Convenient. I'm going the same way myself. We'll take the streetcar together."

She leads me off and I can't help but prick up my ears. The noises seep through the trees. I can hear them. The sound of the city, faint but relentless: the bellow of factories; the trundle of streetcars; the clatter of shoes, boots, and hooves against endless sidewalks; the chirm of countless voices of every pitch and intonation.

Sounds I haven't heard in a long time.

PART TWO
THE CITY

10
AN AUDIENCE OF ONE

BEING CLOISTERED IN ST. REMUS FOR SO LONG, I'D FORGOTTEN WHAT A
madhouse the City can be. All around us, streets teem with
folks of every stripe: plodding hedgehogs, witless mules,
dripping water nixies, pudgy pigs, pensive elves, sloe-eyed
cats, crafty humans, limp-legged frogs, watchful ravens, and
on and on and on. On the streetcar, we're crammed in like
herring, packed and pickled in a rolling jar. The city's a fun
house, an unruly parade, a circus—with Eden hovering high
above like a silent ringmaster.

"So tell me again about this friend of yours?"

"His name's Jack."

Fiona looks at me sideways. "The little hominid?" I
wonder if maybe she's as prejudiced as her brother, but then
she chuckles. "Roy hates that kid."

"Roy hates *everybody*. He can be a jerk sometimes. A lot
of the time."

"I know," she says and then falls silent. I've probably gone
and offended her. "Sometimes," she says, "like with me and

Mom, he can be so sweet." She looks out the window, and since I can't think of what to say next, we ride in silence.

Outside, the city rolls past. Tubes of neon wink at us, even though it's not yet dusk. The buildings are garnished heavily with signs and slogans. One massive billboard for Nimbus beams down. It's a collage of scientific apparatuses—test tubes, beakers, microscopes—all overshadowed by a ropy helix of fairydust, rising up like a mist. In the upper corners, the faces of the Nimbus brothers smile reassuringly down from their experiments. The caption reads, *Coming Soon: A New Way to Enchantment!* It's followed by a list of upcoming products. *Theurgicol. Charmex. Enchanterin. Faericetomol . . .*

"Almost there," says Fiona. We come to a ringing halt and the doors slap open. Outside, the Willow Street Bridge takes me by surprise. It rises up right beside us, blotting out the sky. More than half the streetcar empties and Fiona, granted a little more room, backs away from me. "One or two more stops," she says.

"Uh huh . . ." We're moving under the bridge, right where the accident happened.

"This is you." She points to the bright green arch that marks the border of Elvenburg. As the streetcar slows, she says, "It was nice to see you again."

"Listen," I say. "I haven't been out in the open for a while, so um—well, obviously I don't know too many folks, so . . ." I trail off, hoping she'll pick up the thread.

"You do realize you're about to miss your stop."

I hadn't even noticed the driver putting on the brakes. "Maybe we could hang out sometime. Like before the police catch up with me."

Fiona sighs. "They always do, you know." She opens her bag and finds a pen and a crumpled napkin. Propping one foot on the wall, she uses her knee for a writing surface. She passes me the napkin just as the doors fold open. "That's where you can reach me."

I step backward and stumble onto the pavement. The doors clap shut and the streetcar whines away, the wires above crackling with electricity. I watch until it rounds the corner, then turn to face the enormous green arches of Elvenburg.

Every inch of the sidewalk is so well trodden that the whole neighborhood feels worn down like the carpets of an old hotel. There are folks *everywhere*—elves for the most part, but every other species of citizen is well represented. All of them jostle to out step their neighbors, elbowing for bargains in the market, or merely shoving folks out of the way just for kicks. The address on Jack's note says: 1020 PINE STREET, APT. 7B.

I try asking for directions from a pig and her son, but she tugs the little guy away so fiercely she nearly tears his arm off. The two of them duck into a shop just to avoid me. Old habits die hard, I guess. Next, I try a wearied old mule, clopping up from the opposite direction. With a shaky forehoof, he points me across the street.

"Pine Street" is barely more than an alcove, a narrow recess that widens (somewhat) into a wretched alleyway. I poke my head out of the shadows again to check the sign. Pine Street it is. I'm in the right place, only there certainly aren't any pine trees.

Moving farther in, I'm forced to duck my head to avoid the fire escapes, clawing down with rusty fingers. High above, strings of laundry hang like a million wistful grins.

"*Psst!*"

I look to the left, but there's only an overflowing Dumpster. I'd be surprised if it'd ever been emptied. No garbage truck could squeeze into a clotted alleyway like this one.

"Hey, c'mere."

A thin gray fox steps out of the shadows. He's wearing a ratty anorak with a woolly hat pulled down over his brow, but it doesn't hide his distinctive face. Two streaks of black run up either side, from his snout to the tips of his ears. His eyes are sodium-yellow in the lamplight, sparkling with flecks of violet. In the dimness of the alley, they flash like jewels.

"You wanna buy some dust?"

"What?" I shake my head, trying to stifle my surprise.

"Dust," he says. "Good stuff." His breath hits me, smelling of bile, as if he hasn't eaten in days. "Old Jerry's got the finest of the fine."

I look down the alleyway. Not much farther to the end. Number 1020 must be down there somewhere, so I wave him off. "No, thanks," I say, turning to go.

The fox pushes off the wall and shuffles after me. "I'm talking about the *real deal*. My stuff comes direct from Dockside, direct from them nixies."

"I'm meeting somebody." I keep going but it's pointless—
Pine Street is a dead end, and Old Jerry is with me now,
matching my lope. "This is *old-time* dust. Just like them
fairies could getcha. I'm talkin' about the real deal—*real
magic.* None of that watered down Nimbus junk. This is the
stuff that can fulfill destinies . . . if you know what I mean."

I keep my eyes glued straight ahead.

"Who you meeting down here anyway? Ain't nobody nice
lives down here. Maybe a big, young guy like you—maybe you
think you're fine, but take it from Old Jerry, nobody nice lives
down thataway. You's gonna need something to—y'know, lift
the spirits. A set of horns, maybe. Jerry can do that. How'd
you like to breathe some fire? That'd be nice, huh? Come in
handy. Jerry can do that too."

I keep on loping, scanning the sooty walls for signs,
numbers, anything.

"C'mon!" His voice raises a pitch, sharpened by a whine.
"Give Old Jerry a break."

"I said no. Thank you."

"Don't be like that." He shakes his head woefully. "Old
Jerry ain't got no place to go. Holes in m'clothes and in m'shoes."
He kicks up a foot to show me. Indeed, the sole's coming
loose, flapping like a tongue on a hot summer's day. "All I
got is a little dust here, that's all. Nothing wrong with tryin'
to make a living. Times'er rough, y'know? Maybe a strong,
young guy like you—maybe you can't tell they're rough, but
take it from Old Jerry, *they are.* They most definitely are."

We're getting to the end of the alleyway now. Still no signs, nothing to tell me where I am. "Sorry," I say, "never touch the stuff."

A vulpine grin slides up the side of his face, showing off a row of surprisingly white teeth. "Don't lie to Old Jerry. We all need a little dust now and then. Just natural. And this is nixiedust we're talking about. *Old*-time dust. Fulfills your destiny." He taps his chest. "Whatever you want in here."

"There's none of that left anymore."

"Aw, now don't be like that." He reaches out and places a cloying paw on my elbow. It makes me itch all over.

I spin to face him, baring my teeth and pushing him off. "I said *no!*"

He stumbles backward and I can see I've scared him. He backs away, sheepish. "Sorry, guy. Didn't know you'd take it so hard."

"Leave me alone, okay?"

He nods. "Sure, but who knows? Maybe I'll see you again. Maybe we can do business some other time." He smiles again with his improbably perfect teeth. "Don't forget Old Jerry." He turns his back and moves off toward the lamplight of the main street. The sole of his broken shoe claps against the ground. Strangled applause from an audience of one.

I turn to the dark end of the alley and after only a few steps I find it. A plain wooden door with a number scratched into the frame: 1020.

11
ELVEN INCENSE

THE DOOR ISN'T LOCKED. OR RATHER, THE LOCK'S BEEN SMASHED AWAY, leaving only a splintered wound in the door frame. Inside is a stairway paved in brown carpet that's more like fungal residue than floor covering. Luckily, the smell isn't as bad as I might've expected. The scents in a place like this are too stale to properly offend the sniffer. I start up, step by step. Every one of them sighs, moist with rot.

After seven short flights, I've arrived. 7B. This must be where Siobhan lives. I wonder if she'll remember me. I hope so (as a general rule, folks don't take kindly to a wolf at the door).

I knock. There's a series of clicks as the bolts are unlatched, unhasped, unhinged. There are a lot of them. But they still have one left, because the door opens barely an inch, anchored by a thick chain.

"Yeeees?"

All I can see is one narrow strip of an elf. I look her in what I can see of her face—a bloodshot eyeball, a wrinkled forehead, and a thatch of white hair.

"I'm looking for Jack?"

The eye regards me from behind the lens of a pair of fussy, gold-rimmed spectacles. My snout detects the scent of mothballs emanating from the figure. In fact, the eye is so clouded with cataracts that it might actually *be* a mothball. Talk about cheap prosthetics.

The mothball eye blinks, carefully moistening itself.

"Nobody here called Jack," croaks the elf. The voice rattles like old bones. This is definitely not Siobhan. "You got the wrong place."

"Oh," I say. I hold up the slip of paper. "He told me he'd be staying here."

The ancient elf doesn't bother reading the address. "I can't help you, sonny. But maybe you want my granddaughter." The door shuts with a forceful certainty that doesn't at all jive with the bloodshot eye and the rickety voice.

I wait.

A moment later, the door opens again, but with the chain still on. This time a pair of clear, brilliant-blue, almond-shaped eyes appear, and I hear a voice I remember. "It's Henry, right?"

"Siobhan?"

"He's not here. I don't know where he is."

"Could I wait for him? He has something of mine."

Siobhan doesn't move. She doesn't blink. She looks straight through me. "You don't know where he is?"

I hold up the slip of paper again. "He told me to come here."

Siobhan stares at the paper, and her glare softens. "Okay." She loosens the chain. "You can come in." Siobhan stands aside as I duck under the miniature elven door frame. Inside, the ceilings are low. I'll have to stick to all fours.

"Get outta the way. I gotta lock up." With a sudden jab, Siobhan shoves me farther inside. She kicks a wooden stool against the door to reach the top.

"Here," I say, "let me do that."

Together—me up top and her below—we seal the tiny apartment away from the musty stairwell of Pine Street.

"So," she says, when we're finished. "Henry—?"

"Whelp."

"Henry Whelp." If she's nervous to have a wolf hogging most of the space in her narrow home, she doesn't show it. She sticks out her hand.

"Siobhan Thymus."

My hairy, grizzled, coal-black paw shakes her long, pale, elven fingers. It's like shoving a dirty baseball mitt on a baby.

"Henry Whelp," she says, "meet Pearl Thymus, my great-grandmother." With the flat of her hand, she points toward a darkened corner of the room. I see the mothball eye that greeted me at the door—a pair of them, in fact—shining out of a scarf and a knitted shawl. A pair of old-style elven slippers, coiled into spirals at the toes, peek out from beneath a paisley dress.

"Jiminy," says the old woman. The mothballs gleam with excitement and she claps her hands. "A wolf!"

"*Gram!*" Siobhan glares across the room. She turns to me. "You'll have to excuse her. She's real old. Wasn't a lot of integrating between the species back in her day."

I pad over and put out a paw. "Pleased to meet you, madam."

She blushes, the varicose veins on her cheeks swelling with blood. Instead of taking my paw to shake, however, she turns it over as if it's a piece of bruised fruit in a market. "Hmm . . ." She pores over my palm, nodding like a fortune-teller. Her spectacles slide comically down the bridge of her nose, and when she looks up at me, her face is full of mock astonishment. "Oh, my! What big teeth you have!" She giggles and kicks her slippered feet.

"*Gram!*"

The old elf claps her tiny hands. "I always wanted to say that!"

Siobhan sighs. "Let's talk in the kitchen." She tugs me across the room, ignoring her grandmother's spastic feet. As I'm pulled away, I glance back at the old lady. She pretends to sour her face and pokes her tongue out. It's hard not to like her.

Siobhan's kitchen consists of one large cupboard, one tiny fridge, and a stove with a single burner. It's a sad-looking room, the bare walls stained with generations of steam and grease. Siobhan fills a tiny teapot with water, sets it on the burner, then turns to face me with a worried look. "So you really don't know where he is?"

"I thought I'd find him here. He has something of mine."

"Well, you know Jack," she says with a touch of bitterness. "He comes and goes."

"How long has he been gone?"

"Three days. It's a long time, even for him." She carefully pours the hot water into three porcelain mugs. "It was so nice having him around. He's really good with Gram. She loves him."

"Almost as much as she loves wolves?"

Siobhan laughs. "Almost."

"Where did you meet him?"

"At school, Rowan High. It was one of the first schools to be truly integrated, at least among the hominids—elves, dwarves, humans. Even a few nixies and maybe a brownnosing glob or two, if you can really call either of them hominids. At Rowan there was never the stigma there used to be, like back when Gram was a girl. We elves live a long time, remember. Jack and I had a few classes together. But he only made it as far as the tenth grade, which you probably already know. That's when he started getting into trouble, stealing stuff. It came out that he'd sort of been a kleptomaniac for a long time. But for whatever reason," she shakes her head, "I stuck with him. Now I've just been accepted to Mid-City U, and he's on the run from the cops. Hell, I even helped him escape." She rolls her eyes. "What a pair."

"Siobhan?" Gram's voice crackles from the next room. "Where's my tea? Don't forget the honey. The liquid kind, please! None of that hard stuff! Rots your teeth!"

Siobhan rolls her eyes again. "They *both* rot your teeth, Gram!"

"Then it's a good thing I don't have any left!" The old elf giggles and Siobhan gives me an exasperated look.

A moment later the three of us are sitting around the front room, candles glowing in every corner and elven incense smoldering on the table. It smells sweetly of summer rain and eucalyptus. The three of us sip from mugs of chamomile and milk. I'm hunched on the floor since there's no chair brave enough to contend with me.

Siobhan looks at me. "I'm sorry, I forgot to ask. You said Jack has something of yours. What is it?"

"A file."

"Oh," she says. "Hold on a minute." She puts down her tea, gets up, and paces into the bedroom. When she comes back, she's got it in her hands. "He left it here. I thought it was just another random thing he stole."

"Well, it wasn't. It was something important. And it belongs to me."

She shakes her head, silently admonishing her boyfriend for his thievery. "He never stops. Not even with his friends." Sighing, she hands me the file.

Between my fingers, the manila feels cool and rough.

"What's inside?" she asks.

"Letters," I tell her. "From my father."

12
DEAR HENRY

SIOBHAN MADE A BED FOR ME OUT OF BLANKETS AND CUSHIONS, HEAPED on the floor in Gram's bedroom. But I told her I was too jittery for sleep, so instead I'm loping around outside with Dad's file rolled up in my pocket. I'm looking for a quiet place to read.

Although it's late, the main strip of Elvenburg courses with vehicles, but every shop is closed. I stalk off through the neighborhood's great green archway, dull and blackened by the night. I end up in the only place that makes sense: under the Willow Street Bridge. Off-color trestles ascend from the ground like thick-waisted giants. At the base of each one there's a lonely lamppost and a slatted bench. I take a seat and flip open the file.

Dear Henry,
You must think I'm a monster. I probably am. I didn't write this letter to tell you I didn't do the things they say I did. Because I did do them. And I didn't write this letter to explain

why. Because I don't know. I just walked into that cottage and I killed that girl and her grandmother. I tore them apart like paper. I'm a monster. All those years and years of evolution, they don't matter. When it comes right down to it, I'm still the same wolf I would've been a zillion years ago. I'm a beast.

But that's me, Henry, not you. You're a decent wolf. You don't have any of that old-time bloodlust in you. They told me about what you did, how you caused that accident. And about where it happened. I think I understand why you did it. Maybe you thought it was a kind of revenge. But I know you're not bad, Henry. Not like me. That's all I wanted to say. You're one of the good ones.

Dad

After he was taken away, I cut off all contact with him. I always thought he did the same with me because he understood I wanted nothing to do with a murderer. Now I find out he was writing to me. Why wouldn't Doc want me to know about this?

Dear Henry,

It's been a while. I understand if you don't want to write back. I understand that. But I can't say I wasn't hoping to hear from you. I was. I want to tell you that I started seeing a shrink. He's a new one. And he's a wolf this time. So I think he understands me.

They tell me he has a good reputation around town. He

must have, because they gave him his own office. He's only here part-time, but every time he visits, I feel better. He and I really get along. He's smart, too. He's an artist. He paints pictures in his office, if you can believe it. Mostly trees and water and things. He says it helps him concentrate.

Sounds familiar: A smart old psychiatrist who visits part-time and paints pictures in his office. Maybe that's why Doc never gave me the letters. Maybe treating father and son simultaneously is some sort of conflict of interest.

Life in here isn't so bad. It has its awful parts, of course, but I guess you don't want to hear about that. For the most part, since I'm a big guy, the others leave me alone. I guess I'm telling you because I don't want you to worry. Or maybe you never do. Maybe you hardly think about me at all.

But I was telling you about the shrink. He's really helped me get a handle on things. I never really talked about what I did, about what happened to me leading up to it, but the more I talk to him, the more I begin to understand. That's why I need to tell you something, Henry. About what happened before—

"You wanna buy some dust?"

Instinctively, I slap the file closed and spin around. It's the fox from the alleyway.

"Old Jerry's got the finest of the fine, pure and certified nixiedust." He's staring at my lap, where I had the file open.

How long was he standing there? I was so absorbed I didn't even smell him. But I do now. He smells awful.

He cocks his head to the side and wrinkles up his face. "Have we met?"

"I told you. I don't want any."

Jerry places his two forepaws on the back of the bench and squeezes. "Then what're you doing here? This is my spot."

"Yours?"

"I remember you," he says, pointing at me. "First you say you don't want anything from Old Jerry, but now here you are. Isn't that funny?" He leans forward. "Come sit on this here bench round midnight and it means you wanna buy from Old Jerry, see?"

"I just wanted somewhere I could—"

"Old Jerry can get you whatever you need."

Whatever I need. I think about that, looking up at pillars of the Willow Street Bridge. When I turn back to Old Jerry I can see the hope of a sale sparkling in his eyes. "Okay," I tell him, "if you can get me anything, then how about this? Bring back *my mother*. Because a long time ago, she was killed right here, right under this bridge. Can your dust do that?"

Jerry shakes his head in a kind of disappointment. "You know," he says, "if every fairy there ever was came back right this second, and if *every one* of them waved their wands, it wouldn't do you a lick of good. That's cuz old-time fairy magic is all about *destiny*, see? Once you's dead, that's it. That's your destiny over and done with. Everybody knows dust can only work on the *livin'*. There ain't no magic, old or new, that can do what you're asking."

"Then I guess you can't help me," I tell him.

Jerry nods. "I guess I can't." But instead of wandering away, the old fox tramps around the bench and eases down beside me. "You're just a pup. You don't remember what it was like with them fairies coming down. Sure, it was nice, but they never tell you the truth about real dust, now do they?"

"What truth?"

"There's the good, which they always talk about, and then there's the bad." He pauses a moment before explaining. "Ever'body figures the old-time stuff is all milk and honey. That's cuz nobody looks in the mirror an' says, 'Gee, I think I was destined for something far *worse* than this.' No sir, they all think, 'I was destined for something *better*.' But some folks—maybe Jerry his old self, and maybe some big bad wolves like you—maybe folks like us were never destined for something like that. Maybe our destinies have always been in that *other* category. You ever consider that?"

I shake my head.

"That's why in nearly every fairy story you hear from the old days, it's always them hominids who got the lion's share. When'ja ever hear about them fairies waving their wands for us, eh? For the animalia."

He's right. In all the fairy stories I've ever heard, it's always the humans on the receiving end. It's never us.

"The way I see it, maybe this new stuff is for the best."

Jerry taps a paw over the pockets of his ratty coat. "What I got in here is what you could call democratic magic. Magic you and me both can partake of, y'see? How about it, pup? How 'bout a little whiff?"

I tuck the file under my arm. "No, thanks."

For the first time, Jerry bares his teeth, but as I rise to my full height, his body relaxes. "Damn," he whistles, swallowed up in my shadow. "You're big for your age."

"Runs in the family," I tell him, and lope off into the shadows. My conversation with Jerry has brought back memories, things I haven't thought about in a long time.

Once, I knew a real fairy. Just after my mother died, she visited Dad to offer him comfort. At the time, I didn't realize how strange that was. It was unheard of for a fairy to visit with a poor wolf out in the slums of Darkforest. And although I may not remember my real mother, I do have a few clear recollections about that fairy. Her name was Faelynn, and she's more real to me than my actual mother.

She always came in without a sound, drifting into my bedroom when she thought I was fast asleep. Once or twice, I padded to the top of the stairs, listening to the voices below me. I could hear them, Faelynn and my father, talking, laughing, clinking their mugs of tea. Faelynn had a voice that crackled like a dying fire. It wasn't what you expected from someone who was all delicate limbs and gossamer glow.

I remember the profile of her face. The insectlike thinness

of her body. I especially remember her rings. She wore all of them on one hand, her left. All five were set with deep blue gems, the color of an empty sky just before dusk. My whole life, that particular shade of blue has been my favorite color.

Just before the fairies left for good, Faelynn began to sing to me. She drifted into my room when she thought I was asleep. Her moonlike glow warmed the walls until it felt almost like dawn. When she sang, the roughness of her voice vanished. She sang beautifully, and always the same comforting lullaby.

Sleep, little cub,
and quiet your eyes.
Bottle your tears,
and soften your cries.

Dream, little soldier.
I'll never be far.
I'll find you, my soldier,
wherever you are.

13
THE NTH DEGREE

I LOPE SOUTH, ALL THE WAY DOWN TO DOCKSIDE. PERIPHERY STREET, THE road that rims the city's outer wall, is smooth and silent. I'm looking for a quiet place where I can sit—without being accosted by dust-dealers.

Deeper into the neighborhood, there's more life. It isn't long before a shipping truck comes rolling past. The trademarked Nimbus halo sparkles in the moonlight. The air down here is laden with brine and the chemical stench of refineries. When I get to the far side of the street, however, I pick up something else. It's a mixed-up scent like many things at once. Sunlight and filth; burning hair and melted rubber; still water and old bones. None of it makes sense, and yet it still cuts through all the rest. I've never smelled anything like it, and stranger still . . . *it's moving.*

The scent is coming from down inside a sewer grate. A shadow slithers past. It's *huge.* Could it be a giant? It seems unlikely. Not even a giant as clueless as Fiona's gravedigger would squeeze himself into a sewer. Besides, this isn't the scent of a giant. I prick up my ears to see if I can tune in its shape. What comes back is just as mixed-up as the scent. The hair all over my body rises to stand on end. Whatever's lurking below the street, I don't want to stick around and find out what it is.

I back away from the grate. I've suddenly got a rather strong urge to get out of the shadows, to retreat indoors. Farther down the street, I spot an all-night diner. I lope toward it, grateful for its bright windows. With almost every step, I cast a glance over my shoulder. But there's nothing there.

When I push into the diner, I'm greeted by a sour-faced dwarvish woman. She's boosted up on a rolling stepladder behind the counter, pouring coffee for a nixie. Without even looking up, the woman calls out. "We don't serve runners in here."

I step forward, letting the door shut behind me.

"Didn't you hear me, sugar? *No runners.*"

"I'm not. I'm just a wolf."

"There's a difference?"

"I just need a glass of water."

She points to a sign behind the counter. *Hominids Only.* "There's a tavern up the way, The Fox and Hound. Probably more your speed."

"I just passed it. It's closed."

"Then you're out of luck, I guess."

The nixie in the trench coat ogles me with rheumy eyes. Something dark and gooey leaks from his gills.

"You won't serve me, but you'll serve *him?*"

The nixie belches. "Watcha mowth, boy. I's connected. I's friensh in high playshes. I know *Pa Nixie* hisssself." He fumbles with his coffee cup. The scalding liquid spills over his webbed fingers. "Ow!"

"See?" says the woman. "You're upsetting my customers."

It's not me who's upsetting him, that much is clear. The guy's potbelly is busting through his clothes and the skin's stretched so taut you can see his innards. Something with writhing tentacles slaps about inside, so he swallows another gulp of coffee. The thing in his belly flounders and squeals, and the nixie lets out another belch, this one even juicier than the last. *Well,* I think, *that's certainly one way to settle your stomach.*

"Listen," I say to the woman, "all I'm looking for is a quiet place I can be for a while. I won't cause any trouble."

The woman peers out through the window. She shuts her eyes, tightens her lips, and takes a deep breath through her nose. "Fine," she says at last. "What do I care? I just work here, yeah? It's the *boss's* sign, not mine."

"Thanks." I come all the way in and find a booth at the back. The nixie watches me keenly then stares daggers at the dwarf behind the counter. A moment later, the woman brings me a hot cup of coffee and a glass of water. "On the house," she says, "provided you're outta here quick."

"Thanks."

Down the bar, the nixie sneers at me. It's rare to find one of them out in public. Water nixies: half-man, half-sea serpent, evolved from bottom-feeding angler fish. In the old days, they used their magic to make themselves beautiful, sleek hominids of the sea. But ever since they came ashore to corner the illicit dust trade, they don't bother with the facade. These days, it's nothing but sputtering gills, scaly rolls of blubber, and amphibious eyes like a pair of bursting plums. But I'm not here to admire the wildlife.

I flip open the file and pick up where I left off.

That's why I need to tell you something, Henry. About what happened before I was arrested. As I'm sure you know from the trial, I was never a carpenter. That was a story I made up because you were too young for me to explain what it was I really did. How could I tell you I worked for Skinner, number one bagman for the nixies?

Now, I don't want to make excuses for what I did. I mean, I'm guilty, just like I ended up pleading in court. But listen, I was only supposed to shake down that old woman, get her to sign over her land. That's all.

It was Skinner who drove me to the property. Just before he let me out, he slipped me a hit of fairydust. It was a special blend, he told me. He said it would calm my nerves. Since I was pretty nervous, I took it. I'd never roughed up an old lady out in the middle of nowhere before. So I took it. And it did something to me. I was an animal again. Like a real animal, like a prehistoric wild thing. Next thing I knew I was tearing that poor girl and her grandmother apart.

I'm not saying I'm innocent. I'm just saying I was under the influence of something that day. Something evil. That doesn't make it right, of course it doesn't, but I thought that maybe if you knew, you might see fit to come visit me sometime. We could talk about it. I miss you, son.

Dad

Dear Henry,

I suppose you're not coming, are you? I understand that. I wanted to tell you face-to-face what I'm going to tell you in this letter, but it doesn't seem I'll get the chance. It has to do with what I told you in the last one. And a bunch of ideas I've had along with that shrink I've been seeing, the one I told you about. I better just come out and say it:

The fairies are still here.

They never left us, son. They didn't abandon us like everyone says. That's all wrong. We figured it out, me and the Doc. It's the only explanation that makes sense. There's no dust around that can turn a regular guy like me into a coldhearted, bloodthirsty killer. That's old-time magic. It could look inside you and bring out the best or, like in my case, the very worst. That kind of magic only comes from fairies, right? That's why I need you, son. I'm in here and I'm not getting out anytime soon. And who's ever going to believe a murderous convict like

me? But you, son, you'll be out of St. Remus soon. Then you can help me. You can find them. Because I think I know where they are.
Dad

Dear Henry,
Why don't you come see me? I really miss you, son. If you don't believe anything I've said, that's fine. If you think I'm a crazy old dog, I understand. Forget all that other stuff, and just come for a visit. I'd love to see you. Just once.
Dad

That's the end of them. Four letters in total, undated and written with penmanship that's shakier and shakier with every paragraph. When I look up, I see I'm the only one left. I've been so absorbed in reading, I didn't even notice when the nixie seeped off into the night.

"Sorry, sugar," says the woman behind the counter. "You've been here long enough."

Outside, I find I'm tired and full of questions, but I need to sleep. I need to be sharp in the morning because tomorrow, for the first time in many years, I'm going to see my father.

14
THE EDGE OF A WOOD

THE DREAM IS THE SAME EVERY TIME. THE DETAILS SHIFT FROM NIGHT TO night—the depth of the darkness, the distance from the road to the cottage, the way the wind blows—but everything that matters is the same. I'm always some amalgam of my father and me.

It starts on the edge of a wood, late at night. The trees loom over me. The sky is fevered with fast clouds and the moon hangs like a phantom. I drop to all fours, padding deeper and deeper into the trees. Every one I pass comes alive, electrified with wind. Soon all I can hear is an endless swish of leaves. I still keep going, stalking forward, my belly skimming over the peat.

There's light up ahead, black leaves against a warm glow. Beams of firelight shine out through circles of thick glass. It's a cottage in a clearing. And there's an unlocked door.

Inside, I see a little girl. She's curled on a rug, covered up and warm inside a bloodred cloak. I push in on all fours. The door drags against my flanks. I urge the girl to sleep, hoping she'll remain dead to the world. But each time she wakes up.

Her eyes pop open. She's a thinker, this girl, I can smell it. Before I even see her move, the poker's in her hand, the tip glowing as deep red as her cloak.

She jabs me with the poker, but I don't feel it. The heat against my hide is nothing. I even watch as she tries to beat me, as my clothes and hair are singed and smoldering, as the hook of the poker sinks into my ribs and tears away the hide. I just stand there, letting her do it.

Then, suddenly, I'm exploding with rage. I rise up to the ceiling in this tiny cottage and smother the girl with my weight. I sink my teeth into her throat. She's dead with a single snap. Then, from somewhere behind me I hear the click of loose nails. The creak of old wood.

Someone else is here. It's the girl's grandmother. She's a spare figure, crooked as a winter willow. She also wears a cloak, but hers is black. The hood is pulled over her head so that her face is in shadow. The girl's blood is all over me and I rise again, leaving the throatless body by the fire.

The old woman is silent, standing motionless at the base of the stairs like a heap of rags thrown over a broom. There's hardly anything to her, and I can't even see her face. The rage fills me again and I lunge.

The old woman doesn't flinch. She lets herself be broken inside my jaws—and at first, it's easy. Her body's hollow, just skin and bone. But mostly bone, bones held together with papery flesh and threads of sinew.

Frail as she is, though, I can never finish her. I gnash

at her bones inside the cloak, extracting mouthful after mouthful from the rags, but there's always more. Sometimes her face emerges briefly from the hood. Sometimes I catch a glimpse of a wicked grin.

That's when I realize—too late—that I'll *never* finish her. The bones are growing faster than I can swallow them. The clicks and creaks aren't coming from the stairs or the loose floorboard, but from the woman herself. Every joint has a flinty mind of its own. The old woman blossoms again and again, renewing herself with my every bite.

Sometimes, that's when I wake up. On those nights, I stand half a chance of getting back to sleep.

But there are other times, too, when the dream keeps going, nights when a pain starts in my belly.

It's the bones. I can feel them, still moving inside me. Spidery shards that crawl together to weave and knit themselves into hands and teeth—and they're anxious to escape.

The first ones come out through my stomach. Then one will burst out from between my ribs. Others come through the chinks of my spine.

Soon, I'm on the floor, howling. That's when they really start tearing me apart. They snake up and crackle into my lungs. They puncture my heart, my throat, my face. And if I'm not awake at that point, I can always count on the two great horns that punch out through my eye sockets to do the trick.

15
GEORGE WILLIAM WHELP

THE EAST CITY PENITENTIARY IS A SQUAT COLOSSUS, EMERGING THICK AND crude from the borough of Darkforest. It's built on the crest of Sea Way Hill. From up here there's a good view of the city. Smog grips every building like a fist, while on the opposite side the deadwood forest spreads out over the tundra. The prison reminds me of St. Remus: the high walls, the mechanical gates, the sandstone bastions. The place even comes with poker-faced guards, every one of them a glob.

The ones controlling the gates eye me suspiciously. I have the blazer of my St. Remus uniform turned inside out. It may look like I don't know how to dress myself, but at least they can't tell just from a glance that I'm a juvie on the lam.

"Can we help you?" one of them asks.

"I'm here to visit somebody."

The guard has a face like porridge filled with rotten fruit. He shifts a pair of watery eyes to the clock. "You've got less than half an hour, y'know."

"It won't take long."

He pushes a sign-in book at me. A cool breeze whips up the hill and the pages riffle. I dash down the first made-up name that comes to mind. *Harry Wells*. The guard, meanwhile, doesn't pay attention. He picks up an old black telephone. "Who're you here to see?"

"George William Whelp."

I'm sitting alone at the center carrel in a bare room. A couple feet in front of my face is a glass wall with holes drilled through it in a pattern that resembles a flower. On the far side of the glass there's another room, bare as this one. A buzzer sounds. There's the squawk of an electric lock and the steel door on the far side creaks open.

When my father enters, he's draped in chains. There's a guard on either side of him. Dad sees me and stops. His head hovers, looking too heavy for his neck. He peers at the first guard, as if that bullish face can explain what he's seeing. Me. He looks backward, too, back out the door, but the other guard prods him forward. He hobbles to the glass.

He's nothing like I remember. I really have to search to see him. He's an unfocused image of himself, a faded photograph. They push him into a metal chair and lock him down by the chain around his waist. He's so thin. The hair on his face is molting away in patches. Underneath, his skin is pale and blemished. Several of his teeth are missing.

"You got less than ten minutes," says a loudspeaker.

I put one paw to the glass. "Hi, Dad."

He barely moves. His lips tighten and his jaw opens and closes.

"I came to see you," I tell him. I can hear the clock's second hand, going *sip-sip-sip*, swallowing our time. "I got your letters."

Dad turns and scrutinizes me out of one side of his face. There's a bald patch on his throat. There's a bruise, too. It snakes down from what hair he has left and slithers, mottled and blue, into the neck of his shirt.

"They let me go," I lie to him. "I'm free now. I can come anytime I want."

"Henry," he says. His lips tremble. "You're just in time."

"What?"

"I heard about what they did to Doc."

"He killed himself."

He shakes his head, pulling himself forward. "They made him do it!"

"Who?"

"Same as they made me do it. The nixies."

He's not listening to me. He's wrapped up in his own world. All I want to do is talk to him. "How are you doing, Dad? Are you okay?"

He ignores me. "I knew they'd let you go," he says. "And now you can find them."

"Find who?"

His eyes sparkle. "You *will* find them."

I look at him, trying to gauge how insane he is. "You mean the fairies."

"They're still here, you know."

My dad's face is in the midst of a slow collapse; his mouth is devoid of molars, and his eyes are sinking into his cheeks. "Dad? The fairies are gone. You know that, right?"

He shakes his head vigorously. "Not true," he says. "The nixies have them."

"How do you know that?"

"Why do you think their stuff is so potent? The only ones who could produce a dust like that would be them—the fairies." He's speaking so plainly I almost believe him. "That's how they were able to get me to do it, to send me down the wrong path. Only *real fairydust* could've done that. It could only come from them. Which means—"

"Nixiedust is fairydust."

Dad nods excitedly. "Means they're still here! And *you* can bring them back!"

I almost laugh. "Me?" I point at the guards over by the exit. "Why not the police?"

Dad scoffs. "They're on the payroll. The nixies bribe them. Can't trust them. But if you could get close to Skinner, you could find something. Some proof."

"You want me to be a runner? Like you were?"

"I've got a friend in there, Mattius. We used to run together. I hear he's still there, though I'd be surprised if he's still running. He'll look out for you."

"But—"

"Skinner holds tryouts about once a week. The next ones

97

are tomorrow night." Dad rattles off a whirl of details: a tavern in Dockside called the Woodsman; a secret entrance to an underground warehouse; a midnight race pitting wolf against wolf to find the fastest. "You're fast, son, I know you are. It could be you."

"You realize this is insane."

He ignores this rather astute observation and presses on with his fantasy. "Now, whatever you do, if Skinner offers you dust, don't take it. You understand me?"

"Not really."

"Then listen!" His eyes bulge in their pits. "Skinner's dust can make you do things—*awful* things. But here's what I learned—in the hardest way possible: If he doses you up, there'll be a moment, see? This one moment when you're about to do something awful. That awful thing will fill you up and there'll be a short circuit inside you." He taps his skull with a claw. "For that one moment you'll be in control. I didn't see it coming, so I couldn't do anything, but if you know it's there, you can use it. You understand what I'm saying?"

"Barely."

"Good," he says. "There's a place in Skinner's refinery where all the conveyors of dust come from. No one's allowed in there. I think that's where they've got them."

"I don't know," I say, shaking my head, examining my paws. What I really mean is: *Dad, you are a total crackpot.* Good thing he's too wrapped up in his mad reverie to read between the lines. "Look, Dad, can we just talk? I haven't seen you in—"

"We *are* talking. What else is there to talk about except this?"

I sigh. "Okay, even if any of what you're saying is true, then what?" I move my eyes in a wide circle over the grim room with its guards and its dingy tiles. "Would it mean they'd let you go? Would finding the fairies do anything to help you?"

"Maybe there's someone else it could help."

"What do you mean?"

Dad leans forward until his lips are nearly pressed to the blossom of drilled holes between us. "What if they could bring her back?"

He doesn't have to tell me who he's talking about. "That's impossible," I tell him. "Nobody can do that. Not even them."

On the counter in front of him, Dad lays his forepaws, staring down at the vacant space between them. "You're probably too young to remember this, but after Mom died, there was a fairy who came to see me. I met her in a park one night, on my way home from a dust run. She heard me whimpering to myself about Mom and she wanted to comfort me."

"Faelynn."

He looks surprised that I know her name. "You remember her?"

"A little. Not much more than her scent. The smell of old trees. I remember her rings, too. A whole handful of blue ones."

Dad smiles. "I used to tease her about those. 'How do you fly around with all that hardware?'" He taps the counter with a claw. "We became friends, she and I. It was an odd match—a wolf and a fairy—but somehow we got along. It was so nice to have someone to talk to after Emily was gone." He's calm now, almost solemn. "One night we'd been drinking. We were talking about your mother, and she said something. She said, 'Sometimes I wish we were allowed to bring them back.' And I thought, *'Allowed?'* So I asked her flat-out, and she said it was possible, there was a way, but it was forbidden. It's the first prohibition on the old-time magic. You can't bring them back."

"So there you have it. It can't be done."

But Dad shakes his head, the feral craziness taking over again. "But it *can* be done—all they would have to do is break the rules, just once, and I think they would, too. I know they would—I know *Faelynn* would." He tugs against his chains. *"If* we found them."

The loudspeaker squawks to life. *"Time's up, Whelp."*

The guards step forward and begin to unfasten him. "Midnight tomorrow," he says. "The Woodsman. You can find out what happened. You can find them. Promise me you'll find some proof."

I don't say anything.

"Please, son, promise me." His mouth tightens around his rotten teeth. "They've got Faelynn. She can help us. She can help us both."

Faelynn. All I've got of her are a few smudged memories. A bit of glitter and a song. It's so much more than what I've got of my mother, a wolf I never knew. Could anything my father just told me be true? I can't believe it. But what if he's telling the truth and I don't do anything? Is it really possible I'd be giving up a chance to see my mother again? To change my fate—and hers?

As they're hauling Dad out of the chair, chains clinking, he says, "Not only for me, son, for Faelynn. And for your mother."

What can I say to that? What if he's right?

"Okay," I say. "I'll do it."

16
THE FASTER BEAST

OUTSIDE THE GATES, A DRY HAZE LIES OVER EVERYTHING. I LOPE DOWN THE incline, sinking step by step into the smog. Tomorrow night I'm going to the Woodsman tavern in Dockside.

Behind me, I hear the prison gates clank open for a vehicle. I prick up my ears, tuning in the tires, squishing quietly over the asphalt. I wait for them to accelerate away, but they don't. So I pause—and the car slows, slithering up behind me. I keep going and the car does the very same.

I'm being followed.

Suddenly, a stripe of red light sweeps over the ground. It spins clockwise, the silent, revolving light of an unmarked police cruiser. I hear the whir of an electric window.

"Harry Wells?" It's a woman's voice. Sharp and precise. A stab wound. "Here's a tip. When you pick an alias, choose one that doesn't have the same initials as your real name."

Detective White.

Her car is a sleek but well-used coupe, scarred all over with dents and scratches. One of the headlights has been gouged out. "Folks at St. Remus are anxious to have you back," she informs me through the open window.

I keep on loping.

"Give it up, Henry. You're caught."

I keep going.

"We discovered some, uh—*irregularities* in the office of your pal. The good Doctor Grey."

That makes me slow down. But I don't stop.

"So it's not just the St. Remus folks who want you back. I do, too. I've got some questions for you about Doctor Grey's *alleged* suicide."

The nearest building is a carpet factory at the bottom of the hill. There's an empty parking lot beside it. I could bolt, but there's nowhere to hide. White's little coupe might be dented, but it'd still be a cinch for her to run me down and leave the questions for when I come out of the coma. She might even start shooting. She's hardly known for subtlety.

"Get in," she says. It almost sounds like a friendly invitation. She pops open the passenger-side door. "I don't have time to chase you around."

"If you're busy," I tell her, "you could just forget you saw me."

"I've never once turned a blind eye." The diamond-cutter hardness has returned to her voice. "I won't start today."

The east end of First Avenue is maybe fifty meters off, straight down. The train line runs along First and then over the Sea Way Bridge. If I could get up there, her car wouldn't

ROBERT PAUL WESTON

be able to follow me onto the tracks. On all fours, if I had a diversion, I might make it.

I prick up my ears, tuning in the rumble of a train. It's well out of earshot. Her hominid ears won't hear it. Not yet, at least.

"I saw my dad up there," I tell her.

White doesn't take her eyes off me. "Family's important."

"You're the one who arrested him."

"And now I'm arresting you. Like father like son." She sighs. "Just get in, Henry, I don't have time for this."

"What was it like?"

"Huh?"

"When you found him. Tell me what it was like, and then I'll get in."

"How 'bout I tell you on the way?"

"I want to know now."

"I've taken down guys a helluva lot bigger than you, and I don't bargain with anyone." She shakes her head. "Don't test me."

"I'm not bargaining. I'm just asking you for a favor."

The corners of White's lips flicker. "Fine, but it's only cuz I can tell you're not anything like your pop. It's nice to see, actually. You're a good cub."

"That's what everyone tells me."

The train's coming into view, a freight train, headed up from Dockside.

"It was awful," she says, "if you want to know the truth.

What he did to them. An old lady and a little girl." She glances back at the prison. "Why would he do that?"

"He doesn't know why."

White scoffs. "They never do."

At the bottom of the hill, the train's engine is already on the bridge, slowing to a cautious speed.

"Guess we'll never know what really happened." White hangs her head. "I hate that." Her cherry-red lips part slightly, blowing out a breath. Dad is a mystery she can't solve. It's as much of a diversion as I'm ever going to get.

I leap forward. One step and I'm down on all fours, lashing my limbs into a gallop. White doesn't yell after me through the window. There's no *Hey, stop!* or *Get back here!* or *Why you little!* She merely growls. Then the engine makes a snarl of its own and the chase is on.

I've got the edge when it comes to acceleration. White has to fight up through the lower gears, wrenching howl after howl from the car. I hoof it as fast as I can, haunches straining against the fabric of my inside-out uniform. I can hear the threads popping, the seam along my spine beginning to split.

White's made it up to fourth gear, which makes her coupe the faster beast. Given enough of a straightaway, she would catch me now for sure. There's only a short distance left to the tracks, though. I still might make it.

But the freight train's shorter than I anticipated. The final car is nearly here. It's an old one, rattling and rickety. The slogan on the side—*Nimbus Thaumaturgical ~ Better Living*

Through Enchantment—is barely there, faded and carved up with fractals of rust. The engine has cleared the bridge now. The whole train's picking up speed. This is my one chance at escape.

But White's got me.

She pulls up beside my thrashing limbs and eases off, grinning through the open window, wagging a finger. Her dark eyes sparkle with the thrill of the hunt. She turns her head to face the road and floors it, surging ahead to a spot just short of the tracks. Her rear wheels skid out and bring the car parallel to the train, blocking my way. In the same instant, she draws her weapon. The barrel's perfectly framed in the window.

"Enough." She says it quietly. "Now get in."

But I don't let up. All I can do is hope she meant it when she said I'm a good cub. Maybe that's enough to keep her from shooting as I use her coupe as the perfect stepping-stone. Her mouth goes slack as she watches me leap onto her roof (adding a dent to its collection) and heave off as hard as I can—just as the last car comes clattering past.

There's a freakish, empty moment as I soar up and up and up. Rusty struts crisscross over the side of the train car and loom closer and closer—plenty to grab hold of. Unfortunately, I ram the wall with such force that the whole thing collapses inward. The word *Enchantment*—barely there to begin with—splinters and tumbles into the shadows of the train car, carrying me along for the ride.

I land on something soft. A great heap of blue fairydust—mined, refined, and on its way to pharmacies all across the city. Only now it's got an added ingredient: a big bad wolf. I climb up on the sheet of metal and peek out through the ragged me-shaped hole.

Petang!

A bullet cracks off the train. Detective White has started shooting after all. I duck back and then, stupidly, peek out once more. But she doesn't fire this time. She stands below, getting smaller as the train rumbles north.

"I know you can hear this," she says, speaking only slightly louder than normal, "so I just want to tell you: That was *very stupid.*" She holsters her gun and climbs back into her car, peeling away in the opposite direction.

I lower myself to sit on the sheet of rust I've torn out of the wall. All around, a sea of fairydust shimmers and undulates as if it's the real ocean, rising and falling like waves. Tides of it seethe around me, drawing in and flowing out. It's as if it's examining me, ruminating. Like it's a living thing.

17
THE PRECISION OF BLOOD SPATTER

AFTER SPENDING ANOTHER NIGHT AND ANOTHER DAY AT SIOBHAN'S HOUSE waiting for Jack, I made my way down to Dockside in the late evening. I've been loitering down here since then, loping along the reservoir, watching the tankers wade past one another, docking, laying anchor, having their innards loaded and unloaded by methodical derricks.

My shoulder's been throbbing all day long. I injured it when I crashed through the wall of that rusty train car. Gram stitched up my uniform in all the places it was torn, but there are still bloodstains streaking down my arm. It's less than an hour to midnight. I've got my back against the reservoir railing, staring at a neon sign that flickers on and off: THE WOODSMAN. I amble across the street.

It's a consummate dive, sunken one story below the street with a set of concrete steps so murderously steep it may as well be a cliff. There's a door at the bottom, thickened with hastily applied black paint and propped open with a rock. It suddenly occurs to me that I'm probably not old enough to be here. But since nobody's manning the entrance, I walk right in.

The air inside is beery and humid. The room is populated with a handful of the usual suspects: globs, wolves, foxes, dwarves, and ravens, with a few seedy-looking humans tossed in for variety. In one corner, a band of mangy cats plays melancholy jazz.

My eyes search for a trapdoor, a secret tunnel, anything to indicate this place is a portal to an illegal hideaway. But it's just a sad-looking room full of sad-looking folks. It's an early indication that my father's fairy fantasies are nothing but bunk.

The bartender is a thin goblin (a rare trait). Nobody's ordering anything, so he's standing there in classic barkeep style: legs akimbo, while polishing a glass. I step up to the bar with false confidence. "I'm here for the, uh . . ." I arch my brow suggestively. "You know."

"No," he says. "I don't." Surely he can see I'm underage. Then again, maybe I'm big enough to pass. "My guess," he says, "is that you're here for a drink."

"Uh, sure."

He stares at me, waiting.

"A beer," I tell him.

The bartender smiles. His tusks are polished and sharp. "Good boy," he says and a moment later a smudged mug appears, overflowing with foam. I place a five-dollar bill on the lacquered wood, where it soaks up a spill. "Thanks."

The bartender scoops it up and doesn't bother with the change. He goes off to the farthest point of the bar and folds his arms, watching me. For a while I sit there, passing the beer between my forepaws and wondering what to do next. None of the other wolves look like runners. They're mostly old and lame. Eventually, it is ten minutes to midnight, and there's no point in waiting anymore. I wave the bartender over.

He eyes my untouched pint. "How 'bout you start drinking that one before I get you another?"

"I don't want any more." I lower my voice and lean over the bar. "I'm here to see Skinner." If the name means anything to him, his expression doesn't show it. He blinks at me, slowly—just like a cat. "I'm here to try out," I tell him. "I'm here to race."

He shrugs. Again, it's a practiced, deliberate move. "I wouldn't know anything about that."

I wonder if this is some sort of a test. If so, I've already failed. The condensation on the glass is clamming up the pads of my paws (or maybe it's just me). "I heard if I came here tonight, I could get a job."

"Did you now?" The bartender places his hands on the bar. His forearms are veined and ropy.

"I want to be a dust runner, y'know? For the nixies." I sound like an idiot. An ill-informed one.

"Good for you, but I think I already explained myself amply on this point. I have no idea what you're talking about."

He slides down the bar to serve somebody else—a fox—and I see it's the same one who tried to sell me dust in the Pine Street alley. Old Jerry. He smiles, showing off his incisors. He raises his glass and it looks like he's about to say something, when his face goes sour. He sees someone behind me. In the same moment, a huge white paw comes around to pick up my untouched glass of beer.

"If *you're* not gonna drink it . . ."

It's Roy Sarlat. I turn around and there he is—larger than life, as always. I can sense everyone in the room staring at us.

He downs the beer with authority, his throat undulating with the mere two swallows it takes him to drain it. He slams the empty glass down. "I needed that," he says, slapping a heavy hand on my shoulder. "Never thought I'd see you in a place like this, Hank-man. Not in a million years." He looks absurd in a baggy shirt printed all over with palm trees and sunsets.

"How did you—?"

He opens his mouth wide and laughs loudly, drowning out the sound of everything else, even the mangy music. Then he snaps his jaws into a smile, jamming together his jigsaw teeth. "Whaddaya mean? I've escaped from that place *a bunch* of times. Man, it's easy. You think you're the only one? They couldn't care less either way. Nobody cares what happens to us. We're *wolves*, you and me. Don't you get it?"

Maybe I do.

"Couldn't help overhearing," he continues. "But it sounds

to me like Hank-man wants to try out, huh?" His booming voice overwhelms the room. "'Course with me here, there's really no point. *I'm* gettin' the job tonight. Not you. Just so you know. But since I'm such a nice guy, and you're obviously a glutton for punishment, allow me to show you how to get in."

He leads me toward the band, while the bartender watches with disdain. When the cats see us coming—a pair of huge wolves—the hair on their tails raises, but only slightly. Some of the old instincts kick in for me, too. A ball of tenseness rolls through my gut.

Roy waves. "Hey, fellahs! How 'bout some bebop?" He cocks his head at the bare wall behind them. "We want in."

The trumpet player moves his foot to a button on the stage floor. When he taps it with his toe, a narrow panel in the wall slides open, and not terribly smoothly either. It's an old mechanism. Nobody in the bar appears to care.

Roy booms with false gratitude. "Thanks, fellahs!" He grabs me by the arm and pulls me through the opening, which judders closed once we're inside. It's a long, barely lit tunnel that descends harshly; we're forced to walk heavy on our toes. And it's a long walk.

At the end there's a door that's polished and gleaming and nothing like the interior of the Woodsman. That's because it's completely made of gold. Roy pounds on it and waits. It occurs to me that this is my last chance to turn back. Do I really want to find out who Skinner is? Even if I find a whole flock of fairies on the other side of this doorway, what can I possibly do to help them?

The door clicks.

It's not a dwarf on the opposite side, and it's not a fairy either. It's another cat. He's dressed in a tuxedo that's as sleek as he is. His hair is glossed back from his face in a dapper calico mane. His evening wear is accented with absurd boots, riding up past his knees and flaring out like a pair of upturned trumpets. "I imagine," he purrs, "that you're here to . . . *try out*." Even his voice is slicked down, oily and smooth.

Roy sneers. "'Course we are." He starts to push his way inside, but the cat doesn't move.

"I don't recognize that one." He's talking about me.

Roy laughs. "He's harmless. I can vouch for that."

"What's your name?"

"Henry."

The cat blinks. "And your last name?"

"Whelp."

"Hold on a moment." He shoos us backward and shuts the door. Roy looks at me and shrugs. "That's never happened before."

We wait.

A moment later the door opens again and the cat steps aside. "Welcome," he says.

The building inside is huge. Shafts of incandescent light cut down from hanging fixtures, slicing up the dusty air. It's a huge warehouse of some kind. The ceiling seems like it's miles away, crisscrossed with girders and chains. Foundry basins dangle from them, swaying gently in the drafts. The vast floor is punctuated by ancient refinery equipment, languishing in rusty silence. There're a few wrought-iron staircases too, whirling up to nowhere. It's *huge* in here—it must take up half of Dockside. I can't even see the far end. It's lost in a fog of darkness.

Not far from the entrance is a makeshift throne, a chair soldered together from nuts and bolts, hammers and wrenches, cogs and gears, and a million other bits of junk. Like the door that's just been sealed behind me, the whole thing has been cast in solid gold. All around the base are wolves, ten or fifteen of them, sauntering back and forth, or merely curled up in the shadows of old machines.

Roy nudges me, pointing up at the dwarf who's perched in the golden throne. "That's Skinner," he whispers.

He's larger than I expected. He's a dwarf, sure, and is likely no more than four and a half feet tall, but he's sturdily built. His body presses firmly against the fabric of his clothes, which are impeccable. He wears a three-piece gabardine suit, with gleaming white gloves on both hands and a collar buttoned tightly up to his chin. In fact, it's so tight the skin of his neck bulges over the fabric. Everything about his dress is taut and tiny and perfectly precise. But it's neither his size nor the fastidiousness of his dress that strikes you. What strikes you most is his face.

Skinner's face is a catastrophe.

Down the center is a scar—a shiny, pink river as broad as his mouth, dividing his whole head into two crooked halves. Whatever happened to him must have healed with all the precision of blood spatter. This guy is hideously, *sensationally* deformed. His nose is a rutted, cauliflower-like bloom, his blazing green eyes are entirely misaligned, and his lips are two lumpy piles of mash. Between them, he's chewing on a long stalk of straw.

"Whelp?" he asks. His voice cuts into you, deep and harsh. He plucks the straw from his mouth, confused. "You're not who I expected."

"Maybe you were thinking of my father. He used to work for you."

A cloud passes over his warped face. "Hard to forget." He frowns and his lips tighten into pink puree. "I do hope you're a little more reliable."

Roy throws his arm over my shoulders. "I can vouch for him. We're friends. We go *waaaay* back."

Skinner frowns. "I wasn't talking to you, was I, Mr. Sarlat?"

Roy's tail dips an inch or two. If I didn't know better, I'd say he was frightened, or at least ashamed.

"Well, now," says Skinner, rubbing his gloved hands together. "Why don't we get down to business?" He looks up to the gloom that fills the ceiling. *"Shall we?"*

A great roar of whistles and applause fills the room.

The ceiling is suddenly illuminated. On platforms ringing the ceiling, there are scaffolds covered with bleachers, deep ziggurats laden with countless wooden tubs. Inside every one of them, sloshing in the depths of every barrel, are water nixies. The whole of the Dockside mob must be up there.

"Skinner!" one of them hisses. He splashes steamy salt water down on us. "Start the race! We wanna see some action!" As he says it, the cheering rises, feverish and hot.

But Skinner's not easily fazed, not even by a raft of nixies. "In due time," he says. The lights dim along the scaffolding and the nixies once again fade into darkness. "But first—" He looks at me. "Some of us are new and may be unaccustomed to the way things proceed. The rules are simple: one lap around the warehouse." He points to the floor. "First wolf back here wins."

Some of the other wolves nod, but the majority are merely bored. "Oh," continues Skinner, "and what exactly do you win? The best prize of all, of course. A *place*. A place in my pack." He points to the sloppy, bloodred lines painted on the floor. "And please, I implore you. No cheating. My—*ahem*— 'men' are here to ensure that all of you follow the markers. Aren't you, my boys?" Goblins step out of the shadows. Each one is as big as—if not bigger than—Gunther. They've been lurking in alcoves all along. "You see?" says Skinner, grinning madly. "*Do* try to avoid cutting corners."

Compared to a room full of globs, wolves, and nixies, Skinner looks about as harmless as a child. He's more like a perverted amoeba than an actual dwarf. Why do all these goblins slavishly obey someone like that?

"Oh," says Skinner, "and one more thing: I'm feeling generous today, so I'll tell you what . . ." He tugs at the glove on his right hand, pulling it off finger by finger. With the freshly exposed digits, he takes the straw out of his mouth and holds it up. It's a dirty yellow color, chewed-up on one end and damp with spit.

And then something strange happens.

Skinner pinches the stalk of straw between his bare thumb and forefinger and suddenly there's a cool gust of air stirring through the room. Even from up above, the spatters of the nixies fall dead silent. It's all because of the stalk of straw.

It's been turned to gold.

I put a paw to my pocket. I've got something just like it—and it's enough to convince me: Skinner was there. He was at St. Remus before Doc killed himself. Or worse: Skinner's the one who strung him up.

Skinner tosses the alchemized stick up in the air and catches it with his other hand, the one still sheathed in a glove. "To the winner," he says. Beside me, Roy whistles under his breath and suddenly, I realize something. This is what Siobhan meant when she told me Skinner was untouchable. Not that he's merely powerful and aloof—and surely he is—but it's also that he's exactly that: *untouchable.* He's got some of the old-time magic inside him. Make contact with his skin and that's it, you're done for, turned to gold. No wonder the globs are so well behaved.

"Now then," says Skinner. "There's one last thing we need to take care of before we begin." He smiles at us, which is almost too hideous to look at. Nevertheless, not a single one of us turns away.

"It's time," he says, "to take your medicine."

18
READY TO BURN

BEYOND THE THRONE, THERE'S A TABLE COVERED WITH UPTURNED HUBCAPS.
They're arranged like soup bowls at a fancy dinner. In the pit
of each one is a glistening pile of powder, twinkling in the
shafts of lamplight.

Dust.

This isn't the low-potency, slow-burning medicinal stuff
you get from the likes of Nimbus Thaumaturgical. This
stuff is so bright it looks lit from within, like each little
heap has a whole power station to itself. It's been refined
and concentrated far beyond the legal limit. This is the hard
stuff. This is what foxes in alleyways will try to sell you from
the insides of their ratty coats. This is nixiedust.

Skinner directs us from his throne. "If you want to be a
dust runner, you have to be fast. But fast isn't enough. You've
also got to have—what's the word? *Grit.* Which is the reason
why each of you is going to take a hit of my very own special
blend. It's as close to the old times as you youngsters are ever
gonna get. It's meant to turn your inner self into your outer

self." His mouth spreads into a tortured grin. "Bring out the true 'you,' in a manner of speaking. Which ought to keep things interesting."

A spray of spineless laughter comes from up above. I realize now—too late, of course—that I'm in way over my head. But a glance over at Roy tells me he's feeling none of my apprehension. He's eyeing the dust on the table with unabashed relish. His jaw falls slack and a gobbet of drool falls out, blobbing on the floor.

All I can think about is the last thing Dad told me at the prison. *Whatever you do, don't take his dust.*

"Gentlemen," says Skinner, "choose your poison."

The others scamper up eagerly to the table and start jostling for a hubcap.

"You, too," says the tuxedoed cat. He's standing at the base of the throne, waiting for me to proceed.

I take a step back from the table. "I think I've changed my mind."

The cat frowns. "No," he says, unbuttoning his tuxedo jacket. It falls open and reveals a gun strapped to his narrow chest. "I don't think you have."

Guess I don't have a choice.

Everyone else has picked up a hubcap. There's one left on the table. It's waiting for me. I step forward and the cat re-buttons his jacket. I pick up the cap and raise it to my snout. The dust wobbles in its shallow home, rising out of its own volition, anticipating what's to come.

"Go ahead," says the cat. "We're waiting."

At the end of the table there's a lanky, black-haired wolf. He's a head taller than me, but thin as a reed. I'd be surprised if he weighs half of what I do. I watch him raise the hubcap to his face and inhale. The dust leaps off the metal, snaking up with uncanny speed, clouding around his head. His snout stabs greedily at the air, huffing and puffing. All the while the dust toys with him, swelling and teasing around his head, until finally it pours inside him with a hiss.

For a moment, nothing happens. Then suddenly the wolf buckles over. He's sputtering, his face buried in his paws. When he rises again, his eyes glow red. Curls of smoke scallop from his nostrils like a pair of charmed serpents.

"Interesting," says the cat. He steps backward, leaning casually on Skinner's throne. "Anytime," he says to me.

I look over at Roy. He's got his face pressed to the rusty hub, snorting for all he's worth. The dust geysers up and dances in the air around him before streaming inside. Roy inhales smoothly. He's done this before.

"Man," he says, "I *love* this stuff." He holds a paw up in front of his face and we both watch as his claws begin to grow—lengthening, sharpening—so dramatically they rip the flesh of his fingertips. Every one of Roy's claws is becoming an ink-black sickle. Through all of it, Roy doesn't even flinch. He just stares in wonder at this new and improving forepaw. He's like a massive child with a new toy.

When the claws finally finish growing, he puts the

improved digits to his mouth, mewling and slithering his tongue between them to lick away the blood. And now the same thing's happening with his teeth: fanglike incisors growing and rupturing his gums. He grins at me, more wolfishly than I've ever seen, and bolts of his own blood drip onto his shirt, melding with the gaudy print.

Luminous veils of fairydust cloud the table. Some wolves become bloated with muscle. Others grow spiraling horns. One wolf's tail lengthens and distorts to become like that of a reptile—scaly and whip-sharp. They're all wolves, but now each of them comes with a vicious difference. And they're all staring at me, waiting.

My own little molehill of magic lies shining and quiet. I look up to see Skinner, glaring down at me from his throne.

"Hurry up," snaps the cat. "You either take it . . ." He fiddles again with the button of his jacket. "Or you don't."

What can I do? If I'd wanted a real choice, I should've made it a long time ago and not even come here. Too late for that now. I hunch around the hubcap like it's a fireplace in the dead of winter. And I inhale.

At once, my face tingles with an infinity of pinpricks. I can't help but recoil. I block my mouth with my tongue, but the dust skitters in through my nostrils, through my ears. I try choking it out of my snout, but I only run out of air. So I open up.

The nixiedust has a synthetic sweetness that sears my throat and fills my lungs until they're about to pop. I clutch my ribs and stupidly fight to hold them in. The nixies jeer at me from above. Briny water splashes down in heckling buckets. Then the pain's gone. The dust is inside me. I look at my paws. They're normal. I run my fingers over my teeth and skull. No fangs. No horns. My tail is the shaggy frond it's always been. Nothing's changed.

Roy yawns, showing off his cartoonish teeth. "Too bad," he sneers. "Must've got the placebo."

"Gentlemen," says the cat. His claws beckon. "The starting line, if you please." He lines us up along a red chalk-line on the floor.

"I don't think the dust worked for me," I whisper to him. He lines us up along a red chalkline on the floor. Roy takes a spot right on my left side.

He says nothing and with his scythelike claws, he slices away his tacky shirt. Then he drops to all fours and lopes back and forth, cleaving huge divots in the floor. Braids of muscle roll between his shoulders like dough in a mixer.

Up above us, the nixies spume with impatience. "Get on with it!" one of them screams.

"I got money on the big white one," hisses another. "Don't let me down!"

The cat steps to the line. Clutched in his arms is an ancient musket. He aims it recklessly upward. "On your mark!" he calls.

We drop to all fours, wound up tight.

"Get ssseeeeet!"

He fires the gun and somehow, miraculously, I'm first off the line, but I'm not out front for long. The black, willow-limbed wolf hurtles past. He looks back over his shoulder and barks at me. Flames and smoke blossom from his mouth. *He's breathing fire.* I jostle left, caroming against another wolf—who slashes at me with a lizardy tail. I'm thrown off-kilter, yelping as my ankle twists inward. More of the pack judders past.

Then comes Roy, tongue slavering between his teeth. His every stride floats for miles. He's like a bird in flight, whereas I'm a flawed machine, gears grinding and starved for fuel. My ankle grates with every thud of my feet.

By the end of the straightaway, I'm well behind.

But I still have the leader—the flame-spouter, coughing up fireworks—in my sights. The wolf with ram's horns leaps sideways, clangs off a yellow foundry basin, and butts into the wolf with the crocodile tail, the same one who wrecked my ankle. The two of them ball up, rolling like acrobats. I can hear the cracks of bones breaking. The nixies love it and splash down their cheers.

The heap left by the two broken wolves now blocks the only path. The rest of the runners, unable to swerve, tumble into them. The sudden pile up shunts any hope of getting by. Roy and I are the only ones behind it.

Roy takes the hard way, throwing his head back and howling. He digs his awful claws into the pack and scrabbles over. Hair and flesh tear away under his feet, throwing back a wake of blood and tissue, spattering my face, stinging my eyes.

And then . . . something happens.

My mind goes soft and dreamy. My thoughts rise up, disembodied, like I'm in two places at once, watching from above while my body keeps going. The pain in my ankle is gone. The crowd noise fades away to nothing, but it isn't silent. I can still hear the cheers. Every hoot, every bellow, every insult has become its own compact thing.

I can even hear Skinner, miles away on his throne. He's not cheering. He's muttering. To himself. Under his breath.

"This is my favorite part."

All at once, I know what's happening. It's the dust. It's taken its sweet time, but now it's working. The flaws in my gait are made perfect. My body's broken machine is now finely tuned and revving with speed.

I reach the heap of moaning, broken wolves, and *I leap.* In every direction I see the slack jaws of a thousand nixies, who are wound-up and thrilled, boiling in their pots. Even from my mind's far-off place, I can feel the electricity in my muscles, the sudden voltage of anger and fear and adrenaline. I'm working independent of my brain, which is nothing now but a few pounds of sloppy gray cargo. I land like an ember— glowing and weightless and ready to burn.

Not a second too soon.

Skinner's throne is in sight now. It's the final leg. Roy and the fire-spitter are neck and neck. I'm gathering speed behind them. Roy doesn't waste time. He lunges. There's a pop and a sizzle as he punctures the leader's throat, and he doesn't let up. He sinks his vast canines deep into the flames that flicker and die, doused by a grisly spurting of red. The nixies shriek for it—and they get what they want.

I want it too. Something's gone all wrong inside me. Roy's bloodied teeth make my insides burst with envy. And when his mouth comes away with the remnants of another wolf's throat, I practically swoon. He spits away the papery skin like garbage and runs and runs. Shoulders and haunches rise and fall. Forepaws and hind legs pound the slats. All the while, the nixies wail, sopping it up.

I've almost caught up with Roy. We hammer along in unison. The dust has made me faster than I've ever been. I know I can pass him now. Roy knows it, too. He rears up, sprinting as fast as two hind legs will carry him. He swings wildly with his arms and his huge claws bite into me. A sudden pulse electrifies—my cheek, my neck and down my back—but just as suddenly, the pain is gone. It's the dust, working its magic, fomenting inside me the courage of a lunatic.

Roy falls back on all fours, sprinting with all he has left. An appalling image jumps into my mind—Roy's fresh heart bursting in my mouth. With a cape of my own blood flapping behind me, it's my turn to lunge. My teeth go into his belly, latching onto what is inside. His ribs. Roy sucks in an ocean of air as I gnaw into the bone and feel his ribs splitting between my teeth. I taste his blood and—

It's over. I'm at the foot of Skinner's throne. Roy lies somewhere behind me; the right-hand cat stoops over him, wringing his paws.

There's a twinge in my ankle. The electricity returns to my face and back. The dust, having done its duty, is wearing off. My mind drifts back into my body.

"Impressive," says Skinner. He clinks down his golden steps. "That's precisely the sort of *grit* I'm looking for."

My legs give out, and I sag to the ground. Ten paces behind me is Roy, lying in the very same position. We're mirroring each other, separated by an invisible barrier: me on one side, Roy on the other, a million miles apart. The only difference between us is that Roy's not moving.

Skinner comes and stands beside me. He jabs the golden straw behind my ear, and now I've got a matching set of two. His gloved hand strokes the hair on my head. It's humiliating, as if I'm his pet.

"Congratulations," he says. "You got the job."

19
FLOPHOUSE

SKINNER VANISHED AFTER THE RACE. HE WAS SPIRITED OFF INSIDE A TIGHT formation of loyal globs. At least that's what I remember from before I passed out. When I came to again, the elegant cat was perched on a barrel, ignoring me as I slept.

The refinery was empty. The only thing left were speckles of red on the concrete floor. Roy was gone, too. The stain he left behind was the largest of all. The cat led me out through another tunnel to an underground parking lot.

Which is how I ended up here, packed into the back seat of a long black brougham, apparently just one of several in Skinner's fleet. Back in the lot, they were lined up like soldiers awaiting commands.

"Can I ask you something?" I say to the cat behind the wheel.

"No," he says. He keeps his gaze on the road.

It's a long way to the surface. We spiral up ramp after ramp. It gives you the impression of being in another city, down below the one you know. A very literal underground economy of crime. A black market of black magic.

The cat's eyes meet mine in the rearview mirror. Despite his cool demeanor, I take the eye contact as an invitation to speak. He's a cat after all. When do they acknowledge anyone?

"I guess you know Skinner pretty well."

He nods, a subtle dip of his chin.

"He's pretty tough for a little guy, huh?"

Another nod.

"You know what happened to his face?"

"Not just his face."

That must be why Skinner keeps his shirt buttoned up so high and tight. It's to hide as much of his body as possible. I can't help but wince. "What happened to him?"

The cat's attention returns to the road. Neon lights wash over the windscreen, rinsing Skinner's brougham in a rainbow of lurid light.

"What about the nixies? You know where their dust comes from?"

The cat hits the brakes. We're deep in Dockside now, far from the open air of the reservoir. Refineries and warehouses squeeze the car on all sides. The cat throws a languid arm over the passenger seat. In his other paw, he's got the gun he showed me earlier. "You ask too many questions."

"I was just—"

"You're a runner now," says the cat. "You understand what that means?"

"'Run' isn't exactly the most difficult word in the dictionary."

The cat shuts his eyes and opens them slowly. "I can kick you out anytime," he says. "Skinner won't care. I could tell him you got spooked, changed your mind—just like you told me you did back at the warehouse. I could tell him you jumped out of the car at a traffic light and vanished in the dark." He scrapes his rough tongue along his lips. "No one will ever hear from you again. That's because you'll be at the bottom of the reservoir. We'll arrange for guppies to swim through your bullet holes. At which point no amount of dust—nixie or otherwise—is gonna bring you back. Is that also something you understand?"

"I think so."

"Good." He turns around in his seat. "Now, let's get you to your new home."

After driving in silence for a few more minutes, we come upon a building that slouches in every direction. Located on what might have been an elegant if sprawling apartment block once upon a time, the building is now close to disintegration. It looks to be mostly built out of soot, with only a meager patchwork of sheet metal to cover the holes in the brick.

"Welcome to the flophouse," says the cat, grinning at me for the first time, showing off his fangs.

The foyer is a huge square space, its edges divvied up

by countless corridors and stairways. If the outside was dismal, the inside is worse. The floor angles up and down like a fun house. The ceiling tiles are entirely missing so the lights dangle bare and flickering from exposed wires. Wolves are everywhere: lolling on the floor, swinging from the roof beams, crowded around tables, where even more wolves bark and howl over cards and dice games. As soon as the cat leads me in, the room hushes to a menacing silence.

"Everyone," says the cat, "this is Henry. He was the winner tonight."

Nobody speaks. Off in the corner, there's a small pack of blackhaired wolves. Every one of them frowns at me from around a crooked table, where only a moment ago the dice were clattering freely. One of them scoffs. *"Cheat!"*

"Come along," says the cat. "You can meet your new friends later."

He leads me up to the first floor and down a corridor. There's a hefty door at the end, locked up tight. The cat thumps it with a fist.

"Hey! Got this week's newbie."

No response.

The cat pounds again. "Wake up, ya bum!"

There's a clinking of glass and then the racket of a thousand locks. An old wolf opens the door. He's the light brown color of dead grass. His paw is draped at his side, loosely clutching a bottle, dregs of a pungent whiskey sloshing at the bottom.

"Fresh meat," says the cat. "Show him around."

The wolf shakes his head. His eyes are half-asleep, but in spite of his drunken tilt, there's a kind of regal bearing to him, his head held high on a ramrod spine. "Put him up in, uh—three-oh-nine." He sways a little to the left, then braces himself on the door frame. "Orientation's in the morning, then it'll be his first run."

The cat regards the drunken wolf with disdainfully hooded lids. "Whatever you say, Matt." He looks around at the rotten walls and the dangling fixtures. "You're the boss around here."

The wolf grunts and shuts the door. He never even looked at me.

The cat leads me up a few flights of stairs, past numbers haphazardly scrawled on the doors. Three-oh-nine is a windowless cube on the third floor, furnished with a three-legged chair and a bare mattress. No pillow, and only a thin blue sheet. My only consolation is that the mattress is enormous. It looks almost big enough for me to stretch out in full.

The cat watches me from the doorless entryway. "Better get some sleep." He flashes me an unfriendly smile. "Big day tomorrow."

I lie in semi-darkness, but it's impossible to sleep. The mattress reeks of mold, and intermittent howls of laughter rise up through the floorboards. What am I doing here? How am I ever going to get close enough to Skinner to find out anything at all? And perhaps most importantly, what if my father is completely insane?

No. I know that deep down I want everything he said to be true. I want the fairies to come back. I want my world to be the way it was, once upon a time—even if I can't remember exactly what that means.

Eventually—in spite of the noise, the smell, the worry—I drift off. But my sleep is as fitful as ever. It isn't long before the nightmares set in. The trees. The cottage. The little girl. The blood and the bones . . .

20
A MILLION GLITTERING TEETH

SUDDENLY, I'M AWAKE. ALL THE FOLLICLES I'VE GOT—FIFTY BAZILLION OF them—vibrate like the plucked strings of a symphony (a fugue, no doubt). The room is pitch-black, lonely and empty.

Or not.

I prick up my ears. I can hear shallow breathing. It's not mine.

A voice I don't recognize says, "You really toss and turn, don't you?" It's somebody young, like me, but I can't place it. But I can smell him. A wet scent of licorice and foul breath.

"Who are you?"

"Didn't you hear what Manx said? We're your new friends."

There are more of them—four others besides the voice— clinging to the corners of the room like huge, black cobwebs. Suddenly they're on top of me. Five against one. I lash out against somebody, punching blindly. There's a yelp, and I'm kicked in the gut. A pillowcase is hitched over my head, and suddenly the enormous bed sheet cocoons me.

Whump! Something heavy rams my skull, and I'm thrown back into the nightmare.

The bones pop through my hide. I can't tell which is worse, my dream or my reality. No, that's not true. Nothing's worse than my nightmares. I choose reality. I want to wake up. Happily (or not), that's exactly what I get.

Cold air sieves through the cloth of the pillowcase, chilling my snout. My arms are wrenched up behind me and bound up in the sheet. I'm doubled over something. Feels like a squat hunk of cement. I'm outside. Clanks and rattles rise up from below.

Somebody yanks the pillowcase off. For a dizzying moment I'm blinded by a million pinpricks of light, too many stars to count. Only they're not stars. It's the city, sprawling out below me.

They've got me on the roof. It's not a tall building (buildings made of soot rarely are), but it's more than high enough to give me a sudden shot of vertigo. A fall from up here would kill you.

"You're a cheat," one of them informs me. Looks like five of them altogether. It's the pack of dice players from when I arrived. Three of them have me braced over the ledge, while two more—a big one and a little one—pace behind my back.

"Yeah," says the little one. "A cheat!"

"Shut up, Squitch," says the big one. He comes over to me and leans against the concrete barrier. "There's been some kind of mistake," he says. He almost looks genuinely puzzled. "You see, uh . . . ?"

"Henry."

"*Wrong.* Your name's Newbie, got it?" He glances over his shoulder at the constellation of lighted dust refineries below us. "Nice view, huh, Newbie?"

"Listen," I say. "I just got here, so if I did something to make you guys angry, then . . ."

One of the wolves pinning me down jabs me in the ribs, robbing me of air. I'm sputtering for breath, but the other guy keeps talking.

"In fact, you *did* do something to upset us, see? My cousin was supposed to win today. Name's Zeb. Black hair. Skinny as anything, but fast. *He* was supposed to win tonight. Not you."

"Yeah!" says the little one, leaping up behind his friend. "Tom's *cousin* was s'posed to win!"

"I said shut up, Squitch."

Squitch is obviously an annoyance for everyone involved. Each time they tell him to shut up, my arm gets cranked a little higher. If he doesn't stop yammering soon, they'll rip my shoulder out of its socket.

"Ow!"

"You can shut up, too," says the one called Tom, pointing at me.

"Yeah, you can shut up too!"

"*Squitch!*"

"Sorry, Tom."

"Maybe I owe you an explanation," Tom tells me, leaning casually on his elbow. "My whole family works for Skinner, see? He takes good care of us. This is a good job for wolves like us. *Not* for wolves like you."

Finally, I catch my breath. "Aren't we all in the same boat here?"

"Naw," says Tom, waving me off. "I saw it as soon as you walked in. You're not like us. You're one of them wolves who thinks they're above their species, see? You think you're a hominid, right? But you're not. You're *an animal*. Only you can't see it. That's your problem. Not comfortable in your own hide."

"I know who I am." I say it calmly. Almost as though I believe it.

"Maybe so," says Tom. "If you do, then you'll know that you don't belong here."

"I won that race."

Tom bares his teeth. "You *cheated!*"

"Yeah! He cheated!"

"*Squitch!*"

My arm gets shoved even higher.

Tom looks up at the sky. Eden floats silently above us. Its underbelly is an upturned mountain, one great finger pointing at the city. Up on top it's nothing but glimmering towers of light. Tom squints at it, contemplating. "Them fairies knew it. Never waved the magic wands for *us*, now did they? They knew where to draw the line. Just a fact of life. But you're too young to remember any of that."

I shake my head. "That's not true," I tell him. Besides, he doesn't look much older than me. "I knew a fairy once. Her name was Faelynn. She said things were gonna change."

Tom gives me a pitying look. "You guys hear? *That's* the sort of company he keeps. Not that anybody here believes you." He laughs and spits over the ledge. "Phew! That is a *long way down.*" His features are still, hard as stone. "This won't be pretty."

He nods to his friends and they struggle to lift me over the ledge. But *struggle* is the operative word.

"Damn!" says one of them. "Guy weighs a ton!"

"Help us out, Tom."

"Weaklings."

He gathers up my ankles and heaves. I'm clear off the ground, wriggling as best I can with my arms in a tangle. The city opens up below with its million glittering teeth. Thoughts of my mother and my father flash through my head. Thoughts of Jack, too, of Siobhan and Gram and Faelynn. Of Fiona. Even of Roy.

"Nice knowin' ya, Newbie."

"Hold it, fellahs," says a new voice. "Think you better put him down."

Tom drops my legs. The sheet loosens and I'm able to turn enough to see that it's Matt, the wolf I met when I first came in. He's still draped in his housecoat, bottle in hand. "I doubt Skinner'd be pleased to hear about how you're treating the newest member of the family."

"No part of *my* family." Tom's face remains set in stone.

But Squitch isn't so coolheaded. His bottom lip is drawn back from his teeth in worry. "Don't tell Skinner! Please-please-please, don't tell Skinner."

"Squitch," says Tom. "What've I been telling you all night long?"

Squitch shuts up for once.

Matt slips the bottle into the pocket of his housecoat. "'Kay, boys, get back in your beds in five minutes and I'll consider keeping this little episode between us." He points at me. "And you, the newbie. You come with me. Evidently, I gotta find you a new room." He eyes Tom. "Someplace with a door."

Squitch folds his forearms and pouts. "How come *he* gets a door?"

"Cuz you fidos just tried to toss him off a roof, that's why."

"Good point," says Squitch.

The dark-hairs disperse like nothing happened, as if attempting to throw the newbie off the roof is no more momentous than a dice game. Matt leads me down a musty stairwell and back to the solid door where I first met him. He takes out a massive ring of keys and unlocks it.

I feel a distinct wave of privilege. "You're gonna let me stay with you?"

Matt laughs. "Not a chance."

I peer into the room and see it's a well-furnished disaster. There's not one, but *three* desks, a herd of swivel chairs, couches, armchairs, chests of drawers, and a bunch of bookshelves filled more with empty bottles than books. Everything is askew. It looks like the furnishings were arranged by a bomb blast. The walls, meanwhile, are covered with maps, each one of them dense with fine black lines and arcane notations. Matt opens one of the countless drawers and pulls out a folded blanket, along with a thin pillow.

"Nobody sleeps in here but me," he says, stepping back into the hall. "You can have the room next door."

The room next door, it turns out, is a broom closet. Only there aren't any brooms. It's just vacant shelving and a single dustpan. Matt shakes out the blanket and spreads it on the floor, topping it off with a thin pillow.

"You'll be safe in here," he says.

I stoop in through the doorway. The closet is so squat I fill the whole thing wall-to-wall. I lower myself to the floor in a gambit for more headroom and find it's not quite as uncomfortable as it looks.

"Matt?" I say, looking up at him.

"Yeah?"

"Thanks."

"No problem. They always give newbies a hard time." He shakes his head. "Stupid thing is, all those guys are newbies themselves. Joined the crew in the last couple of months. But don't worry, it's my job to look after you guys. And speaking of which, you better get some sleep. Big day tomorrow." He starts pulling the door shut.

"Can I ask you something?"

"Hurry up," he says. "You're not the only one who needs some shut-eye."

"Is Matt short for something? Like say, Mattius?"

He gives me a puzzled look. "How'd you know that? Nobody calls me that. Not anymore."

"My dad did."

Matt stares at me a long time. My face must look half-baked and cadaverous under the closet's bare bulb. Maybe that's why he recognizes me.

"Oh my God. You're George Whelp's son."

21
THE DEADEST OF ENDS

"HENRY?" SAYS MATT. "LITTLE HENRY WHELP?"

I shrug. "Not so little anymore."

"Why didn't I see it? You look just like him."

"Guess you haven't seen him lately."

Matt looks down sheepishly. "Skinner wouldn't like it."

"He told me you guys were friends."

"We were. But after what he did—*wait!* You can't stay! We gotta get you out of here." He looks anxiously down the corridor. "He made me promise that if you ever showed up here, I would send you packing, but not before giving you a good swift kick in the pants for being so stupid for falling into this stuff!"

"But—"

"A promise is a promise, kid. I stick by that." He checks his watch. "Won't be hard to smuggle you out. We can use the tunnels." He steps into the closet, grabs my shirt, and gives me a sharp tug to my feet. "If George wasn't in the clink right now, he'd kill me for letting those guys nearly toss you off the roof!"

"But *he's* the one who sent me. He wants me to work for Skinner."

"What?" Matt's so deeply baffled he almost stops his drunken swaying. "*Why?*"

I look at him, square in his whiskey-red eyes. "Where does nixiedust come from?"

Again, Matt looks confused. "What do you mean? It comes out of the ground, from all the quarries. That's pretty obvious."

"You've never heard about it coming from somewhere else? Someplace secret? Like a special brand of dust that they get from—I don't know, somewhere else?"

"You're asking the wrong guy, kid. As far as I know, they dig it up—just like everybody." He sighs wearily. "Leftover miracles."

"Oh."

"What's this all about?"

"It's why my dad sent me here."

I tell Matt as much as I know: about a secret brand of nixiedust; dark, impelled destinies that could only come from old-time magic; my father and countless other animals like him, all serving time for sudden, uncharacteristic bouts of violence.

When I'm finished, Matt takes a long swallow of whiskey.

"It's a good story, kid, but who'd believe it?" He sighs. "Your pop was a good wolf—as good as you get on this side of the law. But when he did what he did, he went way over the line. Cooking up a cockeyed fairydust conspiracy is a poor excuse."

"But if it's true, then maybe it would mean he was innocent, because Skinner and the nixies *forced* him to do it—they found a way to make folks live out their worst possible destinies."

"Then there's your proof right there. It can't be true. The fairies would never spin that kind of magic."

"But what if someone made them do it? Don't you think that's possible?"

Matt shakes his head. "In this line of work, I do my best not to think about anything. That's what this is for." He brandishes his bottle. "Now, if George really sent you, then I won't force the issue. The choice is yours. Either we smuggle you out right now, or you stay and go chasing after fairy tales."

"I'll stay."

"You sure?"

"Like you said, a promise is a promise. I made one to my dad."

"Then we both did. I promised to look out for you, and I intend to. But right now, let's hit the hay." Matt pulls the door shut, locking it behind him.

I yank the string dangling from the bulb to switch it off. Surprisingly, with the adrenaline draining out of me and in the relative safety of a locked broom closet, I drift off. It isn't long before I'm back in the forest of my dreams, stalking through whispering trees, belly to the earth, under a moon so bright it's casting shadows.

Things are different this time. The hillside that draws me down into the woods keeps going and going. It's so deep that the moon, radiant only moments ago, has nearly vanished. It's a pinprick now, one point of brightness jabbed through a limitless field of dark. The path through the trees is longer, too. It meanders in every direction, urging me in vast circles. At last, the cottage appears, but when I nudge myself inside, there are too many rooms, hundreds of them, every one devoid of life. There are stairways leading up to nowhere, or down to dead ends. There are tiny, unreachable windows and doors that open up into the bottoms of wells. There are rooms full of cages. Rooms made of gold. There's one I find that crawls with a jumble of chairs and tables, their million legs entwined like the limbs of an endless insect. I stand in the doorway, gazing into the vast space and they begin to move, clicking and cracking their legs, their antennae, their grasping mandibles and—

I'm jolted awake when the closet door opens. Standing in the opening are a pair of globs. They're identical. They look like twins. In unison, they step aside to reveal the cat, still impeccably wrapped in his tux.

"Get up, Whelp."

"Where's Matt?"

145

The cat scoffs. "Sleeping it off, no doubt. No idea why he put you in here. Took me forever to find you."

I sit up, and my body groans, voicing a clear aversion to spending the night on the floor of a closet.

"Henry," says the cat. "It is 'Henry,' correct? I'd like you to meet Skinner's private bodyguards." Without indicating who's who, he says, "This is Adler and this is Baldwin. They're here to get you moving."

Adler (Or is it Baldwin?) hauls me up as easily as if I'm made of crepe paper. The other one snatches my opposite arm and the cat leads the three of us out past Matt's room. The door's shut, without any sign of life. We head down to the end of the corridor. It's a dead end, as if last night's dream were a premonition of things to come. There are no latches. No keyholes. There's not even a door. It's just a bare wall. The cat knocks against it with a finely combed knuckle.

Midway up, a slat opens, revealing an eyeball, which peers up at us in silence.

"Deadwood," says the cat.

The slat closes and the wall slides smoothly open of its own accord. The corridor flips from silence to the thunder of machinery. The cat turns to me, raising his voice over the din. "That's the password, got it?"

"Deadwood?" I ask him. "Like the tree?"

"Pretty much works everywhere around here." He leads the way inside, spreading his arms as he pads ahead. "Welcome," he says, "to the refinery."

It's a *huge* space, many times the size of the derelict warehouse where we raced—and this is certainly not derelict. This one smacks with goblins, cats, dwarves, ravens, nixies, foxes, wolves. Lots of wolves.

They all go about their business, shoveling dust into crates, sieving it into barrels, scooping it off the crisscross of conveyor belts that weave over the floor in every direction. *The conveyors.* They're just as Dad described them. Every one originates from the same place—from behind a single wall that runs the full length of the refinery, all the way down to where it all disappears in gloom.

"What are you looking at?" The cat beckons and the globs push me forward. "You don't have to worry about how any of this works." He sweeps his arm around the refinery. "All you gotta worry about's in here." He pushes through a glass door. I follow him in, but the globs stay put, guarding the entrance.

Inside is an office cluttered with measuring scales, arcane hand-tools, smashed crates, and rusty file cabinets. The mess is built up in hills and gorges of scrap. Awkwardly, the cat wades through it. When his tuxedo snags on a broken barrel, he makes his very first display of emotion. "Hans!" he screams. "How many times do I have to tell you?! You have *got* to do something about all this crap!"

Buried behind the chaotic desk is a hedgehog, but not the meek creature I imagine when I think of that particular species. This guy's massive for his kind. The contours of his arm muscles bulge through a pinstripe shirt. His quills are manicured into glistening blades. If it were ever possible for a hedgehog to appear threatening, this Hans has succeeded in spades.

"Think of it as conceptual art," he says. "This mess is my life's work." Hans scribbles something into a ledger and whips to the following page. "What are you doing in my office, anyway? You need something?" He still hasn't noticed me.

The cat steps forward, casting a shadow over the desk. "This is the newbie. Matt had him sleeping in a closet."

Hans nods but doesn't look up from his ledger. "That old trick."

"It's why I'm late." He swallows. "Skinner waiting?"

"Next door."

"I'll check. Lemme leave him here a second."

Finally, Hans looks up and sees me. "Who's this guy?"

"I told you. The newbie."

Hans squints up at me. "Don't touch anything."

"Okay," I tell him.

The cat stalks out and I'm left alone with Hans. He keeps scribbling. A thick claw on his other hand scrapes down a column of figures on a separate page.

"Um, Hans?"

He doesn't look up. "Hmm?"

"Can I ask you something?"

"Hmm?"

"What's behind that wall out there?"

His claw stops running down the figures. He lifts it up and taps it, once, against the page. Then he looks up at me. His eyes have narrowed to a pair of coin slots. "Why do you wanna know?"

"Just curious."

Hans takes a breath and blows it out. "You're a newbie, so let me give you some free advice." His quills tense up and quiver all over his body. "That is not the sort of thing to be curious about. You got me?"

"I think so."

"But now *I'm* curious," he says. "Why the interest?"

"Just something I heard."

"From who?"

"My dad."

Hans squints at me. "Did I hear that right?"

"George Whelp. Maybe you knew him."

Hans nods. He turns back to his ledger. He keeps writing and clawing his way down the figures. "Prison life can give folks some pretty odd ideas."

Before I can ponder what the hedgehog means, the door cracks open.

"Let's go," says the cat. "Skinner's waiting."

22
HANDS

SKINNER IS PERCHED UP ON ANOTHER ONE OF HIS THRONES, A SMALLER ONE. Another grotesque clutter of alchemized junk.

"Now that we're all here," he says, "it's time to pair you off."

Then I see that standing along the wall, camouflaged by the room's soot stains, are the other wolves. They're all dark-hairs. Five of them. And my stomach flips. They're the same ones who tried to toss me off the roof last night: Tom, Squitch, and three friends.

The cat takes out a clipboard, forepaw hovering over it with a pen. "Whenever you're ready, sir."

Skinner pulls the stalk of straw out of his mouth. "You," he says, using it to point at the wolf who nearly broke my arm. "And you." He points to the wolf beside him.

The cat notes the selection on his clipboard.

Skinner narrows his eyes and looks down the line. "You," he says, swinging the gnawed straw to me. "And . . ."

The other three—Tom, Squitch, and the third—take a pointed step backward.

"I see," says Skinner. "Who shall I choose I wonder?" He points immediately to Tom. *"You."*

Tom shows his teeth, a pearl-white strip of them against his dark face.

Skinner frowns. "Do you have a problem, young Tom?"

Tom manages to pull his lips together, hiding his grimace. "No, sir."

"Good." Skinner points to Squitch and the last wolf. "That leaves you two."

The cat marks it down. Then he says: "All right, boys. Time for your first run."

Hans, the hedgehog, loads us up. Each pair of us is given a pack. Hans gives ours to Tom, but the moment he feels its weight, Tom thrusts it at me. "Here," he says. "You better carry it."

Hans opens a drawer in one of his rusted cabinets. He takes out a series of maps. On each one is an intricate diagram of the City. Only a few landmarks—the reservoir, the cemetery, a couple of the prisons, the skyway to Eden—are labeled with actual words. I recognize Hans's handwriting from when I watched him tally up the figures in his meticulous ledger. Clearly, he's responsible for designing these maps as well.

Hans spreads one of them delicately over his desktop. It's like an artifact in a museum, and that's precisely how Hans treats it.

"Watch carefully," he says.

The map is comprised of two pages. There's the map itself and, at the top, a delicate, tightly rolled overlay of something thin and translucent, like tracing paper. Hans unfurls it, revealing a squirrelly network of lines, crisscrossing all over the city.

"These are the tunnels," he says. "They'll take you boys where you need to go—*without* folks getting suspicious about wolves barreling through the streets." He taps Dockside gently with his claw. "We're here, see? Come up as close to the address as you can. Drop the package at the door and get back underground. Simple, right? Don't talk to folks, don't accept money from them. That's all been taken care of. You're *runners*. That's it. Get back here quick, and we'll have another drop ready to go. Got it?"

We nod.

"Now," he says. "You see some of these tunnels marked in red? Never use 'em. They're off-limits. You got it?"

We nod.

"They don't go anywhere anyway. They're all dead ends. Now, Matt here'll show you how to get in."

We turn around and see Matt, propped up against the door frame. He's wearing the same housecoat that he wore yesterday.

"Follow me," he says.

He takes us back into the refinery, past the conveyors, to a corner near the password-protected entrance. There's nothing here but a defunct furnace. Matt tips it sideways with almost no effort at all. It's just a fake, a shell of the real thing.

Behind it is a hatchway, which Matt yanks open. A stench of staleness wafts out, and we all flinch. There's nothing down there but darkness and the first thin rungs of a wrought-iron ladder. Squitch and the others go first. Then it's Tom and me.

But Matt stops us. "I know you two hate each other, but when you're down there—" He pauses to cough into his sleeve. "When you're down there, be careful. Look out for one another."

"Whatever," says Tom. He pushes past us, but Matt grabs him.

"I mean it," he says. "All kinds of things can kill you down there. All *kinds* of things."

In spite of himself, Tom nods. "Ok, Pop." He claps me on the shoulder, a little too hard. "We're a team."

Then down we go.

The chamber's damp and nearly pitch-black. Even with wolfish acuity, it's a long time before our eyes adjust enough to be of use. The tunnel smells like the scent that clogs your snout just before you get sick.

Tom's galloping ahead. He hasn't said a word since we left. With a hefty sack of nixiedust on my back, it's a struggle to keep up. The only thing Tom's carrying is the map. Now and again, he pauses to consult it with one of the small flashlights we were given. Then he rushes on.

Most of the tunnels are extremely narrow. The walls bulge with outcrops of stone, thrusting out at random. They pepper our faces with chalky whiteness and moisten our clothes with drips of condensation.

On occasion, we jog along the bottoms of chasms, the walls rising up on either side. Other times we're high on a ledge with a claustrophobic ceiling above us and nothing but a thread of rotted rope to keep us from tumbling into the old sewage below. The wastewater here is so stale and ancient it hardly gives off a scent.

We stop to catch our breath.

"Almost there," Tom tells me, speaking at last.

"Who do you think built all this?"

Tom shrugs. I can't see much more than the outline of his body. "The nixies did, when they first arrived. Came up through the reservoir."

"Can I see the map?"

Tom shakes his head. "No time," he says. "We're almost there."

Eventually, we ascend again to the surface. When we come up behind a derelict building, the smog-filled air is like a lungful of countryside. We follow a few side streets to a block of terraced homes.

"It's number thirty-one," says Tom. "Right up here."

"Why's the door open?"

"Who cares?" He looks up and down the street. It's deserted. "Drop off the package and let's go."

I pad up the crumbling steps.

Tom whispers nervously after me. "Hurry up!"

I can see all the way down the corridor. Who would leave their door open like this? Especially around here. As if to answer my question, a woman appears at the far end, deep inside the house. She's in a dress with long white sleeves that flap like wings. She walks toward me with a slow, methodical gait.

"Come in," she says.

I turn to Tom. He's shaking his head wildly.

"I can't," I tell her. "I, uh—have another delivery."

"Please," she says. "I need your help."

She asks me with such plaintiveness that I can't resist. The corridor looks worse on the inside. All along the ceiling, wallpaper strips away like dead skin. I hear Tom come pounding up the steps. "Henry! Let's go!"

"This woman says she needs our help."

"No kidding." He takes one step inside. "What do you think the package is for?"

The woman reaches the end of the corridor and turns to face us both. Her voice is wisp-thin, but she manages to project it down to Tom. "It's what I need your help with," she says. She looks at me and raises her arms. Her billowy sleeves fall away to reveal her—*nothing*. Not hands. She doesn't have any. There's only a pair of shining stumps.

"Please," she says. "It's better if you do it."

She steps to the left and vanishes into a room. I look back at Tom. He doesn't say anything. His eyes are wide.

"C'mon," I say to him. "I'm sure it'll only take a second."

23
ADDICTED TO BEING WHOLE

THE WOMAN LEANS AGAINST THE STOVE. HER FACE IS AS PALE AS DETECTIVE White's, but she's got none of White's vigor. Her arms are folded tightly, stumps wedged up into her armpits. I place the package on the table.

"Open it," she says.

Tom thumps all the way down the corridor and peeks his snout into the kitchen. "We're not supposed to be here," he growls. His face isn't as shocked as it was a moment ago. Now he just looks sour.

I use a claw to cleave away the tape. "I've never done this before," I tell the woman.

"Well, *I* have," sneers Tom. "Better let me do it."

The woman points at me with her narrow chin. "I want him to."

Tom throws up his arms. He stands near the doorway and glares at me. "If we're late getting back, it's *your* fault."

I turn my back to him and face the woman. "What should I do?"

"Put some in your hand."

I pick up the package and pour a little molehill into my palm, just like Mrs. L would do.

"More."

I tip the paper until dust fills the whole of my palm. The woman says nothing until a few flecks overflow onto the table.

"Okay, that's enough." She comes and stands near me. From here I can see the lines on her face. She's got a lot of them. She's older than I thought.

"Go ahead," she says, staring a the black pad of my upturned paw. "All you have to do is blow a single breath. The dust knows what to do. It always does."

I bring my paw up to my mouth. The instant I exhale, the dust fans out to cocoon the woman's head. She hardly moves. Her body goes rigid as the magic roils and hisses into the slackness of her mouth.

She backs toward the window, haloed in the bright sun. Eyes shut, she leans against the glass and lets her head fall back. She raises her arms, elbows pressed together. She's so pale I can actually see the dust swirling beneath her skin, coursing up toward her wrists. The stumps ignite with strange blue flames—licking, fluttering, silent—and shaping themselves into hands, knitting together into perfect palms and perfect fingers.

She opens her eyes and smiles at me. "Thank you," she says, her face sweating. It appeared to be painful to regrow a set of hands, but I can hardly blame her for dabbling in street magic. Anyone can see she's addicted to being whole.

She holds her new hands up to the light, wriggling her enchanted fingers. I want to ask her what happened. How did she lose them? But that's her business, not mine. She moves across the room to the corner where two shallow countertops meet. "Must be hard work," she says, "running all over town."

"It's my first day."

Tom scoffs. "No kidding it is!"

"Would you like something to eat?"

"*No!*" says Tom.

"He's right," I say. "We have to get back."

But she's already slapped down a chopping board and gathered utensils. It's only when she uses them that you can tell the hands are enchanted. Faster than I can follow, her fingers slide over the board, gathering vegetables and meat, slicing them impossibly thin.

"I hope you like soup," she says, smiling weakly.

"I do."

"No," says Tom. "We have to go."

But I can see he's as mesmerized as I am. The woman's hands move so fast, you can barely see them. In an instant, the meat's deboned and sizzling in a pot. Onions are diced, carrots julienned, potatoes perfectly cubed.

But then her grip on the knife falters. Her mouth tightens in concentration. There's still more to chop, but she's already slowing down. And then, almost miraculously, she cuts herself.

It's a clean slice across the back of her thumb, and although she's in pain, she doesn't make a sound. She merely stiffens her grip on the knife and hardens her eyes, struggling to finish. The wound leaks an ethereal kind of blood. Not a fluid, but a gas, ribbons of smoke that scatter in the stagnant air.

"I need some more," she says.

At this rate, the nixiedust will hardly last her through the evening. It'll be gone by nightfall.

"Can you give me another hit?"

Tom grabs me. *"No way,"* he says. "Do it yourself this time. We gotta go."

He pulls me away and the last thing I see is the woman tearing open the packages, frantically scooping up dust even as it trickles through the holes in her vanishing hands.

24
WARP AND WEFT

THAT'S HOW IT WENT FOR DAYS, A BLUR OF BREATHLESSNESS AND PITY AND nervous sleep. Tom and I shuttle under the streets, galloping back and forth between Skinner's refinery and an endless stream of random addresses. We never know where we're going until the moment Hans the hedgehog furnishes each of us with a tightly bound brick of dust.

Every time we return to the refinery, I watch the conveyors. From behind that wall they trundle out with a seemingly endless supply of dust. The way to get back there is perpetually guarded by a pair of enormous globs. But I'm also learning the tunnels, garnering a keen, wolfish sense of how they hang together beneath the streets. When I get the chance, I study the maps—and I think I've found something. I think there's another way in, from the reservoir.

Oddly, most of our drops are made during the day. This is because, in the middle of the night, the only folks awake are the night-shift dust miners and the cops. A pair of dustrunnners—even if we're only aboveground for a couple of blocks—nevertheless look pretty suspicious. In the daytime, however, there's the bustle, the traffic, the construction noise—all the things you need to blend in.

Which is why I'm so surprised to be shaken awake at three in the morning.

"Henry, get up."

I'm too bleary with sleep to see who's in my room-slash-closet, but I don't need to. It's Matt. I recognize his scent. There's a boozy cloud that follows him wherever he goes. "Outta bed," he says. "You got a drop to make."

He stands by the door of my closet while I'm getting dressed.

"How are you doing, Henry?" he asks me. His voice is clear and even despite the fact that his breath is so full of whiskey I'm buzzing on the fumes. "Tom giving you trouble?"

"A little, but I can handle it."

"Good. You let me know when you want out. I'll see what I can do."

"Who said I wanted out?"

"You will."

Once I'm dressed, curiosity gets the better of me. "You want to explain why I'm up so early?"

"Let's just say Skinner likes you. C'mon."

When we get down to Hans in the refinery, I notice something. The place is practically deserted. There's only one guard and he's rocking himself to sleep in a creaking metal chair. Three in the morning. One guard. Duly noted.

Tom's waiting for us in Hans's office. "I was wondering when you'd get here," he says. "This place is lonesome in the middle of the night."

Hans, apparently, doesn't sleep. He's bright-eyed and active behind his desk, same as ever, poring over figures in his ledger. Loaded into the archaic scales on his desk are several bricks of dust. Tom plucks one of them up, waving its chemical tang under my snout. "Special delivery," he says in a whining, singsong voice.

Hans rises and swipes the brick from Tom, replacing it on the scales. "Which is why," he declares, "you gotta take this seriously. No fooling around, no dawdling, and"—he glances pointedly up at the wall clock—"there and back quick as you can." He points a curled claw at us. "You screw this up and Skinner'll murder the both of you. Literally."

Tom glares at me. "Or maybe he'll just murder *one* of us."

Matt steps in and clips Tom behind the ear. "Yeah, and he'll do Hans and me in the bargain. So pay attention."

"Ow!" Tom rubs the back of his skull like a peevish cub.

"They specifically asked for our biggest guy on this run," Hans informs us, and then he points at me. "Which means you."

Tom turns to go, but Matt blocks his way. "What?" says Tom. "If they want *him* so badly, I say we let him go on his own. That way, I can get some sleep."

"I don't think so," says Hans. "Runners always run in pairs."

Tom snorts but turns back to the desk.

Hans hands us the bricks one by one, somber as a hangman. "This is top-grade stuff. Takes years to refine it properly. Closest thing to old-time magic you're liable to find anywhere. Few folks are rich or stupid enough to afford it. So whatever you do, don't screw it up."

"Okay, okay," says Tom, zipping up his pack. "We'll be careful."

After Hans drew our attention to how special—not to mention expensive—this dust is, I expected to come upon something a little more grand. But not so.

We surface on a side street, one of the broad alleys where folks living in meager townhomes park their cars. Even in the dark, you can make out the leopard spots of rust. The homes are shouldered together in one endless array, and I can tell from the wooden slats and metal siding—just beginning to fade and buckle—that this is a newer subdivision going to pot. In short, it's not a slum, but it will be soon. How could someone living in a place like this afford several bricks of the nixies' most exclusive dust?

"Stop staring," says Tom, striding up the alley ahead of me. "It's not like there's anything to see." He points. "Should be right up here. Number forty-seven."

When we get closer, I see something I recognize. It's a tree—the same tree Doc was painting in his office back at St. Remus, the last time I saw him alive.

"I've seen that before," I tell Tom, slowing my gait to take in the tree's stooping, Doc-like posture and lolloping roots.

Tom doesn't care for it. He reaches for the back gate, sneering. "Ugly," he says. "They oughta cut it down."

"Maybe they are." As we enter the backyard, I point to a hole in the ground at the base of the tree. "Looks like they're planning to dig it up."

"Good for them."

In one of the rear windows of number forty-seven, there's a light on. A shadowy figure moves behind the curtains. A moment later, a blowzy, middle-aged woman steps out on the back porch, her hair tied under a head scarf that matches her faded, flowery dress.

"Come," she whispers, waving us toward her with both hands.

"We're just dropping something off," says Tom, a suspicious growl creeping into his voice. "That's all."

The woman glances back and forth down the alley. "Come in, please!"

Tom shakes his head, unzipping his pack. "No way." He stacks the bricks delicately on the bottom step of the porch. "Our job ends right here, lady."

"Please," she says, "one of you." She's looking at me. "I need your help."

"No," says Tom.

"I need you to bring him back."

When she speaks the words, I freeze. It's an echo of what my father told me at the East Pen.

What if they could bring her back?

"Tom, wait."

He's already on the far side of the fence. "Either you come back to the refinery with me right now, or I go back alone and tell them you were too slow to keep up."

If Tom returns without me, it'll mean one of two things: One, Skinner and his goons will turf me out and I'll lose whatever chance I have of finding out where they're keeping the fairies; or two, they'll save themselves the trouble and kill me.

I jog up to Tom. "Don't forget what Hans told us." I point back toward the stoop, where the pudgy old woman is gathering up the packages. "He said this stuff was special. He said it was *expensive*. A customer like her is valuable, so you gotta figure Skinner, Hans, the nixies—they'll want us to make her happy. Right?"

Tom squints at me, searching my face. Then he looks past me at the woman, the bricks of dust piled in her arms. "Fine," he says. "Go see what she wants. But hurry up. In ten minutes, I'm gone."

25

A CLOUD ON A WINDLESS DAY

INSIDE, THE HOUSE IS A MUSEUM OF BRIC-A-BRAC. FRAMED PHOTOGRAPHS clutter the walls; small plinthlike tables fill the corridors; and every surface is awash with cups, saucers, figurines, dusty glass baubles, every sort of knickknack you can imagine. The same goes for the wallpaper. The pattern is a twine of roses in every color, thorny stems mangled together.

"This way," says the woman, waving me toward a locked room at the end of the hall. "Hurry." When we arrive at the door, she fishes through her pockets for a ring of keys.

"What did you mean," I ask her, "when you said you wanted to bring him back."

Without turning around, she shrugs. "I meant just what I said. I need to bring him back."

"Who?"

"My brother." She slides the key into the door, opens it, and releases a puff of warm, stale air—air that reeks of illness. It's a bedroom, featuring a high, four-poster bed and a further clutter of collectables. On the floor, pushed against the baseboard, there's a hefty wooden chest, locked with tarnished brass fittings. Even though it's smaller than the bed, the grim darkness of the trunk dominates the room.

At first, I can hardly see the man lying under the blankets. He's buried so thickly in quilts and pillows that his body is a formless blob. Only his face is visible—skeletal, pale, with papery skin that collapses into deep hollows. He looks as old and fragile as the figurines that fill the house. I assume he's dead—*I need you to bring him back*—but then the man coughs. It's a hopeless rattle.

Now I realize what the woman meant. She *did* want to bring her brother back, but not from death. Merely from the brink of it.

"So this is your brother?" I ask.

"No," says the woman. She goes to a table under the room's frosted window, tearing open the bricks and pouring all of them into a large ceramic bowl. "This is Papa."

"But I thought—"

"Yes. My brother. He died when we were only children, and now my father wants to see him again, one last time." She lifts the bowl, heavy and brimming with all the nixiedust. "Hold this," she says, handing me the bowl. "I'll need your lungs if I'm going to get it off all in one blow."

"Okay," I say, hesitating. "But where? Where are we supposed to aim it?"

With several other keys, the woman unlocks the chest at

the foot of the bed. "In here," she says. When she opens the lid, I feel my heart thump heavily against my ribs. Inside, the wooden chest is empty save for a pile of bones. They're in such a jumble it takes my mind a moment to put them together.

Then I realize what I'm looking at: the skeleton of a hominid child. The torso is curled up like a baby in its mother's womb. Beneath the bones are a few clumps of moist earth. I remember the hole in the ground, out in the yard. Worst of all is the tiny skull. It gapes up at me, severed from the spine and lying empty at the child's feet.

"What happened to him?"

"I can explain later," the woman says, taking the bowl back from my paws. "Right now, I need you to take a deep breath. You understand?"

I nod dumbly.

"Good. Now on the count of three. One, two, three . . ."

We both exhale, long and slow and even. There's so much dust inside the bowl, it's hard to believe we'll get it all out. But we do. It spirals up to fill the room, sparkling and still, a cloud on a windless day. For an instant, I wonder if it knows what to do. Could it be confused? If it believed it was meant for me, what would happen?

All at once, the full weight of the hovering dust reels and hisses and blows down into the wooden trunk. The whirlpool of air is so fierce that it buffets the lid and slams it shut. The room falls silent, save for the weak sputterings of the old man.

The woman steps around me and goes to her father's side. "It's okay, Papa," she says. "I did it. You'll see. He's coming now."

There's a wet thump from inside the wooden chest and then, very slowly, the lid is pushed open. Rising up is a small boy. He looks about four or five years old, with deep brown hair to match his eyes. His skin is as pallid as his father's, but unlike the sickly old man, the boy's skin glows as if lit from within.

"Mama?" he says, looking around, blinking and bewildered. "What happened?"

"She's not here," says the woman. "But come." She lifts the boy out of the box and carries him to the bed. "Come and see Papa."

But instead of regarding his father, the boy buries his face in his sister's shoulder. "I'm frightened," he whimpers.

"Don't you want to see Papa?"

The boy nods, grinding his forehead against his sister's neck.

"Okay," she says. "Then why don't you let me put you down?"

"No!" the boy cries. "I'm frightened!"

"Why? Why are you frightened?"

The boy's nearly in tears. "There's a wolf," he says quietly. "There's a wolf here. I saw him. A wolf."

The word stings me, but I understand. Sometimes it's easy to forget what you look like to the rest of the world. Sometimes you need a child to remind you.

The woman clutches the boy and looks at me with sad, apologetic eyes. "Tell you what," she whispers to her brother. "If you let me put you down and you have a nice visit with Papa, then I promise to chase the wolf away. Does that sound okay?"

The boy nods, and is promptly plunked down on the bed beside his father.

Out in the cluttered corridor, the woman thanks me. "You can go now," she says.

But I can't leave yet. "What happened to him?"

"I've never told anyone."

"I'd like to know."

Without meeting my eyes, the woman tells me. "His mother died when he was born, and Papa remarried—that was my mother. But somehow, after marrying Papa, my mother became a madwoman. Something changed in her, I don't know what, but she was suddenly filled with an all-consuming jealousy. She envied the boy, you see, the attention my father doted upon him. And so—" The woman's voice catches in her throat. "So my mother killed him. She used that chest in there to do it, slammed it down on his tiny neck until he was dead, until his head was severed from his body. And worse, she tried to make me believe it was my fault, that I had caused it. She convinced me that I'd go to prison, that I'd be punished, and so I helped her." The woman covers her mouth, remembering. "To hide the crime, my mother led me as we cut up his body and boiled the flesh. We buried the bones in the yard."

"You could have told the police."

The woman nods. "When I was old enough, I thought of that. But by then, my mother was gone. She had already died herself, you see."

I don't know what else to say, so I let the woman speak for me.

"You read about these things in the paper all the time. It's horrible, the things people do." The woman's eyes are welling up, full of regret and sadness. "I swear, there's something very *rotten* at the heart of this city."

Rotten. Maybe so. The woman's story reminds me of my father, of what he told me in the East Pen, how dust could cause a murderous shift in character. It also reminds me of what Jerry told me. That dust could go either way, good or bad.

"If you don't mind my asking, was your mother a user?"

"Dust?" The woman asks. "Of course. Who isn't? It's not so bad, really. In moderation. Look what it did for my father's boy."

"It brought him back. But I need to know something. Is it permanent?"

The woman puts her hand on the closed bedroom door. "Papa doesn't believe in a life after this one. I told him they'd be together soon, but he's not a believer. So we saved and saved for this." She looks at me. "To buy your nixiedust. The man I spoke to—a dwarf with a terrible face—he promised it would last. He said it was fairy magic."

"He said that?"

She nods. "He promised Papa would have his boy back for as long as he wanted."

The woman's brow furrows. There's a soft knock on the door. It's coming from inside the room. She pulls the door open and there's the boy.

"Something's wrong with Papa," he says.

The woman rushes to the bed, kneeling beside her father—who lies dead and still beneath the blankets.

Meanwhile, the little boy is frozen in the doorway, staring up at me in fearful wonder. The darkness of his eyes appears to be seeping into the rest of his face. Gray circles begin to pool in his cheeks. Then, slowly, a deep red bruise spreads across his throat.

"My neck hurts," he whispers.

The woman looks up from the bed, coming to comfort the child, but already I can see what's happening. Skinner lied to her. The effects of the dust are wearing off. He's beginning to decay, beginning to return to the dead.

"It *hurts*," he says, louder this time, tears in his eyes.

The woman kneels in front of him, hugging and squeezing, hoping her embrace can keep him alive. But the boy screams in pain, which makes her hold him even tighter. Too tightly, in fact, because the body is coming apart, the solidness of the boy's pale skin is beginning to shred. The pressure of the woman's embrace is all too much and the boy screams—*"Papa!"*—as his head is once more wrenched from his shoulders. It thumps on the bedroom floor, and yet still the boy's mouth is open wide, wailing in pain.

The woman turns her despair at me now. "Get out!" she shrieks, clutching the tiny, dissolving body. "You *beast!* Look what you've done! This isn't fairy magic! It's rotten! It's *evil!*"

So I run. I run out to where Tom is waiting, racing past him without any answer to his questions, galloping down the alleyway, leading him back into the echoing safety of the tunnels.

26
SUNLIGHT AND FILTH

DAWN IS ON ITS WAY. SPORADIC SHAFTS OF EARLY MORNING LIGHT CUT through the grates above us. We're going as fast as possible— at least without tripping over the loose stones or killing ourselves by falling over an edge. The passages, the gratings, the pockmarked walls, the unforgiving ceilings, the vicious inclines, the slim bridges over rancid waters—they all flash past like half-asleep dreams.

But none of it fazes me. All I can see in my mind is that resurrected boy. Is that what my father meant about bringing Mom back? It can't be, because that woman back there was right. It's an *evil* kind of magic—dark, fleeting, morbid. Maybe that woman was right about something else, too. At the heart this city, something's rotten.

Suddenly, Tom stops and I nearly slam flat into his haunches. "Wait," he says. He flicks his flashlight on, blinding me. "Hold this." He hands the flashlight to me as he flips the map open.

"What are you doing?"

"I figured out a shortcut." He points to the map, where the reservoir is marked off as a cloud of black. His claw traces the border with Dockside. "If we go left up here and cut under the cemetery, we can bypass all of this."

It makes sense for about a second, until I see it's one of the red tunnels. "We're not supposed to go down there," I tell him. "Besides, it's a dead end."

Tom squints. "Prob'ly a typo."

"It's a *secret map*. Who makes a typo on a—"

He snaps it closed. "I listened to you back there, and you made us late. So now we're gonna do things my way. C'mon!" He takes off and I've got no choice but to bound after him. This tunnel is larger than the others, which allows us to really get our speed up. The padding of our feet and the raggedness of our breath echo everywhere. Then, suddenly, the echoes get louder. We slow down.

"I *told* you," I say, but without satisfaction. A vast black wall looms up ahead of us. It's a dead end.

"God*damn*it!" Tom slaps the rock face. He turns to me, his dark hair melding with the blackness of the wall. All I can see is the dim glow of his eyes and his bared teeth. *"You did this."* He takes a step forward. "All you wanna do is give folks a helping hand. But that's *not our job.*"

"Don't you get it? That's why she asked for someone big, like me. She needed someone who could—"

"Shut up." He says it quietly, twisting the words into something sinister. "It oughta be my cousin standing where you are right now. He's fast, even faster than me." He takes another step. "But Zeb didn't make it, did he? Instead I'm stuck with you. And because of that *we're late*." Another step. "Bet you don't even know what Skinner does to latecomers." Another step. "Which means now I gotta come up with a story, see?"

I'm bracing myself for a fight. But I can hardly see him.

"How's this? Newbie trips and falls off a ledge. I try to save him, but I can't and that's why I'm late. All I could do was watch him get swept off, slapping and howling on a river of shit." He smiles broadly, a white slash hovering in the air like a crescent moon. I can sense him about to lunge when he stops. The grin vanishes, and I know why.

I can smell it.

A mixed-up scent fills the chamber, something like sunlight and filth, burning hair and melted rubber, still water and rotting flesh.

"You smell that?"

"I think I've smelled this once before."

"What is it?"

"I didn't stick around to find out."

Tom points at me. "This ain't over," he says quietly. "But, uh . . . maybe we oughta head back to the other tunnels."

So we do, loping warily back the way we came. But the mixed-up scent whirls and spins all around us.

"It's moving," he whispers.

"I know."

"Keep going," he says. "We passed an alcove back there with a slope to it. It'll head back to the surface. I don't care who sees us."

One more step and something huge and dark comes out of the very alcove we're trying to get to.

Tom leaps backward, tripping over his legs. *"Run!"*

We both backpedal toward the rock face. Tom pants with fear. "What is that thing?"

It roars, the sound echoing off the walls. It's enough to flatten us against the stone.

"Gotta get around it," says Tom.

"It's too big."

Could it really be a giant? Surely, it'd never come down here, and the shape of it—it doesn't seem right. I can't tell where it starts and where it ends. How do you get around a thing like that?

The roaring stops. It's sniffing the air. It's coming for us.

Tom sets out to run, but I grab him. "Wait," I say. "Not yet. Wait 'til it lunges."

"Are you insane?"

"That's how we'll get around it," I whisper.

The creature swings its shadowy head at us and rushes forward. Tom and I dart away from each other, sprinting along the wall. The creature's body slams into the rock. It howls a shriek of frustration. The whole chamber quakes as though it's made of nothing but pressboard.

Then it gets worse. The whole cave starts crumbling.

Chunks of rubble fall from the ceiling. It's even harder to see than before. But my plan worked. We got around the thing. We're on the far side, running blind through a shower of falling rocks. But it's still back there, still wailing, still coming for us.

"Gotta get outta here!" Tom barks at me.

We meet up again in the middle of the chamber, galloping back the way we came. I glance over my shoulder. It's still following us, booming forward in a kind of grotesque hobble, moaning and roaring.

"There," says Tom. He veers left and the chamber narrows, sloping upward. Ahead of us there're a few stripes of dim light coming through a drain. "As soon as we get—" He yelps when a large stone thumps down on his back. I, on the other hand, keep going.

But then I stop. I don't know why, but I do. Maybe it's because of what I did to Roy. I can't let that happen again, so I turn back for a wolf who was just trying to kill me—for the second time. He's lying dazed on the ground. A line of light from the grating above cuts him squarely in two.

"Henry," he whimpers.

"I'm coming."

Then, out of the darkness beyond, comes a hand—a black, cloven claw, like the forehoof of an enormous mule. But even as I watch it come out of the darkness, I think, *That's impossible. It's too big.*

It rakes into the back of Tom's hide and hoists him up, drawing him into the shadows.

"Tom!"

I slip the empty pack off my shoulders. A large chunk of stone thumps down at my feet.

"Here," I say, speaking to the darkness and waving my forearms. "You want some dust, don't you? Everybody wants dust. I've got some." I hold up my empty pack. "It's in here. Put Tom down and I'll give it to you."

The creature grunts at me but doesn't move. "Okay," I say. I pad farther into the shadows. I can see the outline of both of them. Tom, dangling in the air above me, clutched in the grip of a great black beast.

"Put down my friend," I tell it, "and I'll give you some."

The creature roars.

"Okay, okay—" I start unzipping the pack. I have an idea. I toss it at the thing's feet. "There you go," I say. "Take it, it's yours." I take out my flashlight.

As the creature bends to reach for the bag, I flick the light on. Suddenly, I can see the creature's not a mule. Not a giant either. It's not a goat. Not a wolf. Not a raven or a pig or an elf. It's not even a hedgehog. It's *all* of them. I beam the light dead into its enormous eyes. Blinded, the creature screams and drops Tom, recoiling into the dark.

Tom rushes past me and up the slope.

"You're welcome!" I yell, chasing after him.

There's a ladder at the end of the tunnel. Tom's already climbing up.

"Where's this lead?" I ask.

He doesn't answer me. He keeps scrambling toward the light. I grab hold of the ladder and it trembles in my fist. I can feel it slipping away from the wall. The whole tunnel is collapsing.

Tom throws the hatch open and the blue light of morning floods in, shooting through the rain of rubble. When I reach the top, the ladder drops off the wall entirely, but I manage to grasp the edge of the cement just as the cavern buckles completely. I clamber out and narrowly avoid being crushed alive. I roll onto my back, staring up at Eden.

My heart's pounding. Tom's on his back beside me, his breath ragged and his eyes wide. I look around and see we're lying right in the middle of the street. We've come up through a manhole. There's a traffic jam freezing cars in both directions. Families on the sidewalk stare and point at us. I tune in the sound of sirens, but I'm too dazed to tell if they're coming this way.

"C'mon," I say, helping Tom to rise. "We gotta get out of the street."

Tom nods, and I usher him to the side of the road. I see now that the families are dressed in black. We've come up on a street right beside Earthwood Cemetery, not far from the place where we put Doc in the ground. The trees are thick beyond the fence. I point my snout in that direction and take a deep breath, trying to clear out the scents of the underground. I'm grateful for the cemetery's trees, but my snout picks up something else, too. It's a strong whiff of cigarette smoke.

Tom stumbles over and shoves the map at me. "You take it! I don't want it anymore!"

Begrudgingly, I crumple the map into my pocket.

A few mourners on the sidewalk hug their children close, drawing them away from us. Tom lays his paw on my shoulder catching his breath. "What *was* that thing?"

I can only shake my head.

"When you flashed the light . . ." He trails off. "It looked like—like . . ."

"I know. What *did* it look like?"

There's no time for Tom to answer, because the ground starts shaking. The mourners scream and all at once, the collapsed hole we just climbed out of erupts in a geyser of asphalt and cement. The creature itself bursts through the ground, coughing and roaring and pulling itself into the light of day.

27
TITANS

THE CREATURE ROARS, LOUDER THAN EVER, SHATTERING THE GLASS OF A SHOP window across the street. Even though we can see it clearly now, it is still impossible to say what this thing is. Though one claw is huge, black, and mulish, the creature's other hand is long and thin, with the amphibious sheen of a frog. Halfway up the same arm, quills begin punching through the oily skin, bristling thicker to cover its back, which is streaked with the fins of a water nixie. The legs and the head are wolfish—save for the globbish tusks that burst out like sabers. And everything—every mixed-up bit of this thing—is blown up to the scale of a giant. It's a freakish chimera of everything in the city. Maybe this is what happens when you thrust all of us together. You get something awful.

The creature rears up, its huge eyes trained on us. A massive set of raven wings extend from its back, heaving and dragging its bulk along the ground.

Tom screams and gallops past me, off along the edge of the cemetery. I chase after him as fast as I can, and the iron bars of the fence become a blur. The creature hobbles and flaps, shedding a trail of jet-black feathers, revealing patches of white flesh.

Meanwhile, Tom and I are running in tandem, scampering like a pair of crabs, tossed off-balance by the quaking earth. From behind me, I hear something that sounds like the pulling of a thousand teeth, the cracking of a thousand bones. It's the cemetery fence, as the creature rips it out of the ground. The fence undulates along its length and crashes down, knocking us to the asphalt. No, not us. It's just me who's crushed under the fence.

"*Tom!*" I call to him. "You gotta help me! You gotta lift it!"

He stops, but he doesn't make a move. "It should've been Zeb," he whispers. "Not you."

The creature thunders closer.

"But just now in the tunnels! I *saved* you!"

"I know," he says. "Zeb never would've done that." He stoops and grips the fence, straining to lift it while I press up with all four limbs.

"Come on!" Tom screams at me. "Slide out! Hurry!"

"I can't. I'm still—"

There's a whoosh of air as the creature's claw sweeps over us, batting Tom away like an insect. He shoots across the street, tumbling into the shadows of an alley.

The creature roars, baring teeth and tusks. It picks the fence up with ease. I try scampering out, but it's got me and as I'm raised into the air by the scruff of my neck, I get a good view of the deserted street. Everyone has run for cover. I can see a family of elves cowering in the cemetery trees.

The creature hauls me up to its face. Up close, it's less wolfish. The hide and hair are a kind of mosaic, patches stitched together and looking loose, puffy, and ready to crumble.

"I know," I say, speaking as calmly as I can, "that I lied before about having some dust in my bag. I don't have any, but I could get you some." But I'm giving this thing too much credit. It doesn't understand a word of what I'm saying. Its other hand latches onto one of my ankles. I think to myself, *This is it. I'm about to be torn in two by a giant, mixed-up abomination from the pit of the city.* Then I sniff something on the breeze. Cigarette smoke.

"YOU ARE HURTING HENRY FRIEND!"

All at once, the throbbing pressure in my limbs vanishes. The creature drops me. It drops me because it's defending itself—from David, the gravedigger, who has come thundering out of the cemetery in a blind run, toppling trees and kicking over mausoleums. I've never been so happy to see a giant in my whole life.

I land on all fours in the cemetery bushes, right in the midst of the startled family of elves. They huddle together, backing away. Instantly, we're all thrown to the ground by a new earthquake, this one caused by David and the beast tumbling to the ground, wrestling and punching and taking cars and lampposts along for the ride.

"Henry!" someone whispers.

The elves flinch like they've all been shot.

"Henry!"

"Fiona?"

"Over here." She comes crawling through the hedges, down on all fours with her camera swinging low between her forepaws. She tosses it around her back and lunges for me, throwing her forearms around my neck. "I thought that thing was gonna kill you!"

"So did I."

"Had to convince David to come to your rescue. It wasn't easy."

"Guess I owe you my life." I'm beginning to hug her back when she sees the quivering elves ogling us. She pulls away, embarrassed.

Fiona brings up her camera, snapping a few pictures. "What is that thing?" she asks.

"I have no idea."

The fight's moving down the street, wreaking all kinds of havoc. David's slightly bigger, and well-muscled from a life of digging holes and lifting gravestones. But he's only got his arms and legs to battle with. The creature has wings. And that mulish claw. And that snout full of goblin tusks. It's using them, too, cleaving deep into David's shoulder.

Fiona covers her mouth. "Oh, David!"

Police cars scream past. Instinctively, I hunch down to hide myself.

"I see you're still a wanted wolf." Fiona moves to shield me from view.

"They're gonna send me back to St. Remus."

Fiona lowers her voice. "Maybe you should go. Let them finish with you." She shakes her head. "How does running away help? Look what happened to Roy."

My throat tightens up. "W-what happened to Roy?" As if I don't know.

"They found him a couple nights ago. In Dockside. He'd been left in a gutter, under a pile of trash."

"Oh, no."

"He was nearly dead."

"Nearly?"

"They have him in the hospital now, pumping him full of dust. But it's not enough. They can't wake him up."

The cops are out on the street now, trying to surround the thunderstorm of two grappling titans. All of them are armed with rifles, and they are taking aim. David's heel kicks a parked car and sends it scudding across the street (and there goes the local pool hall).

"*Fire!*"

The police let loose. Tranquilizer darts loaded with sedative dust *thwip* through the air and *pop-pop-pop* into the giants' bodies. Each one explodes on impact, barbs hooking into the skin and puffing out clouds of riot-grade fairydust.

The creature prods its snout curiously into the cloud. David, meanwhile, is startled. He fans his huge hands, trying to escape the fog of dust. But escape is impossible. The dust knows what—and who—it's for. David screams as the cloud swarms inside him.

Almost instantly, the giants' feet falter and their knees buckle. A moment later, the two of them are slumped on the asphalt, dead to the world and snoring in a bruised and bloody heap.

"You should go," Fiona tells me, "but I'm gonna stay. In case David wakes up. He's not so good at explaining himself."

"Okay," I tell her. I reach out to squeeze her paw. "Thank you."

She laughs. "Don't worry about it. I doubt it'll be the last time I have to save your butt."

I drop to all fours and scamper off into the trees. I follow them along the wall and come out near one of the cemetery's less conspicuous exits. Before heading any farther, I consult the map. I'm hoping to find another entrance to the refinery, one that will take me in behind the wall where the nixiedust is made. If Dad is right, then somewhere back there I'll find—

"Hello, Henry."

I close the map and crumple it into my pocket. Standing at point-blank range behind me is Detective White. She's got her weapon drawn, leveled squarely at my chest.

"Relax," she says. "I probably won't shoot you, but just in case you're wondering, this isn't loaded with tranquilizers." She waves her gun in the air. "I've always preferred real bullets."

28
THE WAY THINGS ARE

WHITE NODS AT THE POCKET WHERE I STUFFED THE MAP. "CARTOGRAPHY," she says. "It's good to have a hobby."

I raise my paws to show her I mean no harm. "Listen," I say, "you have to let me go."

She laughs. "Why would I have to do that?"

"Because I know where the fairies are."

Her face goes grim. "You shouldn't joke about that."

"Who's joking?"

"You are. Obviously."

"I'm telling the truth."

"No, kid, you might *think* you're telling the truth, but you're not. Nobody knows where the fairies went. They're just gone. I oughta know. I was on the squad assigned to find them and bring them back. Only we didn't find squat. Eden was a ghost town." She spits on the pavement. "They're gone. It's just the way things are."

"What about that thing back there—that thing that came out of the ground?"

"What about it?"

"You ever seen anything like that before?"

She shrugs. "No."

"That's my point. Maybe sometimes 'the way things are' isn't the way they are at all."

She raises the gun until it's level with my snout. "Enough philosophizing. You'll make me forget I'm still ticked off about how you gave me the slip last time around. So be a good little pup and do as I say. Sit, roll over, and play dead. It'll make things easier."

"But don't you—"

"Do it."

A shadow flashes between the trees and springs out of the hedges.

White manages to mutter something like "Wha—?" before she's bowled over by Fiona. The gun goes skittering up the path and into the bushes. Fiona snarls and struggles to pin White to the ground. "Told you," she says to me through gritted teeth, "I'd have to . . . save your butt . . . again."

But White's as slippery as they come. She's fast, too. Every motion has the practiced calm of a martial art. All Fiona can do is hope to outweigh her. Unfortunately, as I've already seen, a weight advantage isn't much use against Detective White.

She slips out of Fiona's grip, spins low to the ground, and sweeps her leg into the back of Fiona's knees. Fiona falls flat on her face, while White flips to her feet without any effort at all. She spends an instant roving the path with her eyes. When she can't spot her weapon, she hunches into a grappler's stance. Her pale hands, still spotted with scabs of countless brawls, curl into fists.

"Two against one," she says. "That's okay. Try *seven* against one sometime. That's more my speed."

My own eyes go to the bush where the gun skittered away. I don't think White saw where—

Fast as lightning, she's on me, throwing punches and kicks that seem to come ten at a time. She snatches one of my fingers and chicken-wings me just like she did Gunther, shoving me to my knees. Then, suddenly, she eases off. She steps back with her head cocked to the side.

"You're not very good at resisting arrest, are you?"

"I've never had to before."

"The least you could do is make it interesting." She shrugs. "Aw, never mind. I've wasted enough time on you already." She approaches casually, as if it doesn't matter what I do. That makes me mad. I rise up to my full height and rotate my big, thick skull, smoothing out the kinks. Fiona rises up, too, a pair of big bad wolves against one puny hominid.

White smiles. "Now that's more like it." She rushes me, but this time I've steeled myself, and I block as many of her blows as I can. A few still hit their mark, but she's got to contend with Fiona now, as well. Only White's ready for her. She seems to get better—swifter, more accurate—when she's in an unfair fight.

She chops me one in the throat that sends me coughing and reeling backward, and then deals Fiona a backhanded punch followed by a leaping kick to the ribs. Fiona goes tumbling into the bushes, which makes me even angrier.

White lunges for me and lands a heel on my thigh muscle. The promise of a bruise resonates all the way into my gut. But she has taught me a thing or two in this fight, namely, diversion and speed (in that order), so I fake with one paw and lash out with the other. She's fast, but my knuckles catch the curve of her chin.

She staggers, dazed and shaking some sense back into her head. I can't help regretting what I just did: punched a woman half my size square in the face. But in a second she's steadied herself and is regarding me with something that looks a lot like admiration. Cherry-red blood trickles from her cherry-red lips. She doesn't bother dabbing it away. "Nice one," she says. "Nobody's hit me that hard in weeks." She smiles, spreading her lips so the flow widens and dribbles from her chin. "Maybe I misjudged you. Maybe you're more like your father than I thought. Maybe someplace deep down, you really *do* have that killer instinct."

I roar at her, and for the first time, I see real fear in the eyes of the infamously hard-bitten Detective White.

Then there's a gunshot.

It's Fiona. She's standing in the bushes, White's gun cocked straight up at Eden.

White looks her up and down. "I know you," she says. "Or

rather, I know your brother." She nods thoughtfully. "How's he making out, by the way?"

Fiona points the gun at White. "Where're your handcuffs?"

The detective narrows her eyes. "In here." She points to a pocket. "Why don't you come and get them?"

Fiona shakes her head. "Get them yourself. But first, throw me the keys."

Reluctantly, White does as she's told.

"Good. Now cuff yourself to the fence."

White doesn't move.

Fiona takes a step forward. "I'm not kidding," she growls. "Do it."

White takes out a pair of hefty cuffs and stands by the fence. "I hope you know you're about to get yourself into a whole lot of trouble."

Fiona smiles. "Guess it runs in the family."

"Evidently," says White. She looks at me. "A lot of that going around lately."

"Hurry up, Detective."

White locks one wrist to the fence.

"Thank you." Fiona's clearly pleased with herself. "I'm going to leave your gun here in the bushes. You can get it later, okay?"

"I'm gonna get *you* later is what I'm gonna do." White looks to me next. "You, too, Whelp."

I do my best to ignore this comment. Instead, I turn to

Fiona. "Why are you helping me like this? You're just making trouble for yourself."

Fiona shrugs. "You said you knew where the fairies are. If anyone can help Roy, if anyone can wake him up, it's them."

"Oh."

"I know they never really granted wishes for animalia before, but if we saved them—you and me, a pair of wolves—they'd have to, right?"

"A pair?"

"Wherever you're going next, I'm coming with you."

29
A BAD DESTINY

WE'RE STANDING ON A BRINE-RUSTED PLATFORM OVERLOOKING THE reservoir. Across the street is the flophouse and the underground refinery. There's a high wind off the reservoir and the water's choppy. Tankers full of fairydust look like toys, bobbing gently in a vast concrete bath.

On the way here, I explained everything I know to Fiona, namely, my father's theory about the perversion of old-time magic and the enslavement of the fairies. She seemed as skeptical as I was, but she's still here, which means she's as hopeful as I am, too.

The platform we're standing on is two floors below street level and, according to the map, opens onto a tunnel that will lead us to the refinery's forbidden rooms. On the paper, it's red—one of the tunnels we aren't supposed to use. I can only hope there's not another giant chimerical beast lurking inside.

"You sure you wanna come with me?"

Fiona takes my forepaw in hers. I can feel the hair on the

back of her fingers. Not coarse like mine. It's like silk. "Of course I'm sure. I want my brother back, and besides—" She holds up her camera. "We'll need pictures, right?"

Thankfully, the tunnel is empty. At the far end, we climb a ladder that leads up to a hatch similar to the one Matt used when he first introduced me to the tunnels. I push it open slowly.

Silence.

The hatch opens onto a large, empty room. This place has the somber austerity of a library—and the shelves to match. Aisle after aisle of them. But instead of books, these shelves are packed with fairydust, glimmering in buckets and packaged into bricks like the one Tom and I delivered. It's more dust than I've ever seen in one place, but there's nothing unusual about that. The nixies are dealers and smugglers. This sort of room—little more than a fortified stash house— is exactly what you'd expect to find behind closed doors.

"Is this it?" Fiona whispers. "Maybe you should check your map again."

"It's the right place." I can see the conveyors entering the room over our heads. Looking up, we see that second-story scaffolding rims the walls. Every ten feet or so, there are doorways.

"Up there, maybe," I say, pointing at them. "In those rooms."

Just as we're about to climb the stairs, our ears prick up. We hear a *click*. Silently, I lead Fiona behind the shelves to hide. We watch through the gaps between them as one of the doors opens. It's Skinner. He's talking to someone.

"—as fast as we can," he's saying. "Isn't that right, Pa?"

Skinner stands aside and ushers out the person he's addressing. It's Pa Nixie. I can't believe it. Few folks have ever laid eyes on him (and have lived to tell about it, that is). But I recognize him from the handful of grainy photos they've been printing in newspapers all my life. I can feel the image of his rubbery mass branding itself into my brain. Fiona snatches my paw and squeezes it.

"Yes," says Pa. His lower fins shuffle over the floor, carrying his great blubber with careless effort. He casts a glance over one sloping shoulder, back into the room. "We're still on schedule for, uh—how shall I put this? Market saturation." He's speaking to someone else who's still in the room. My insides flip when I see who it is.

The Nimbus Brothers, Karl and Ludwig, CEOs of Nimbus Thaumaturgical. They come strolling out as if they belong here, in this dingy place. I've only ever seen their faces blown up on billboards or plastered across the sides of streetcars. There's something eerie about seeing them in real life.

Karl, the younger and thinner of the two, looks at his brother, grinning happily. "*Total* market saturation," he says.

"Indeed," says Ludwig.

Skinner shuts the door and the four of them move to the staircase that swoops to the floor. They're coming down.

"You're certain the new strain has no effect on hominids?" asks Pa.

Karl nods. "Elves, dwarves, you nixies, all of us up in Eden, even those insufferable goblins. We isolated a common gene. There aren't many, but we found one. I can assure you both this is an enchantment for animalia alone."

"Excellent," says Pa.

They've reached the bottom of the steps. They're about to move directly in front of us. Skinner grins like a carnivorous plant. "I trust we can count on the fairies to provide enough to go around, yes?"

Ludwig nods. "As you well know, the fairies have been very good to my brother and me over the years."

"Indeed," says Karl. He and his brother glance up at the rooms above. "Very cooperative!"

All four of them laugh.

Now it's my turn to squeeze Fiona's paw. She looks at me in wide-eyed silence. My father was right. It's even worse than he suspected. Skinner, the nixies, Nimbus Thaumaturgical. They're all working together. They're planning something.

"Won't be long now," says Skinner. He unlocks the door to the rest of the refinery and leads them out.

We wait and listen to the door being locked. Once the clicks have died away fully, Fiona nuzzles into me. "So it's all true," she says.

As much as I like the idea of having her in my arms, I push her away. I can't forget where we are. Or why.

"C'mon." I take her by the paw and lead her up the stairs. An image of Faelynn flashes into my head. Her lithe arms. Her delicate wings. She could be up there right now. What will she look like, after all this time? What will I say to her?

We choose the same door we saw Skinner and the others use. It's locked.

"Of course it is!" I whisper harshly. I step backward to the railing. "I think I can knock it down."

Fiona stops me. "They'll hear you." Her eyes search the scaffold. "Look for some loose metal. I can pick any lock."

"You can?"

She smiles at me. "You're forgetting who my brother is. He taught me years ago. It was kind of a game we played when we were kids." She crouches down, running her paws over the metal. "I need something long and thin. Preferably two."

"What about these?" I fish into my pocket and come out with two rods of gold, the one I found in Doc's office and the one Skinner gave me at the race.

Fiona takes them from me, staring. "Are these gold?"

"It's a long story."

"Never worked with gold before, but I'll try." She slides in the chewed ends, marred with imprints of Skinner's teeth. Her face loses all expression as she feels her way. Then a thin smile grows on her face. "Got it," she says. She twists the rods simultaneously and the lock spins, shifting the dead bolt.

"Let me just say," I tell her, "I am *so* glad I brought you with me."

"I'm glad I came." She passes the stalks back to me and I pocket them both.

I don't know what I'm expecting to find in here. A fairy prison? A sweatshop full of enchanted creatures? An army of dull eyes and clipped wings? Whatever I'm expecting, it's not this.

Fiona has opened the door onto nothing more than another room full of fairydust shelves and arcane refinery equipment. In the center is a large, stainless steel table, something you'd expect to find in a thaumaturgical laboratory. Suspended above the table is a bright white lamp, glaring down on a single object.

"Is that a branch of deadwood?"

"Looks like it," I whisper.

"So where are all the fairies?"

"I don't know." I reach out and touch the branch that's lying there, gnarled and twisted. I run the pads of my fingers over the hard white surface.

"Henry," Fiona whispers. "I found something."

She's over in the corner near a door. It's hidden on the far side of a cabinet and it's not locked. As soon as she opens it, we're hit with a terrible stench. It smells like—like—well, there's no other way to put it. It smells like *shit*, a whole room of it. For some reason, the smell frightens me more than anything else I've ever sniffed. There are noises, too. Frightening, unintelligible grunts. Fiona goes in first and I follow, keeping a firm grip on her shoulders.

"Oh my God," she whispers.

The room is full of cages. But there are no fairies. Behind every set of bars, there's a—*wolf?* Maybe that's what you'd call them, but none of these are like me or Fiona or any other wolf I know. These things are primitive beasts. Naked, mindless animals. These are primordial creatures, the animals you only see on the posters in Mrs. L's biology class, posters used to teach us about evolution and our primitive ancestry.

Wolves like this don't exist anymore.

I crouch down for a closer look. I'm fascinated and repelled. These are savages. Their forepaws and hind feet look almost identical, with fingers and toes that are little more than clawed nubs. Yet still, there's something majestic about them. The way they move, the way they pace in their cages, circling round and round. Imagine being down on all fours, all the time, unable to stand up. Just from looking at them, I know that if we were out in the open, racing through a field, any one of these creatures would beat me every time.

"Henry, look."

Once again, Fiona's found another door, this time behind a different cabinet. It seems all the rooms are linked along rear passages.

"There are more of them," she says.

The next room stinks with a wetter, tangier kind of excrement. It's also full of cages, but smaller ones, shaped like bullets standing on end. Each cage imprisons a tiny raven, no taller than a pumpkin. When they see us, they flap

and squawk. Dull black eyes flit with terror as we lope past
their bars. We must look like monsters to them.

We keep going. Every room houses another species.
There's a room for mules, one each for cats, frogs, pigs, goats.
There's a room full of foxes. I notice they are much like the
wolves, only smaller. But they're just as fierce with energy,
padding in cramped circles on primitive paws, careful to
sidestep the piles of their own waste.

Fiona's taking rolls of pictures. It feels like we haven't
said a word in ages.

"Wait," I say. I crouch down in front of one particular
cage. Inside, there's a gray fox, lurching in circles on four
ancient legs. Two shocking black streaks slide along either
side of its snout, and its eyes—they're sodium yellow and
shot through with flecks of violet.

"I know this one."

Fiona comes closer. "What do you mean you know it?
How can you—?" Her voice breaks up as it dawns on her.
"You mean?"

"His name was Jerry. He was homeless, I think. Sold dust
on the street."

"It's a coincidence. It only *looks* like someone. It's not
possible."

"It's his eyes."

We both peer into the cage, into Jerry's distinctive face.
In response, seeing the hairy mugs of these two enormous
wolves looming over him, Jerry growls. He bares his tiny

perfect teeth and coughs up a bark so small and meaningless it makes me feel nothing but deep sadness.

"But Henry, how? If they used dust—if they used magic—to do this to him, it would've worn off by now. It's impossible."

"Not for fairies," I say. "Not for old-time magic."

"Fairies would *never* do something like this."

"What if they didn't have a choice?" I think about what Jerry told me, when he caught me reading Dad's letters. Good destinies and bad destinies. Old-time magic could send you either way. That's what this is. A bad destiny. The worst kind of all. A destiny that doesn't push you forward to some unfulfilled potential, but backward, devolving you to savagery.

Fiona covers her mouth. "So that means . . . in all these rooms?"

"What else can it mean?"

She lets out a tiny cry. "Remember what they said? 'Total market saturation.'"

Of course. "That's why Nimbus is down here with the nixies. They control Dockside, and that means the reservoir. Let's say Nimbus produced a dust potent enough to use in the water system . . ." I gaze around the room. Everywhere, tiny foxes scratch hopelessly against iron bars. "We could all end up like this."

For a moment, neither of us can speak.

"But then . . ." Fiona looks around. "Where are the fairies?

When they talked about them just now, they were looking right up here. But all that's here are these—I don't know—these *animals*."

"When they talked about the fairies, they were looking up, but not up here. They were looking up to—"

"Eden."

We both flinch. It wasn't Fiona who completed my thought.

It was Skinner. He's standing in the exit that leads out to the scaffolds. We were so shocked by what we were seeing, we never even heard him open the door. Behind him stands a whole army of globs.

"Good," he says, chewing on yet another stalk of straw. "Just the wolf I was looking for." His disfigurements crack into an ominous grin. "I have a job for you, Mr. Whelp. And I know you'll do it, too. After all"—he looks at Fiona—"you were kind enough to bring me a hostage."

Fiona growls from deep in her throat and the foxes respond in kind, braying and barking and leaping in their cages.

"That reminds me," says Skinner. "We shall have to find you two *animals* a cage for the night."

30
PROOF

TO SAY THINGS ARE NOT LOOKING GOOD WOULD BE A NASTY UNDER-statement. I'm sitting in the rear of Skinner's brougham. Manx, his right-hand cat, is piloting us through the early morning streets. Skinner's beside me in the back, his bare hand on my knee—a natural deterrent when it comes to running away. But attempting to escape isn't even an option. Fiona is still locked in Skinner's demented idea of a kennel.

Outside, the houses fall away as we move farther west, out past the edge of the city. The last vestige of urban life is yet another billboard, the Nimbus Brothers beaming down on the highway with their smocks and test tubes. The slogan cries, *Enchantment for All!*

Manx steers us onto a turnpike that leads out through the vast wall hemming in the western edge of the city. The lights turn everything inside the tunnel a jaundiced yellow. Once we exit from the far side, it isn't long before we're driving through the quarries, endless pits that pucker the desert like honeycombs. Huge derricks and diggers and machinery litter

DUST CITY

the edges, the walls, and the floors of countless canyons. Conveyors spew chunks of sparkling stone into towering silos, where they wait to be crushed, sifted, refined, bottled, and shipped. These are the dust mines.

Manx accelerates past them, peering at me in the rearview.

I turn to Skinner. "You killed Doc, didn't you?"

He pretends he didn't hear me.

"You made it look like he killed himself, but I found this in his office." I take the rods of gold out of my pocket. "See? Just like the one you gave me yourself."

"Not much in the way of proof, is it?"

"So you did kill him."

He purses his twisted lips until they resemble the blossom of a cauliflower. "Please, don't get me wrong on this point. I'm not offering you a denial. I'm merely observing that what you're holding there in your paw is—I don't know . . ." He considers for a moment. "Rather weak. In terms of proof."

"Why did you do it?"

Again, the cat glances at me in the rearview. His eyes are narrow and suspicious.

Skinner shrugs. "Your friend, the good Doctor Grey, was an inquisitive old wolf, wasn't he?" His uneven eyes blink slowly. "There's a lesson to be learned there, I think."

"Inquisitive," I say, more to myself than Skinner. I think about Dad's letters and something clicks. I know why Doc held them back, why he never gave them to me. He was

205

keeping them for himself. He was using them. They were clues. "He found out about what you were doing, didn't he? He knew you were planning to send us all back to the dark ages. Or some of us, at least." I look back into the rearview, catching the cat's eyes. "Don't you know what he's got in store for us? It'll happen to you, too."

"Maybe you ought to pipe down." Skinner regards me solemnly. "There's no need to worry about what we're planning. It's perhaps a tad too complicated for primitive minds." He looks out the driver's-side window. "Ah, you see? We're already here." He points to a road that's barely a cobbled foot path. "Up ahead, Manx. Take the next left."

We glide off the exit ramp, leaving the city. It isn't long before we hit a dirt road. Gravel spumes out behind us. A small number of agriculturalists live out here, the hardnosed ones who haven't yet been lured into the city by the promise of smoggy infrastructure and meager-but-steady wages.

Apparently, we are headed to an arid farm that is nothing more than a few acres of emptiness pressed against the river. Seen from the main road, the farmhouse is a coffee-colored smudge.

The driveway is long, straight, and lined with sun-bleached ceramic pots. A few of them are planted with neglected begonias, all dead, shriveled to brittle strings. The fat wheels of Skinner's brougham crackle over the dirt. The sun is bright this morning, splashing down, flooding the dry land, leaving no shadows. Manx stops the car.

"Look at me," says Skinner.

I do as I'm told.

"A family of goats lives here. The mother's a pain in the ass. The *man* of the house agreed to will us the property once he died, and we gave him the benefit of the doubt. But the old nanny went and had the papers annulled, says she wants to keep the place, will it over to her sons." He sucks on his twisted lips, licking in some fugitive spit. "I've tried asking nicely. I warned her of what would happen if she didn't fork over the land, but she refused. So now you're gonna go in there and convince her. And if you can't convince her then I think you know what to do." His crooked eyes drill into me. "You are a wolf, after all. You understand?"

I try swallowing, but my throat's too dry. Manx stares out through the windscreen, arms folded over the wheel.

Skinner pats my knee with his bare hand. "Nervous?"

"I, um . . ."

He reaches into his jacket and takes out an unmarked vial of fairydust. It writhes inside the tube like swarming bacteria. "I happen to have something for nerves right here." He rubs his thumb around the cap. "It's something special we've been working on. It'll calm you down. Keep you focused. Make sure you get the job done."

The words echo all of my father's warnings. *He'll say it's for nerves, something to calm you down, something to help you get the job done right.*

I reach for the door handle and pull. "I'm okay." I hurry

out, fighting down the urge to run away. "I can do this for you. No problem."

Skinner's visibly disappointed. "Are you sure? I think this would really help you."

Manx mugs at me through the window, expressionless.

"I don't need anything." I try chuckling with confidence, but it comes out all wrong. "I'm not afraid of some old goat."

Skinner repockets the vial. "Suit yourself." He looks at me calmly. "There'll be other opportunities." He sits back in the seat. "We'll be waiting for you on the main road."

I push the door shut and Manx coaxes the car into a three-point turn. The wheels pop so loudly over the dry earth it sounds like gunfire.

31
BROKEN GHOSTS

THE FARMHOUSE IS A WRECK. THE ROOF SAGS LIKE A HAMMOCK AND EVERY wall cants badly to the left. The mailbox out front is marked by a rusty number five and a name: THE CAPRAS.

The land surrounding this place is grooved and waterless, coated in a layer of windblown sand. If anything had ever grown here, it long ago dried up and died. It's not the sort of land you'd think anyone would be willing to kill for. Yet still, here I am.

My foot breaks through the wood of the porch as soon as I attempt to step on it. I stand like that awhile, one leg buried in the coolness. Maybe I could make a run for it. Maybe I could get back to the city somehow and rescue Fiona. But what chance do I have? Instead, I pull my foot free and knock on the front door. A moment later it opens, just wide enough to squeeze in a credit card.

"Nobody's here," says a voice, speaking from about the height of my knee.

"So who're you?"

"I'm just a kid." The door opens a little wider. "See?" He sticks his head out through the gap. His horns are barely there, just a pair of pink thumbs budding from the top of his skull.

"Is your mother home?"

"You mean my grandmother. My mom's dead."

"Your grandmother. Can I speak to her?"

"I told you, there's nobody here." If the kid is intimidated by a wolf at the door, he doesn't show it. "No wait," he says, thinking hard. "She's down at the well. She's getting water." He points one cloven finger through the gap. "Down there."

There's a gazebo-looking building off in the distance, among a thick copse of deadwood trees. A figure shambles around it, indistinct in the haze.

"That's her?"

The kid opens the door a little wider. "I can—um, take you there if you want."

I tell him no. I can find my own way.

As I approach, I see the gathering of deadwoods is denser than it looked from the farmhouse. The gazebo is roofless and falling to pieces. Beyond it is the well the kid mentioned, in the dead center of the trees, invisible from the house. It's a simple cylinder of stone, shaded by a sheet of corrugated steel. There's a hefty pulley suspended over the opening, coiled with thick rope and presumably tied to a bucket far below. But there's no one here.

"Hello? Mrs. Capra?"

Silence. Just the creak of the deadwoods, straining up against a bright sky.

"Hello?"

A goat steps out of the copse, but it's not an old doe. It's a young buck, about my age. I'm still a good head taller than him, but he makes up for height with horns—huge coils of bone that wrap round his ears like enormous seashells.

"Who're you?" he asks.

"I'm looking for the lady of the house."

"She's not here."

"I was told that—"

"Shouldn't listen to the little guy." He spits on the ground. "He's a liar. But I got other brothers. Maybe you wanna meet them instead?"

They emerge from the trees like spirits. Five more. Six in total. All I can see are the horns. All twelve of them.

"I only need to talk to her."

"You can talk to us," says the one who looks to be the oldest. A scouring-pad beard points due south from his chin. "Wha'ja wanna say?"

I try explaining that I've been sent by the nixies, that this property belongs to them, but my explanation doesn't fly. The goats laugh in my face. One of them has a pitchfork. He stamps on the prongs and sinks them deep in the empty earth. "Them mermen don't own nothing they di'nt steal, and they's never gon' steal this land. This land's ours. So best you scram. We never liked you canids comin' round here."

"If I could speak to your grandmother, I'm sure she could—"

"You're not the first one they sent, you know." It's the eldest again. He's holding a stout shovel. "Send 'em all the time."

One of the younger brothers steps forward. "Usually we just run 'em off the property before they even get to the house."

"But we're tired of them sending you guys," says the eldest. "We thought this time we'd try something different." He smirks. "No offense meant to you personally, but we gotta send a message. If you catch our drift."

They fan out. It occurs to me—much too late—that they had all this planned. One of them swings a rake. I dodge it, but he wasn't really trying. It was a diversion. One of the other brothers swings a shovel at my back. It clangs into my side and I double over. Seizing the opportunity, they pile on, hammering down blows from shovels and horns and bony fists. One of them raises the shovel over his head, sharp edge aimed at my throat.

Then it happens again. Like in the race with Roy. Only this time I don't have any dust to blame. It's only me, in the firm grip of a natural, homegrown brand of fear and rage. Just like before, the pain vanishes. I'm a slick, impervious machine.

My paw whips out. I catch the shovel as it swoops for my gullet and I yank it from the goat's hooves. With the handle

I strike back, whipping the kid at the base of his neck. He's down and my arm flings the shovel around again. Its flat metal face slams another one against his broad, billy-goat chin. There's a crack and a gurgle, and then he's down too.

But there're four of them still pounding me. I break the shovel into pieces and lash out. My claws tear gouges into the legs of two more. Their pants sop with blood and they collapse on severed sinews. That leaves two.

The first one charges pitchfork-first, but I dodge him. I grab hold of the fork and snap off the prongs, pulling the goat to me with the handle and punching him dead in his snout. He crumples like all the rest.

The oldest and wisest, however, takes me by surprise. He's given up his tools to go with what he knows: his horns. The coils of bone ram my ribs. The momentum hurls me into one of the trees. It buckles under the meat of my back, hand-like branches clawing my face.

It takes a second for my vision to clear and when it does, I see the eldest brother standing over me with something in his hands. A chunk of loose stone. It crashes down onto my head and the rock explodes, blinding me with its fragments. The goat lifts what's left for another blow, but before he can, I lunge for his hands. The rock shatters in my teeth and I feel his goatish fingers snapping like twigs.

My paws clench murderously around his throat. His eyes bug out of his head, pleading with me. He's beginning to go limp, when I realize I can't breathe. My lungs are full of gravel and dirt and everything he hit me with. I drop him, choking and weak, and then my ears prick up. They're tuning in something new. Footfalls. Scampering feet.

It's the youngest kid. He's run down from the house to join the fight. But without air, I'm useless. The kid hits me square in the belly, hard enough to force the grit from my lungs. I vomit up a thick sludge and falter backward. My knees buckle against something. The edge of a wall?

No, it's the well. I see the sky, sagging with blue. It slides away like quicksilver. I see bricks, rough-hewn and getting darker and darker. I'm falling. And then it all goes black.

Deeper into the trees. They're alive in the wind. All I can hear is the swish of leaves. I still keep going, stalking forward, belly skimming the earth . . .

It's cold and quiet now. I feel queasy, seasick. It's dark. It's nighttime. High above me, the full moon blazes brighter than ever. My body is soft and slow. I can hardly feel my hide, but slowly, my senses reignite. Things begin to make sense.

It's not nighttime. It's the middle of the day. The moon's no moon at all. That white disc is the brightness of the well's mouth, and I'm at the bottom. I beat against the surface, and suddenly I'm choking as briny water pickles my throat. I can just about reach the bottom with one foot, enough to keep my snout from going under. My nostrils flare for breath, and I freeze like that, inches away from being drowned. I wonder how long I can keep this up.

I pop one ear above the surface; maybe I can hear something—anything. I hear whimpering from up top. It's the youngest kid, sobbing over his fallen brothers. The crying goes on and on. It echoes down the walls. I wouldn't be surprised if they're all up there dead and dying. Maybe I'm just like my father, after all. Only I'm worse, because I never took Skinner's dust. I don't have any excuse.

I shift my eyes away from the moonlike patch of sky. I relax. I float. I'll probably drown down here. It's only a matter of time before the water sucks me under, starts dissolving me in its darkness.

Near the top, the well walls are scabrous brick, but down here in the depths, it's all rotted away. Soil and clay are exposed in patches. Patches of earth that seem to sparkle. Maybe it's the water, catching light from the surface and throwing it up the shaft. But no, it *is* the soil. It's glimmering faintly.

It's fairydust runoff from the old days. I'm down with the leftover miracles. This land is full of it. That must be why Skinner sent me here. This is how they claim their land. With wolfish muscle.

The whimpering above me has died away. Either the kid recovered from my carnage or he slipped into catatonic shock. Or else he's gone for help. Sure enough, off in the distance, I pick up the squeal of sirens.

My body throbs in the water. My eyes are playing tricks. The glittering streaks buried in the soil become morbid shapes. Frayed, disjointed skeletons; cracked skulls; bony, grasping hands, and the splintered wings of angels. They clutch and spin and flap around me, an army of broken ghosts. While inside my head, an old voice sings . . .

Sleep, little cub,
and quiet your eyes.
Bottle your tears,
and soften your cries.

Dream, little soldier.
I'll never be far.
I'll find you, my soldier,
wherever you are.

PART THREE
EDEN

32
A FAIRY STORY

THERE'S A ROW OF HOLDING CELLS IN THE REAR OF THE MID-CITY POLICE
Department. They come in all shapes and sizes. Little cabins
for elves up to great caverns for giants. I've got my wolfish
one all to myself.

Gunther and Mrs. Lupovitz are here. They're on the far
side of the station, filling out forms with a police administrator.
Mrs. L looks overwrought, edgy as a cliff. Gunther just looks
bored.

I was in pretty desperate shape when they fished me out
of that hole. They hoisted me up with a lungful of well water
and a spine that felt like it was bending the wrong way. The
goats had pummeled my face into a disaster that would've
given Skinner's a run for its money. Detective White, however,
was unfazed. She was content to have me languish in a cell
rather than take me to a hospital. In her experience, she told
me, it makes for better interrogations when the felon (in this
case, me) is given a night to "stew in their own bruises."

So it's lucky Mrs. L always carries a few vials of fairydust in her handbag, ready to patch up hooligans at a moment's notice. For obvious reasons, I balked at the sight of the Nimbus halo, but I was in such bad shape I didn't say anything. I just sat there like a junkie and breathed it in. The dust did its best, but it was just some basic over-the-counter stuff. I'm still sore and still a little crooked from the waist up, but overall I'm not too bad. I'm a passable version of myself.

Only it's not me I'm worried about.

"Hey!" I yell across the room, rattling the bars. "When's somebody gonna *listen* to me?! They've still got her, Mrs. L! It's Fiona! It's Roy's sister!"

Gunther rolls his fat eyes. I've been going on about Fiona so much he's drawn the obvious conclusion that I went on the lam because I had a crush on a girl. He's half right.

"I can show you where they've got her," I say. "I can take you to the biggest nixie refinery of all. I know exactly where it is. I can tell you all about it."

Detective White rises from her desk and stalks over, sucking her teeth. "You like telling fairy tales, don't you? Just like your pop."

"He didn't do it. He was forced to do it. I mean, when he first—"

"Oh, so now you're *both* innocent. That *is* a fairy tale."

I grip my bars. "It's not a story. Everything I've told you about—my father, the fairies, what I saw at the refinery—*it's all real.*"

White shakes her head. "We've raided Dockside I dunno how many times. Never found any fairies, that's for sure."

"That's because they're up in Eden."

"Ah," she says. "You want us to raid Eden?"

"If that's what it takes. You have to believe me."

White shakes her head. "I believe what I see, kid. I saw what you did to those Capra boys."

"I was defending myself."

"Save it for your statement—which you can give me in the morning. Right now, I'm too tired to listen. I'm going home." She trudges off and grabs the leather jacket slung over the back of her chair. I see her wince as she slides it on.

Mrs. L's done with the paperwork. She comes over. "Oh, Henry," she says, and I'm enveloped in her peppermint breath. "What am I going to do with you?" She massages her handbag like it's an aching muscle. "Honestly, this is so unlike you. You'll end up in a cell next to your father. Is that what you want?"

"Maybe he's not as bad as everyone says. He was *forced* to do what he did, you know. The nixies have this awful new kind of dust, and Nimbus is helping them. They've got the fairies locked up in Eden."

Reaching in through the bars, she gives my paw a reassuring squeeze, but it's clear she doesn't believe me. "I'll do everything I can to help you," she says.

"Thanks, Mrs. L."

She nods and waddles across the station, tugging Gunther away with her.

All that's left for me to do is slump on the tiny cot. My bruised back is tender against the cold cement wall. All I can think about is Fiona. Is she going to end up like that dealer, Jerry? I imagine a gorgeous, chocolate-brown wolf, sea-green eyes flashing with an ancient ferocity, pacing back and forth inside a cage bedded down with her own excrement. It's all I can think about for hours, watching the cops slowly trickle home. Eventually, only the night guard remains. I can't see him, but I can hear him, drowsing quietly down the hall.

There's a single barred window in the holding cell. Outside, I can see Eden floating up there with the moon. One's a hovering suburb, peaked with bristling spires of light. The other one is a luminous, bone-white disc. They couldn't be more different, but somehow, seen from where I'm sitting, they're the same—bound together in freedom and flight.

Suddenly, there's the sound of smashing glass. It's followed by a growl and a scream. Sounds like it came from the night guard. I can't imagine who caused the commotion. But someone is strolling into view, tapping the bars one at a time.

It's Matt, from the flophouse.

"C'mon," he says. "We gotta get you outta here."

"But how?"

He holds up the guard's jungle of keys. "How else?"

"No," I say. "I mean how did you get in here?"

Matt starts trying key after key. "You kidding? Nixie tunnels go everywhere. Even here. *Especially* here, if you see what I mean." He finds the key we're both waiting for, and the lock clunks open. "The nixies, the cops—they're practically in bed with each other."

I pause in the door to my cell. "You mean Detective White?"

Matt waves away the suggestion. "Not her. She's barely in bed with the police half the time. If she wasn't a hominid, I'd call her the ultimate lone wolf. Now come on," he starts down the corridor. "We gotta go."

At the end of the hall, the guard's lying face up in a pool of black coffee. The white handle of a smashed mug is clutched lovingly in his fist. Matt leads us to an open ventilation shaft and we climb inside, headed back into the world under the streets.

33
THE STATUARY

"I KNOW THIS DARKNESS BETTER THAN I KNOW MYSELF."

That's how Matt explained the fact that he doesn't require any map. He led us through every twist and curve, under every overhang and over every crossing, without any hesitation at all. Which is why it's so strange that he would lead me here. To a dead end.

"Where are we?" I ask him.

"Under the statuary," he says. He's running the flat of his forepaw over the wall, searching for something. When he finds it—a crag that juts out a millimeter too far—he struggles to spin it clockwise. "No one's . . . used this . . . in a while," he says. "It's stiff." Finally, the rock twists a half-turn and a door cracks out of the bare rock face. A secret entrance.

"This way," he says.

Once I'm inside, the door cleaves shut behind me. It's a new kind of dark in here, miles beyond pitch-black. Matt takes me by the elbow. He leads me forward blindly. Even here, he knows his way. My ears pick up a shift in the echo. I sense we're approaching another door. Matt grabs my wrist and places something cold and metallic in my palm. It's a key.

"You'll need this," he says. "They've got her locked up."

Without a sound, Matt opens the door. My stomach sinks a little when I see where we are. It's the defunct refinery where I nearly murdered Roy.

Matt shakes his head. "Can you believe this is where he lives?"

He means Skinner. This empty ruin is his home.

"It's down there," says Matt, pointing down the wall. "I'll create a diversion. You get her out. The door to the statuary is behind the yellow foundry basin at the end."

"Thank you, Matt."

"Hey," he says, "a promise is a promise." He hunches over and stumbles into the open. "Ssshkinner?!" he yells in a drunkenness that's probably only a mild exaggeration. "You hearin' me, Ssshkinner? I wanna talk to you! I worked for you a *loooooooong* time, but now I'm thinkin' of quittin' and you know what? I want a package! I want a retirement plan!" He picks up a bent wrench and starts clanging it against the machines. "*Wakeup-wakeup-wakeup!* Get your hideous butt down here!"

I hope he knows what's he doing.

The door behind the basin isn't lavish or gilt with gold. It's as grimy and dilapidated as the rest of this place, and it clings to its jamb by a single hinge. The only lock is a length of chain, tied in a loose knot. Thinking of Skinner, it makes sense. When you've got the power of alchemy budding in your fingertips, displays of wealth lose their meaning.

Matt clangs across the floor, throwing his limbs against everything he can find. I take advantage of the noise, using it to mask my work as I untie the chain. The room inside is like the rest of Skinner's makeshift home—bare concrete walls, cracked glass, ragged light—but instead of a room haphazardly strewn with derelict refinery equipment, this one is thick with the golden statues of Skinner's victims.

Every species is represented—ravens, elves, foxes, humans, dwarves, mules, cats, goblins, nixies, and on and on. There's even a single giant, a young one, his boyish features vast and perfect. The giant's head reaches all the way above the scaffolds that line the ceiling. Each one of the victims wears a frozen expression of bewilderment or fear or pain. Goose pimples raise the hair on the back of my neck as I wander through the statues, surrounded on all sides by terrible expressions: eyes popping, heads thrown back, mouths wide, tongues raised in silent screams. Others are less dramatic, with eyes and teeth clenched, steeling themselves for the inevitable. Then there're those who're merely stunned, doomed to an eternity of quizzical disbelief. A few of them are completely calm, accepting their fate. They even wear the faintest hint of a smile as if to say, Yes, I suppose I had this coming.

"Henry?"

I see her in a cage in the corner. She's still herself.

"Are you okay?"

She's trembling. "Get me out of here."

The cage is locked, but I've got Matt's key. It grates when I punch it into the mechanism. It turns, but hardly.

"Come on, come on!"

Fiona pulls on the bars. I shimmy the key some more, yanking again and again on the lock. Fiona's looking past me, back toward the door. "Hurry! The only way out is way back there." I shake the key harder, twisting with all I've got, growling with the effort, and *presto*—it's either worked or I've broken it. Who cares which? It opens.

She's been cramped in there all night, so she's wobbly on her feet. We stick to all fours, weaving through a forest of gold. I see Matt through the gaps between statues. He's leaning in the doorway, swigging from his whiskey bottle.

"No diversion required," he says. "Don't think anyone's here. But that's no reason to stick around." He eyes the statuary. "'*Specially* in here. This place gives me the—" His eyes widen slightly and lose focus. His mouth opens in tiny increments, like the cogs of his jaw are sticky. Slowly, his face takes on the expression of an empty scream, agonized and silent.

"Matt?"

An acrid odor seeps into the air. I recognize it, something like burning soap, jagged and hot and scorching the insides of my snout. Matt's struggling to breathe, but it's not working.

"Matt! What's going on?"

He doesn't answer. His eyes beg for air. The bottle slips from his hand and explodes on the floor. His tongue bobbles out his mouth and all over his body his hair quivers and bristles and then—it all stiffens. Every follicle shimmers. He's been turned to gold.

"Matt!"

Skinner steps out from behind his newly minted statue. "Hello, Henry," he says, out of breath. His face is bright red and sheened with sweat. Twisted blood vessels pop out all over his disfigured face. "Glad to have you back," he says, dabbing his brow with a silken glove.

"What have you done?"

Skinner laughs. "I'd say that's fairly obvious." He spreads his arms, waving them across the room. He lightly kicks Matt's frozen leg. "He was getting old, wasn't he? Outlived his usefulness. But look at him now. Matt here is worth *much* more dead than alive."

A growl rises in my throat.

"Easy now," he says, wagging a finger. "I wouldn't want you to do anything foolish."

"We know what's going on here," I tell him.

"Do you now?"

"You're working with the Nimbus brothers. We saw you all together."

Skinner says nothing. For a tiny moment, he looks concerned, but on a face like his, it's difficult to tell.

"We know all about your dust experiments. What you did to my father, and all the others. We've seen what you're hiding upstairs at the refinery."

Skinner raises his eyebrows.

"We even know about the fairies. Up in Eden."

For the first time, Skinner loses his composure. His face goes pale.

"It's true isn't it?"

He smiles and his color returns. "I must say, you've certainly uncovered a great deal. I can see now you're a tad swifter than your father ever was." He toys with the fabric of his glove. "I wonder if there's anyone who would believe you. I frankly doubt it, but I'm afraid you won't be able to find out."

He steps into the room to allow enough space for his bodyguards, the two twin goblins, to enter.

"I'm sure you remember my friends, Adler and Baldwin."

"Henry . . ." Fiona grabs my arm and in tandem we take a step backward.

"Don't worry," says Skinner. He's grinning like a fool. "The procedure is almost completely painless." He chuckles and waves his empty glove in the air. "It happens just like magic!"

Fiona lets go of my arm.

"There's nowhere to run," Skinner says, and I realize he's speaking to Fiona. She's dashed off behind the statues. One of the globs—Adler? Baldwin?—moves after her, while the other one comes for me. But I don't care. I just want to stop either one of them getting to Fiona. As the first makes a swipe for me, I resort to the only thing I can think of. I bite him.

My teeth sink deep into the glob's spongy flesh. His blood fills my mouth, thick and rancid. I'm retching, coughing, ready to puke, but I don't let up.

The bite takes him by surprise. He yawps once and tries to shake me off, but he only throws himself off balance. I leap off the floor, free my jaws, and shoulder into him as hard as I can. He stumbles into his twin, and the three of us go toppling over the statue of an elf. I land on the soft cushion of a goblin belly, while the glob on the bottom gets crushed painfully against the statue. Before the one on top can grab me, I roll onto my feet.

Without a doubt, it's the most impressive piece of improvised combat I've ever come up with. And it works. I spit out the goblin blood and smile. Which, of course, makes them angry. They rise up with a pair of matching scowls and lumber after me. At least they're ignoring Fiona.

"Henry!" she calls out from somewhere (*where?*). "Get outta the way!"

I have no idea what she means, but I run blindly for the corner of the room. In the upper peripheries of my vision I see her, hanging from a scaffold, feet clamped against the head of that boyish giant, pushing with all her might.

Skinner gasps. He looks terrified for once. "Don't!"

There's a slow creak and then a terrible crash. I keep

running. Countless statues go falling, sliding, battering into one another. The ground shakes and a gray cloud of long-settled filth plumes up to fill the room.

Someone runs for me—I can't see who it is—and grabs my arm. "C'mon," says Fiona. "Let's go while we can." She drags me away, and we clamber through a grimy mist and over countless fallen statues. I can't help but feel pity for them, especially when I see Matt. "Sorry," I tell them, though not a single one can hear. "That was *her* fault."

"Come! On!"

Near the door we see Skinner and the globs pinned under the statue of the giant, under its oppressive weight in gold. The first glob is staring blankly at the ceiling, cradling his bitten hand and taking slow, deep breaths. The other one's facedown, not moving.

But Skinner is all action. He's struggling uselessly to free a pinned leg. He spits at us angrily, but the saliva gets stymied between his twisted lips, dribbling down like the spew of an infant. "You, " he says bitterly, pointing at us with his only weapon, a bare finger. He strains against his leg to reach us, but we veer wide of him. There's nothing he can do.

Skinner and I regard each other. His eyes flash with hatred. There's something deeply wrong with that dwarf.

"Let's go!"

Moments later we're out on the street. We run through Dockside until we're out by the periphery wall. The edge of the city falls away, a sheer cliff to the desert below.

"Okay," pants Fiona. She's leaning on her knees, the adrenaline of our escape subsiding. "Where to now? The police?"

"No."

"But we have to tell them."

"I already tried, but Skinner's right. No one believes it. Besides, I just busted out of jail to come here, I can't exactly go running to the police."

"Oh," she says. She cocks her head sideways and stares at me. The lamplight makes her curls glow all over. "You busted out of jail? To come save me?"

I shrug. "Matt helped."

She throws her arms around me and gives me a long, wet kiss. I return the compliment and when we pull ourselves apart, all I can do is stare happily into her face, tail wagging like a fool. "Thanks," I tell her. "It was *definitely* worth it."

She takes my paw in hers and we lean on the wall overlooking the emptiness. Not too far off is one of the deadwood forests, where countless branches jut upward like broken teeth. The trees glow a cool white under a moon that is just now past its apex, miles above Eden.

Fiona nods to herself. "We're gonna have to go up there, aren't we?"

"As soon as we figure out how. Right now we need someplace quiet where we can plan our attack." I pull her away from the wall and start off in the direction of Elvenburg. "But don't worry. I know a place."

34
BAG OF BEANS

GRAM'S EYEBALL SWIVELS SUSPICIOUSLY THROUGH THE GAP.

"Siobhan!" she yells back into the apartment. "There's a wolf at the door again! And this time he's brought somebody with him!" She whistles quietly, and in a lower, lascivious voice she says, "A *lady* friend!"

Fiona snickers behind me, but I'm all nerves. "Let us in, Gram, we're in trouble!"

"Sorry, I can't reach the chain," she sings. "Have to wait for—*aha!*"

Siobhan throws open the door. "Jack?!" But when she sees that it's Fiona I've brought her hopeful posture collapses. "Okay," she says quietly. "Come in."

Fiona and I lower our heads to squeeze through the door. We end up on all fours, the two of us filling the kitchen. Gram squeezes into the corner and takes a perch in her rocker, coiled slippers dangling over the edge. Fiona and I search each other's faces as our snouts fill with the scents of this humble elven apartment: floral incense—rose hip and blossoms of spatterdock—and the lingering steam of brewed tea. We pick up subtler scents, too, ones only a wolfish snout could detect. Siobhan's dimly iridescent skin, for instance, which smells of an evening breeze. It's practically the scent of moonlight.

"You haven't seen him, have you?" she asks us. "It's been two weeks now."

"Jack can take care of himself," I tell Siobhan, although I'm not sure I believe it.

She nods. "Maybe, but what about you two?"

Only when she says it do I notice how wretched we look. Our faces are blotchy with grime, our clothes are torn in too many places to count, and—with me especially—fresh bruises are swelling up all over the place.

"We've had a rough couple of days," I say, which inevitably leads me into a lengthy explanation of what's happened to us.

When I'm finally finished, Siobhan's only response is, "I better put on some tea."

Gram, meanwhile, has been bored to sleep. She's dozing in her rocker.

"So," says Fiona, "what it comes down to is this. We have to find a way—"

There's a wet *thump* against the apartment door. It's followed by a slow, hard pounding, like whoever's out there is using a baseball bat instead of knuckles.

Ba-doom!

"Quick," Siobhan says. "That could be the police. You two gotta hide."

"Where?!" says Fiona. "We're too big."

Siobhan points at the window. "The fire escape. Can you fit through there?"

"We'd better."

Ba-doom!

It's a struggle to get us through the window, but we make it. Beneath our weight, the web of black metal complains with creaks and groans. We huddle together, making ourselves as small as we can (easier for Fiona than me), and watch through the glass as Siobhan stands at the door.

Ba-doom!

The wood shudders visibly. Siobhan cracks the door open and peers out. Instantly, she slams it shut again—and then undoes the chain and hauls it open.

It's Jack.

Only there's something wrong with him. He looks . . . *strange.* He falls into Siobhan's arms, but she's unable to support his weight. The two of them crash to the floor and it sounds like someone just dropped an anvil. I squeeze myself back in through the window and find Siobhan on the floor beneath her boyfriend, gasping for breath.

"Get him . . . off me," she rasps.

I reach down and roll him over, and all I'm thinking is,

Why is he so heavy? His eyes gape wide at the ceiling, glossy and bulging. Then I see what's wrong with him. The left side of Jack's body shimmers. It's made of gold.

His left arm is stiff. It sparkles yellow. The color spreads under his sleeve to his neck, stretching his skin with its weight, pulling so hard it looks like his flesh is about to tear away.

"Siobhan," he rasps, but he can't say any more. His voice is grainy and coarse, like his throat's full of sand. Fiona comes in through the window and the three of us kneel around him. He nudges his head against Siobhan's knee.

"Don't worry," she says, stroking Jack's face. Her voice is bare. "We'll get help for you." She turns to Fiona. "Call an ambulance. There's a phone in my room."

Fiona nods and hurries off. Siobhan gives me a serious look. "You can't be here when they come."

From the corner of the room, Gram comes to life. "The cabinet in the bathroom has some of my old fairydust. It's for my arthritis. I get so stiff!"

"Gram, no!" Siobhan screams. "This is serious!"

"Skinner did this, didn't he?"

Siobhan nods. "Skinner."

At the mention of the word, Jack's eyes open. He manages to peel his head up from Siobhan's lap. The skin about his neck cracks like old leather. There's a dribble of blood. It runs over the gold and blots into the collar of his shirt.

"Henry," he says. "You're here." His forehead is sticky with sweat. It's hopelessly pale. "That's perfect," he says, smiling weakly.

Siobhan pushes his damp blond hair off his forehead. "Don't talk, J," she says. "Take it easy."

But Jack's stubborn. "I read your pop's letters," he says to me. "I'm sorry, but I did. When he talked about the fairies still being around, I thought I could find one myself." He sputters and an eddy of spit foams from the corner of his mouth. He smiles. "I figured I'd find myself my very own fairy godmother. You know how it is, get myself a brand-new destiny." He rolls his eyes to Siobhan. "I don't want to be a thief anymore."

"You don't need a fairy godmother to stop that."

"Maybe," he whispers.

Gently, Siobhan lowers his head back to her knees. She places one hand on his cheek. "Aw, Jack," she says. "I never cared either way."

Fiona returns from the bedroom. "They're coming," she says.

Jack shuts his eyes. "I've seen some weird things," he says. "Awful things."

"So have we," I tell him.

Jack's eyes pop open. "I know. I think I was one step ahead of you guys the whole way."

"You were?"

With his one good hand, Jack reaches into the folds of his

shirt. He comes out with a familiar object. An oiled leather pouch, tied with a dirty shoelace. It's his bag of beans. He rolls it into my lap and smiles at me. "You're gonna need these."

Fiona puts a hand on my shoulder. "We gotta go." In the distance, we're both tuning in the clamor of sirens. They're coming this way.

The leather pouch is heavier than it looks. It has a strange weight to it. And I know exactly why Jack gave it to me. There's only one problem.

"I don't know how to use these."

Jack shuts his eyes again. "Don't worry," he whispers. "They're magic."

35
BIG AS BEDSHEETS

WE'RE STANDING ON THE NORTHERNMOST EDGE OF THE CITY. THE PERIPHERY wall falls away at a ferocious incline, nearly straight down to the desert below. This end of the city is notorious for its secluded streets, its quiet, vaguely middle-class neighborhoods. After a certain hour, these streets are as deserted as the badlands that lie beyond—which is precisely why I chose this place. Even the wind has forsaken it; the air's got the stillness of dawn.

I lead Fiona to the bulwark. "C'mon," I tell her. "We're going over the wall."

I still haven't explained what's in the pouch Jack gave me, but for some unfathomable reason, Fiona seems to trust me. She follows me to a gap in the wall. The stairs beyond it are barely there, just a series of slim blocks cantilevered into a dizzying brick face. The only barriers offering a pretense of safety are the wooden poles pounded into the end of each step. They're strung together with a balustrade of dry rope.

It's an entirely unreliable barrier against an accidental (not to mention deadly) plunge over the side.

"Stay close to the wall," I say, but Fiona doesn't need advice. I can hear her paw sliding down the rough surface, pressing tight to the bricks. It starts getting cooler as we descend. By the time we reach the bottom, we're both shivering.

I explain to Fiona that we need to find some open space, and then I lope into the darkness. After only a few minutes of walking, I stop.

"Oh, no."

"What is it?" she asks.

"We need water. Maybe a lot of it. I should have thought of that."

Fiona's silent for a moment, but she's looking around. She points to a gathering of deadwoods, standing in an eerie puddle of moonlight. "What about over there?"

"Why there?"

"If the trees are surviving, there must be groundwater of some kind. Maybe we could dig for it."

It's a good idea. We change our tack, heading for the copse.

"Are you going to tell me what this is about ever?"

"If we find water," I tell her, "I'll show you."

Up close the deadwoods reveal their age. The bark is stretched like old parchment. Fiona and I fall onto our knees to rake away the soil. It isn't long before the theory bears fruit. The lifeless topsoil gives way to a boggy mud. Soon, eddies of dark water seep up to fill the pit. I stop digging and fall back on my heels. "That's enough. I think."

Fiona watches me. "Enough for what?"

I take out the sack of beans. I can see she's still puzzled and unimpressed. I'm nearly as confused as she is. *How much should I use? How much will get us there?* I pass the sack back and forth between my paws, gauging the weight.

I gaze up at Eden, a vast airship on a static voyage. Jack used the sliver of a single bean to escape over a thirty-foot wall. Now then: Exactly how far away is Eden? Of course, it doesn't take long for me to give up the calculations. "What the hell," I whisper, emptying the whole bag into the pit.

Fiona cringes. "You sure you know what you're doing?"

"Quick," I tell her, ignoring the question, "cover it over again." We shove the soil back into place as if refilling a grave, firming it down with a few hard smacks. "When you see a good strong vine," I say, repeating Jack's words, "grab hold tight and it'll pull—"

Before I can finish the ground swells up with enough force to chuck me sideways. Instantly, the rising earth is as tall as I am. It spreads fast, separating me from Fiona.

"Forget what I said! Just run! Get outta the way!" I skitter backward, crabwalking myself into the trunk of a deadwood. I can't see Fiona at all now. A mountain of earth is climbing higher and higher between us. I shout her name, but there's no answer. Or if there is, I can't hear it, not over the growl from beneath my feet.

The first sprouts tumble and burst from the ground like serpents, already thick as saplings. Half of them rocket straight up, while others coil down, weaving themselves into mangrove-like roots. And the *noise* of it—the earth-shaking, skull-rattling noise—it's immense. The ground's quaking so much I can't get to my feet. I'm down on all fours, not for speed but for stability—I need both right now.

The mound of earth widens in a flash; a wave of soil chases me, uprooting the trees as it comes. I hear them creaking and toppling behind me, gnarled dominoes falling by the hundreds. I'm out in the open now at full gallop. Ridges crackle up and snake out in every direction, the lightning-fast forks of an instant root system.

Maybe using the whole bag wasn't such a good idea.

"Hen . . . are . . . you?!" Fiona's voice is clutching at me through the gaps in the noise. I see her, wobbling toward me on all fours, stumbling drunkenly over exposed roots and shifting earth. All the while, a monstrous column of deep green is erupting behind her.

". . . crazy . . . I . . . and . . . is that thing?!" I can easily guess the beginning of her question.

"It belongs to Jack!" I scream at her.

At last, the growth is beginning to stop, the bone-shattering thunder is subsiding. But the thing's still rising.

Tendrils whip upward, twining themselves into the main stalk. Leaves as big as bedsheets quiver in the wind. We stand and watch, and I see this thing for what it is: the beautiful otherworldliness of magic. Looking at it, rising up into the clouds, I'm hit with a strange nostalgia. *What if this is it?* I used up the whole bag. Could this towering thing before me be the last of it, the end of the old magic? *But no*, I think. *There's more up above us—and we're about to go find it.*

Fiona, however, isn't pleased. There's a scowl on her face when she punches me in the shoulder.

"Ow!"

"I don't *believe* you!" she cries. "Did you really think I could actually *grab hold* of one of those things? It would've torn my arm off! I would've been killed!"

"How was I supposed to know? It's not like I plant one of these things every day! What exactly were you expecting?"

"I don't know. Fair warning, maybe."

A furrow of clouds gathers above us. The moon, the peaks of the city's buildings, the top of the stalk itself—everything is obscured from view. Eden has been swallowed up entirely. There's no way to tell if Jack's enchanted plant will get us where we're going. But there's one way to find out.

"We'll have to climb it," I say.

"No kidding." Fiona points her camera straight up and flashes off a few pictures. "This way," she says. "When they find me splattered on the ground down here, they'll know what killed me."

As we move closer, we're forced to climb over uprooted deadwoods lying everywhere. The plucked-up roots resemble skeletons, with moist soil clinging to them like rotting flesh. Up and down the huge stalk, tiny vines and more conventionally sized leaves blossom sluggishly. The ground bubbles with roots, burrowing after precious water. There's a low creak from the stalk itself, as the huge thing finally comes to a stop. Its trunk is a mosaic of shadow, brightened here and there by spillover from the city's neon. There's plenty to hang on to. I grab a hefty vine and pull. It doesn't sag, not even when I lift myself off the ground.

"Seems pretty solid, but we should hurry."

"Wait," she says and gets out her camera. "I'm never gonna get another shot like this." She snaps a picture of me, hanging from the base of something that can barely be explained.

"Perfect," she says. "Now let's go."

36
A THOUSAND OCTOBERS

THE TUNDRA LIES FAST ASLEEP BELOW US. IT'S DIFFICULT TO TELL HOW MUCH farther we have to go because of the ceiling of clouds fanning out above us. Fiona's climbing higher, her clothes buffeting in the wind.

"This is crazy!" she yells back at me. "I can't believe we decided to *climb* to Eden! I can't even see where I'm going!"

My arms are beginning to tremble, but Fiona looks strong, pulling herself up with a determined steadiness. "Keep climbing!" I call up to her. "We can't stop now!" What I don't say is that we have to get there before this thing crumbles like it did back at St. Remus.

Fiona growls at me and yanks herself up, climbing even faster. I take a moment to rest, straightening my arms and hanging off the stalk like a fly—tiny and eminently swattable. The city looks peaceful from up here, a quilt of twinkling lights, silent as the stars. When I look up again, Fiona's gone, vanished into the clouds. I follow her, letting the mist swallow me up.

Inside, it's cool and surprisingly wet. The air is calm, the clouds acting as a blanket against the wind. Suddenly, the serenity of the place is shattered by a scream.

"Fiona?!" I search the clouds above me, but all I can see is a dim white mass. I pull myself up as fast as I can. I'm frantic. I'm climbing recklessly.

Then, fluttering into view is what appears to be a slip of paper. It curls and tumbles down and all I have to do is reach out and . . . catch it. It's blue.

Steadying myself against the stalk, I flip it open with one paw. There's a smattering of words written on the page in a childish hand:

DER SIS,
THANK YOO FOR TECHING ME REEDING.
I LUV YOO,
ROY

It's the letter Roy didn't want anyone to see. He just wanted to thank his sister for teaching him to read. He was trying to better himself.

"Fiona?" I call up to her again. No answer, so I keep climbing.

The underside of Eden emerges lazily from the fog. It fills the sky, gray and craggy and silent. The stalk begins to tilt, leaning backward slightly to rise over the clifflike lip of Eden's edge. Then it twists again, until it's horizontal, broad and firm enough to walk on.

"What took you so long?" There she is, sitting cross-legged with her face in her hands.

"You okay?"

"I lost something," she says. "On the way up."

"Could this be it?" I take out the note.

She stares at it, dumbfounded. "You caught it?" She throws her arms around me like she did before, and I'm rewarded with another kiss. Then our faces slide forward, and we cradle our heads on each other's shoulders. "Thank you so much," she says. We sit there like that a while, the exhaustion of the climb setting in. We're simply too tired to move.

"I was there," I tell her, pointing to the note, "when Gunther took it away from him."

She nods, beaming at the slip of blue paper. "It's the first thing he's ever written to me. Prob'ly the first thing he's ever written in his whole life."

I take a breath. "I need to tell you something. It's about what happened to Roy."

"I think I already know."

"You do?"

"It wasn't hard to figure out," she says. "Roy told me he was planning to audition for Skinner. So when you told me you got the job, I put two and two together. If you won the race, you must have been at least partly responsible."

My tail dips as low as it ever has. "Maybe more than just partly."

"I know they dose you up beforehand. It wasn't the real you." She almost laughs. "Anyone can see that."

"I hope so, but that's not how they explained it. They said it would bring out our true selves."

She shakes her head. "It was *bad dust*, that's all. They can design it that way. Which is why we're gonna find the fairies. Right now. And we're gonna bring back the good stuff."

Down below us, there's the glow of lamplight. It's rising up like steam. "We should keep going," I say. "We need to find a place that's close enough to the ground to jump off—and quick, too. Before it's too late."

Fiona lets go of my face. "Um, what's that supposed to mean?"

As if in answer to her question, the stalk begins to tremble.

"Hurry," I tell her. "It's starting!"

"*What* is starting?"

"It's how Jack covers his tracks. This whole thing is gonna disappear!"

But Fiona isn't moving. She crosses her arms and pastes a stubborn expression on her face. "You do realize that's *Eden* down there, right?"

"Where else did you think we were?"

"If this thing we're sitting on disappears, how're we supposed to get back? You have more of those beans, right?" The trunk sways beneath us. There's a crackling sound like a newly set fire. The spongy green we're sitting on is turning brown and brittle.

"I thought if I used the whole bag it'd last long enough for us to get back!"

"The whole bag? You mean you don't have any more?"

"You were there when Jack gave them to me! All he told me was—" But I can't finish. The trunk's melting all around us. It swings over the fancy lampposts, over an empty street, over the Eden treetops.

"Hang on!"

We both try, but the swaying is too violent. We pitch sideways with enough force to throw us over the side of the stalk. We're left hanging from the thickest vines, and there aren't many of them left. Everything is fading in our grip. Huge leaves—red, orange, brown—wrinkle and curl and break away, fluttering to the earth like a thousand Octobers.

Then it's our turn.

The final vines wither away and we tumble down. Instinct pitches us forward to all fours, cushioning the fall. We land on grass, close-cropped and irrigated so thoroughly it's springy as a mattress. We're in some sort of park, more clear and quiet and beautiful than any I've ever seen. We're safe.

One flame-red leaf, big as a newspaper, snows down from above. It shatters at my feet with a hushed magic, moldering to nothing before my eyes.

"Idiot!"

Fiona punches me again—same arm, same place. She turns in an aimless circle, her arms at first spread wide and then collapsing angrily at her sides. "This is *just great!* What're we supposed to do now? We're stuck!"

We *are* stuck. We're stranded a mile up in the air in the one place the city's animalia are never allowed to be. We're in Eden.

37
CREEPING DISEASE

A CAR, A BIG ONE—AN ENORMOUS ONE—THUNDERS DOWN AN ADJACENT street. The headlights strobe through the trees, blinding us both. It's a giant's car, overwhelmingly huge and rumbling as loud as a thunderstorm. We duck behind a dense row of hedges to let it pass (not that whoever's driving would notice us).

When the air's silent again, Fiona stands up. She lets out a low whistle. "Look at this place. It's gorgeous!"

I have to admit, Eden has an austere beauty, with its pillowy earth and finely cropped grass, its ornate lampposts and coiffed greenery, its polished benches with silver fittings. Rising above it all are the tapered cones of fairy palaces, places we've been told all our lives are devoid of fairies, places I've wanted to see ever since I was a cub.

"No wonder the Edenites keep all this to themselves," says Fiona. "It's beautiful."

Breathtaking. Majestic. Eerily perfect. It's all of these things, but there's something missing. It's as if you have to hold your hand out in front of your face to make certain it's got three dimensions, that it's not just a painted backdrop. Then, when your senses tell you it's really there, you can't help feeling like you're standing in the midst of a full-scale model railway set, everything cast from plastic and pressboard.

"I don't know," I say. "It doesn't smell right. It smells like—actually, it doesn't smell at all."

Fiona laughs. "That's because it's clean. It's not that Eden doesn't smell, it's that the City *stinks*."

I take Fiona's paw and lead her past perfect trees, tiered fountains, huge firebrick urns that erupt with blossoms.

"Where are we going?" she asks.

I point to the highest spire of all, dead in the center of Eden. We both know it from the Nimbus TV commercials. It's the hub around which the whole corporation spins. And we know the story that goes with it, too. Once upon a time, it belonged to the fairy queen, the first of her species. They said she could still communicate with moths and butterflies. But now it's the epicenter of Nimbus Labs.

We stick to the trees and shadows along the edges of the street, but everywhere is deserted. There's none of the bustle you find in the rest of the City. The only sound is the cool buzz of electricity. It comes from the lampposts, each hung with a squidlike chandelier, the tentacles tipped with bluish bulbs.

The homes aren't homes at all. They're castles and palaces. Everywhere you look, you see spires and ravelins, steeples and domes, all of them rising high above the trees that seclude them from the street. It's lonely to think there're folks buried deep inside all that stone and glass.

Soon, we're nearing the center. We turn a corner onto a street that looks like all the rest—rows of palaces, well removed from the sidewalk and buried in blue shadow. But then I notice a difference. They're all connected. And there's a raised concrete monorail running between all the buildings. A signpost reads: *Nimbus Thaumaturgical ~ Better Living Through Enchantment.* It's topped with the familiar halo.

Farther along the street we see it's more than just a monorail that links these buildings. The palaces are ancient, but they're connected by a thoroughly modern network of pipes, towers, platforms, exhaust vents, storage tanks—all of them glistening under the moonlight. High-voltage wires sag from everything. It's as if the laboratory modifications are a creeping disease, a gleaming virus spreading from the foundation upward.

Fiona shakes her head. "Look at it all. They're ruining this place."

"We have to find a way in," I whisper.

All around the compound, there's a tall fence, crowned with loops of razor wire. If worse comes to worst, we could scale it, but not without leaving a good few snags of ourselves behind. There ought to be another way.

"We'll keep following the fences," I say. "Maybe we can find a lock you can pick."

We stay behind a hem of bushes and keep going, circling

the palace-cum-laboratory. Eventually our search pays off. We find a door in the fence fastened with a huge padlock. It's massive.

"You think you can beat that one?" I ask Fiona.

She sucks in a breath. "Might be beyond my capabilities."

"See if you can—" I stop. I grab hold of her shoulder and pull her back to the bushes.

Someone is coming.

Fiona pricks up her ears. She hears it, too. Muffled footsteps through a door. The jingle of keys. We watch through the bushes and through the fence as a man comes out from an unmarked door in the building. He's dressed in a set of gray coveralls and he's stumbling badly, zigzagging toward the fence. He falls onto the links, grabbing hold to steady himself.

"He's drunk," Fiona whispers.

With one hand, the man is covering his face, wearing his palm like an eye-patch. He struggles to open the lock and then comes through, heading straight for us.

Fiona flinches beside me. I'm about to leap out, when the man stops and turns and plops down on the grass, right in front of us. He's muttering to himself. "No way, no way, this cannot be happening . . ."

Fiona stares at me. I put a finger to my lips and point in the opposite direction. Maybe we can sneak off. Gingerly, we raise ourselves to all fours and tiptoe away.

"*Who's there?*" The man leaps to his feet, shining a

flashlight into the bushes. All the while, he keeps one side of his face covered with his hand.

"Who—" The man peers into the bushes. "You better come out now." He takes a step closer. "You're—" He stops. "A *wolf!* There's a w—"

I lunge out of the bushes, bowl him over, and pin him to the grass. I clamp his mouth shut and he's too shocked to put up a fight. Besides, he seems more worried about covering his face. His one hand is still glued there, cupping his eye.

I bare my teeth. "You're not going to scream, okay?"

He nods. There's a blue badge pinned to his coveralls. It says: *Richard Froschler, Shipping and Receiving.*

Fiona comes out of the bushes, crouching behind me. "We're not going to hurt you, understand?"

He nods again, so I take my paw from his mouth.

He gapes at me, wide-eyed. "And I thought *I* had it bad."

"What? What are you talking about?"

Finally, he takes his hand away from his face. It's his eye. It's *huge*—the massive, glossy, bulging eye of a frog. It's popping grotesquely out of its socket, rimmed with lumpy green skin. "See?" he says. "I'm changing back."

"Huh?"

He sighs heavily. "They never tell you about the fine print, do they? *Sure,* it sounds good at the time. Get the girl, fall in love, and we'll make you a hominid. You can live up in Eden, get seats at the theater, get into the country clubs. 'Sounds great,' you tell them. Damn fairies! So you say, 'Sure, wave your wand, sprinkle your dust, do what you gotta do.' But what they *neglect* to mention, is what happens when things go south. When you fall *out* of love, I mean. Suddenly, they up and disappear, and by the time you figure out you're screwed, there's nobody around to fix it." He lolls his head back and forth. "But what am I telling *you* for? Obviously, you know *exactly* what I'm talking about. Looks like the magic ran out for you and your lady friend a *looooong* time ago."

Fiona's first to figure out what he means. "Sorry to burst your bubble," she says, standing over the pair of us, "but Henry and I have never masqueraded as hominids. It's not like we've lost our sheep's clothing. We're just wolves, plain and simple. We're looking for something."

The man blinks at us, with one normal eyelid and one huge, translucent mess. "Wolves! There are wolves in—"

I slap his mouth shut again. "Okay, already. We established that." I lean in close. "Now, listen—*Richard*. Judging by that eye of yours, do you really think it's a good idea to start drawing attention to yourself?"

He stares for a moment, thinking. He shakes his head. So I do him a favor and let him speak.

"Sorry," he says. "Force of habit. They sort of train us up here to cry wolf. But you certainly have a point there. Can't have anyone finding me looking like this. Right now, all I wanna do is to bail on this whole crazy place." He sighs, gazing wistfully into the sky. "I thought it'd work out, y'know? Thought I'd be able to fake it, even after things went sour for Lily and me—that's my wife, by the way. Ex-wife. Obviously, it *did not* work out." He points to his amphibious eye. "It's getting worse now, too—and fast. Believe it or not, I didn't look like this when I started my shift. All I had was this little green patch on my temple. But the divorce was finalized today, so I think that's why. Figure I've got another twelve hours, maybe a day, before I'm back to my old hippity-hoppity self." He squirms to look back at the Nimbus buildings. "Sure as hell can't be up here when *that* happens." He looks back at Fiona and me. "Just like *you* shouldn't be here, either."

"Sorry," I tell him, "but we came here for a reason."

"Better be a damn good one."

"It is," says Fiona.

"Wonderful. Congratulations. And now that we've settled that, would you mind letting me up? I'm gonna have to get past security going down the Empyrean, and the sooner I do, the better."

I give him another glance at my teeth. "You're not going to tell anyone about us, right?"

"I promise," he says. "Look at me. Who am I gonna tell?"

"Okay." I help Richard to his feet and take special care to brush him off, picking crumbs of grass and dirt off the back of his coveralls. "There you go," I tell him. I give him a friendly slap on his back. "Get going, and good luck."

He looks at me oddly for a moment, like he's astonished I didn't chew his face off. "Thanks," he says. "Uh, you too." Then he scampers off down the street.

Fiona watches him. "You sure it's wise to just let him go?" she asks. "You seemed awfully nice cleaning him up like that. Maybe sometimes you're a little *too* nice to folks."

"Or not." And I show her what I mean, holding up the ring of keys I picked from Richard's pocket. "A little trick I learned from Jack."

38
LEFTOVER MIRACLES

INSIDE THE GROUNDS, WE'RE SUCKED INTO A SWAMP OF LABORATORY works. We head toward the center, toward the largest, most forbidding tower of them all. The nearer we get, the denser the shafts and wires become. Around the base, you can't even see the walls of the palace.

We jam the stolen keys into door after door until we find one that works. It's a service entrance, leading to a corridor with walls of painted breeze blocks and a ceiling lined with pipes. There are noises down the corridor—whirs of machinery and clanks of metal. We follow them. It brings us to the entrance to a warehouse full of enormous shipping containers. Keeping to the shadows outside the entranceway, we watch.

There are several workers in uniforms like the one the frog-eyed man was wearing. Two of them control a pair of cranes, lifting the containers from here to there. Parked in the corner are several trucks—just like the one that killed my mother. The cranes swing the containers from the trucks and into an enormous freight elevator. When the elevator's loaded, the doors shut and the containers (unaccompanied by any of the workers) get spirited away to some other part of the compound.

I cock my head in the direction of the elevator. "Bet that goes somewhere important," I whisper.

"Yeah," says Fiona, "but where?"

"One way to find out."

Slipping to all fours, I lead Fiona from container to container until we're beside the elevator doors. When the crane swings past we lope in its shadow—and right inside. The floor of the elevator is oddly soft and rubbery. We're squeezed into the rear when the doors shut, casting us into pitch darkness.

Fiona moves close to me. "You think this is a good idea?"

"It's the only one I've got."

I take Fiona's paw in mine and for a moment, nothing happens. Then the elevator buzzes and clicks and starts moving upward. Distant winches and cables strain to lift us, creaking with the weight. At last, we stop, only the doors don't open.

Fiona's grip tightens. "Now what?"

I prick up my ears, hoping I'll hear something. But I don't. This may've been a mistake. We might be trapped. Who knows if—

There's the crackle of electricity behind us. The elevator wall we're leaning against slides away, taking us by surprise. There's another set of doors on the opposite side of the freight car; and as if that weren't enough to throw us off balance, the floor starts moving. I realize that's why the floor was rubbery. It's all automated, a huge conveyor belt.

Fiona and I are spit into a hall and onto another conveyor belt. It pulls us sideways along with the containers, all of which trundle in single file, geometrically perfect. We travel down a barely lit shaft toward a rectangle of light. As we get closer I see the claws of another crane reach for a container and pluck it off the end, swinging it into space. There's a hydraulic hiss and a loud click, and the bottom of the container pops open, spilling its cargo in a smoky blur. It looks like—*like what?* Giant skeletal hands?

Fiona grabs me. "What *was* that stuff?"

Before I can offer an answer (which I don't have) I realize we've got a much more pressing problem. When the conveyor ends, it's a dead drop-off. That crane is the only thing that stops the containers from smashing on the floor—which is exactly what we're going to do in about ten seconds.

"Quick," I tell Fiona. "Grab on!"

We latch onto the container beside us, dangling off the side, just as the crane lifts it from the conveyor. There's the hiss and the buzz and then the bottom of the container opens up, releasing its cargo. Up close, I see it's not a pile of giant bones. It's something else.

Deadwood trees.

Whole trees plummet from the container and land on top of an enormous heap. It's piled so high, the branches are grazing the soles of our feet as they hang down.

"Jump!" I say, and I let go, reaching for a thick bough. I catch it, but of course the tree isn't rooted to anything, so it lurches under my weight and I nearly lose my grip. Which is fine until Fiona leaps off herself and goes for the very same branch. With both of us hanging on, the tree tips to the side, suspending us over a drop that must be sixty feet to the floor.

"Hang on!" I shout.

"What do you think I'm doing?!"

At the last moment before I think the whole tree's going to lose its grip and come tumbling down on top of us, the roots find purchase, hooking into the pile, holding us steady.

As gingerly as we can, we scale down the trunk and continue climbing, down the expanding pile, careful to avoid the rain of more trees from the containers. Finally, we reach the floor of this cavernous place, a warehouse bigger than anything I've ever seen. It's a vast, windowless corridor, as tall and broad as an airplane hangar. The remains of uprooted trees are everywhere, all of them deadwoods. The concrete floor rises and falls with dunes of bone-pale branches and roots and—

Roots.

I see something I've never noticed before.

"Oh, God. Look at that."

"What is it?" asks Fiona.

"I think we found them."

"What?"

"Look at the roots."

Seeing them here, far removed from the desert, laid bare under bright artificial light, it's clear what the roots are really made of. *Bodies.* Bones. Thousands upon thousands of delicate frames, each one blessed with the arcs of moth-like wings. It's the army of ghosts I saw at the bottom of the Capra well. Only that wasn't a hallucination. Those weren't spirits I saw. They were skeletons.

Fiona grips my arm. "But how?"

"This must be what happens to them. After they die. Look at the branches—they're made of hands. Every one of them rising up, grasping for the sky." I look at her. "It's because they want to go home."

"Why bring them here?"

"Leftover miracles," I say.

"What?"

"This must be how they make it," I say. "It's why Nimbus-brand dust is more popular than the rest, and why nixiedust is so potent. They aren't using the fairies for labor. They're using them as . . . *raw material*. It's processed from the bodies of their dead."

"But if they vanished all at once, it would mean . . ."

I nod. "They killed them."

Suddenly, Fiona swings into action, bringing up her camera. "Pictures," she says. "We need pictures of this." She starts snapping away, close-ups to show the vertebrae, the wing structures, the delicate skulls. Other shots reveal the scope of the place, the horrendous volume of bodies. When the clicking stops, she flips open the camera.

"Here," she says, handing me the film. "Hold this for me. I need to reload." She hurries in a new roll of film and keeps going. "How could they do this?" she asks me, over and over. "How could they do this?"

"I think *we* could answer that question." Fiona and I spin around. Fiona's heart is pumping so fiercely I can hear it. She can probably hear mine, too. Standing side by side a ways down the storehouse, dwarfed at the bottom of a mountain of bones that reaches the distant ceiling, are Karl and Ludwig Nimbus.

"But before we do," says Karl.

"We're going to have to shoot you," finishes Ludwig. He raises his arm until he's pointing some sort of antique pistol at us.

He pulls the trigger and a dust dart whips into Fiona's ribs. She yelps and spins, trying to pluck it out, but before she can, it releases a cloud of fairydust that sparkles like the sun. It's stronger than anything I've seen, pluming around her in a silver sphere, and then compressing all over her body. There's a sizzling sound. This dust doesn't bother with your mouth, your nose, your lungs. This strain is ground so fine it seeps in through your pores.

"Fiona!"

She howls and falls to her knees, raking her claws over her hide, trying to get it off. "It burns!" she screams.

I kneel and hold her, but it's too late. Her eyes roll back and her tongue flops horrifically from her mouth. She slumps into me, lost in a bitter sleep.

"Better living through enchantment," Karl chuckles.

"Now it's your turn," says Ludwig.

Each brother raises a pistol at me and fires.

39
TOOTH AND CLAW

THE TREES FORM A CANOPY OF DARKNESS ABOVE. THROUGH THE BRANCHES I see flashes of clouds and a ghostly moon. I drop to all fours, padding into the forest. Every tree I pass comes alive, electrified with wind. All I can hear is the endless swish of leaves . . .

I emerge from my nightmare in a room all too similar to one of the cells in lockup. It's got padded walls, a bare floor, a domed lamp hanging from the ceiling, too high to reach. There's the distinctive lack of windows and the single door—heavy, thick, and presumably bolted from the outside.

Briefly, I wonder if this whole thing is a bad dream, my worst (and certainly longest) nightmare of all. Maybe I dreamed up everything while I was conked out in a cell back at St. Remus. But that can't be the case. There isn't any furniture in lockup—and I'm very clearly sitting in a chair.

It's something you'd expect to find at the dentist. But my teeth are fine, so I try to get up. Only I can't. I'm strapped in. Silver clamps pin down my wrists, arms, and legs. There's another clamp around my throat and one around my forehead.

From the neck up, I'm completely immobile. I've also been fitted with a muzzle.

If I strain my eyes downward, I can make out a low table beside my chair. It looks like the place where a dental hygienist stacks those little paper cups you spit into. Only there aren't any paper cups. The only thing on the table is a large pair of pliers.

The door opens. It's Karl Nimbus. He comes in carrying a stool and sets it beside the table. But he doesn't sit down. Instead, he stands close to my face and puts his thumb against my eyebrow, pushing upward for a closer look.

"Good," he says. "I'll get my brother."

He leaves again, locking the door after him. I make an attempt to get to my feet, but it's useless. I prick up my ears, but I can't hear anything. The padded walls sap away all the sound. It's as if they've muzzled my hearing, too.

The door opens again. This time it's both of them, Karl and Ludwig.

"Welcome back," says the elder brother. "It's Henry, isn't it?"

As if I can answer him.

"Yes, sorry about the muzzle, but you know how it is with you animals." He wags a finger in my face. "Prone to biting."

Karl takes a seat on the stool he brought in earlier. He lays one hand over the pliers, but he doesn't pick them up.

"Did you really believe you could come here, to our little paradise in the sky, to the very headquarters of our corporation, and simply waltz in and out?"

I glare at him between the straps of the muzzle.

He shakes his head, apparently mystified. "Since you're here, I can only assume that yes, that is precisely what you thought. Only a beast like you would be so foolish. I'll take it as clear proof of your inferiority as a rational species."

I try to let out a growl, but the muzzle strangles it in my throat.

Ludwig steps behind me. "Now, I'm going to ask you a question. It's a simple one, and I want you to speak nothing save for the pertinent answer. Do you understand?" He unbuckles the muzzle from the back of my neck, and gently, he frees my jaws.

"Where's Fiona?! What have you—"

Ludwig clamps the muzzle back over my face.

"I know what you're thinking," he says. "Torture is so inhumane. How can two esteemed men of science such as Karl and Ludwig Nimbus resort to such grisly techniques of interrogation?" He pauses. "The answer is simple. It is our belief that it is impossible to be inhumane to a creature that is, by its very nature, inhuman." He lightly pats my shoulder. "Karl?"

Ludwig's brother picks up the pliers. They're huge and heavy. They gleam as fiercely as the pipes and chutes we navigated through on the way in. Karl holds them out in front of his face, opening the jaws and then snapping them shut. "What's that expression?" He's addressing the tool in his hands. "Tooth and claw." He looks at me. "You must have fought 'tooth and claw' to get here, Henry. It's an interesting expression, is it not? It refers loosely to the modus operandi of all animalia, of beasts such as yourself. It's the way you prefer to do things. By tooth and by claw." He lowers the pliers until they hover above my fingers. "Some might say that's who you are, nothing more than an overgrown set of teeth and claws."

I squirm as best as I can against the restraints, but it's useless. Karl clamps the pliers onto the claw of my baby finger. "I'm going to remove your fingernail now. There's a good chance I may break one or two of your knuckles in the process. This is merely meant to impress upon you the seriousness of this interrogation."

He begins to pull. At first, there's only a dull pain at the tip of my finger. Karl's clearly the younger and fitter of the two, but he's still more or less an old man. Maybe he's incapable, I think. I hope.

Then he starts twisting. The size and weight of the pliers give him ferocious leverage. Bullets of agony shoot through my finger, up the tendons on the back of my paw, and the pain swells all the way up to my shoulder. The center joint in my finger grinds and pops and finally bursts. It snaps just as Karl predicted. He's broken my finger. The pain is more than I could have imagined. I feel faint, like my whole body's floating away.

Karl rises off the stool, spreads his legs, and then he *really* starts pulling. Every time he yanks, the whole chair judders on its bolts. The pain is hot and terrifying, but it's mostly in the joints of my paw and in my wrist. But then, when the roots of my claw finally begin to tear, the misery concentrates in the very tip.

Karl wrenches one last time and the claw comes free. I've lost it—along with a chunk of hair and flesh.

Ludwig puts his hands on the sides of my shoulders. "I hope you understand how serious we are. This will end as soon as you answer our questions."

Karl drops my claw on the little side table.

Again, Ludwig unbuckles the muzzle. "Now, I want you to tell us everything you know about our operation in Dockside."

I grit my teeth, grinding them together as I speak. "If you hurt Fiona, I'll ki—"

On goes the muzzle.

"Henry, Henry, Henry," says Ludwig, shaking his head. "How stubborn you are. Do you really wish this to continue?" He sighs. "Alas, I can only imagine you do."

Next, Karl goes to work on the middle digit of the same hand. It's a much larger claw and he has to use all his strength to tear it free. I shut my eyes tight and gnash my teeth inside the muzzle. It feels like he's taken off my whole finger, but when I open my eyes, I see that it's still there, although the end looks like it just came out of a blender.

Karl looks exhausted. His forehead glistens. My claws have printed a little map on the surface of the side table: a pair of black, volcanic islands in a lake of blood.

"Perhaps we're not taking the most productive approach with you," says Ludwig. "We could certainly continue, wearying as it is, to remove your claws, then your teeth, and finally strips of flesh."

My head spins.

"*Or*—since you clearly possess little in the way of self-interest and appear to harbor nothing but great sympathy for your companion—it might be more fruitful to threaten these same procedures against *her,* instead."

Despite the pain throbbing up and down my right arm, I rage against the metal bands locking me to the chair. The frame rattles and creaks, and for an instant, Karl looks concerned that I might actually bust loose. But it's all for nothing.

"Ah," says Ludwig, enjoying my display of strength. "I think we may have discovered a chink in your armor." He steps around to face me. "Can I assume you're ready to tell us what you know?"

If I could speak, I would say, "Yes, I'm ready. I've got nothing to lose, nothing except Fiona."

Ludwig moves behind me again and unfastens the buckles.

"Okay." My voice sounds as shredded as my fingertips. "I'll tell you." And I do. I explain how I found my way behind closed doors at the nixie refinery; I tell them about my father's theories; I tell them about my vain search for the fairies and how Fiona and I uncovered the truth.

"You killed them."

Karl chuckles. "Not Ludwig and I personally, no. The nixies did it. There was no road to Eden back then. The nixies used to be the only ones who could get up here. That's why we seduced them out of the sea and put them under our employ."

"That makes you responsible for the deaths of—"

Ludwig claps his hands. "Enough of this! We're not finished. There's something else we need to know." He lays the muzzle in my lap and looks me in the eye. "Who have you told about this?"

"No one."

Ludwig gives his brother a stern look. In response, Karl picks up the pliers and pulls his stool over to my opposite arm.

"Wait, I'm telling the truth. I haven't told anyone."

"We find that hard to believe," says Ludwig.

"It's true." Except that it isn't. I told Mrs. L and Detective White. Of course they didn't believe me, but that's beside the point. No matter what these guys do to me, I'm not going to mention either one of them. Who knows what they'd do if I did.

"You told *no one* else?"

"That's right. No one." It's a fight to keep my voice from cracking. "I'm telling the truth. Just don't hurt Fiona."

Ludwig picks up the muzzle and returns to his place at my back. "Very well," he says, an odd kindness in his words. "We won't hurt her."

"Thank you."

"But we have to be certain." He foists the muzzle over my face.

Karl grips the claw of my left thumb with the mouth of the pliers. I mewl through the muzzle, but he doesn't let up. He starts pulling and as my joints begin to buckle, as the flesh begins to tear, everything goes fuzzy. My vision reels and the room shrinks into a pinprick of darkness.

Thankfully, I've fainted.

40
PAPERWEIGHT

CONSCIOUSNESS RETURNS IN A DRIBBLE. ONE DROP ADDS TO ANOTHER UNTIL I'm trembling in a humid puddle of candlelight.

"Henry?"

Fiona's face hovers off to my side. It looks strange, not like her real face but an image on a mosaic wall, faintly interrupted by a million cracks. But it's not the factures between broken tiles. It's wire. There's some sort of metal mesh between us. I lift my head and the light caroms wildly, everywhere at once.

"Careful," she says. "It's wobbly up here."

I roll onto my side and vomit. The meager contents of my stomach sieve through the cage, dripping onto a plush carpet.

"Nice one," says a voice from the opposite side. "Good distance." I turn and see Richard, the man-slash-frog whose keys I stole. He's locked in a third cage, and his face is worse than before, the jade-green skin spreading down his cheek, his hair balding on that same side and his once-hominid ear retreating into his skull. "Hey," he says quietly. "We meet again."

"Henry," Fiona asks, redirecting my attention, "are you all right? Your fingers . . ."

My pulse drubs slowly in my paws. They hurt so much I can barely move them. I have them curled like crab claws, cradled in my lap. "I'm okay," I tell her, but I can see she doesn't believe me.

These cages are nothing like the rusty kennels Skinner keeps in his refinery. These are gilded beauties, works of art. We're in somebody's study, one that reminds me of Doc Grey's roost in the old rectory building. But where Doc's office was cramped and cluttered, this one is expansive. Every inch is done up in plush red, sparkling gold, and deep, studious brown.

"Where are we?"

"This is where they live," says Fiona.

Richard nods. "Helluva lot nicer than my wife's place, I'll tell you that much. She ended up with the palace, you see." As he speaks, I notice his lips have grown thinner and his mouth wider. The corners are drawn back nearly to his jawbones. He sighs to himself. "Who knows? She might be proud to see me here, rubbing shoulders with the likes of these guys."

There's the sound of several footsteps from beyond the door. The first to come in are a pair of globs. They're dressed in gray uniforms and caps—chauffeurs. They stand on either side of the doorway and clasp their hands in front, not saying a word. Next, Ludwig comes in, and then Karl. They're in their familiar lab coats, the same ones they wear on their billboards and on television. Karl is pushing a metal handcart shrouded in a white sheet. Something pointed and angular lies underneath, pitching the fabric into hills and valleys. The last to enter is Skinner. He's limping, his one leg tied in a splint from where we crushed it under the golden giant. He comes straight for me, standing before the cage. "I owe you," he says. He raises one of his hands between us and starts to remove his glove.

"Uh-uh-uh," says Karl, waggling a finger as if admonishing a child. "We told you: look, but don't touch."

Skinner spins to face him. "I *owe* him," he growls. "For this!" He pounds a fist against his injured leg.

"Don't worry," says Ludwig. "Everyone will get what's coming to them in due course."

"You too," spits Fiona, speaking to everyone there who isn't locked in a cage.

"I quite agree," says Ludwig, smiling back at her. "My brother and I expect to get what's coming to us. Wealth, influence, prosperity—more of the same, I suppose."

Skinner has moved to the corner of the room, sulking in an armchair. His injured leg spills out sideways at an awkward angle.

"They killed them," I whisper, trying to flex my fingers. I look up at Ludwig. "And now you grind them up, don't you? You grind them into *dust*."

"It's more complicated than that, I assure you," he says. "But ultimately yes, we do. We grind them up." He bends to open a drawer in the side of the handcart. When he rises again, he's got some sort of machine in his hands. It looks like a shortwave radio, complete with technical readouts and illuminated dials. On top there's a wooden flap. "It wasn't always that way. Initially, killing the fairies was merely a sound business decision. If the thaumaturgists were the city's only purveyors of magic—even a lesser, basically medicinal brand of magic—then we'd corner the market. But we failed to anticipate that without the fairies, the leftover dust we mined would someday run out." He places the machine on a nearby desk and starts fiddling with the dials.

"Then," says Karl proudly, "we hit on the idea of digging up *the bodies themselves*—which by that time had grown into those ghastly deadwood trees. We wanted to see if we could refine them into a new brand of fairydust."

"Sadly," says Ludwig, "our experiments never turned out properly. They only revealed that dead fairies make for bad dust, as you'll soon see."

"Experiments," I say. "Like on my father."

"And the others, too," says Fiona. "Those animals we saw at the refinery."

"And yet others still," adds Ludwig.

An image of that creature from the tunnels flashes into my head.

Fiona growls. "That's what you want, isn't it? That's your

plan. You want to use dust from dead fairies to turn us into those—those *animals*."

"But, my dear," says Karl. He waves a finger in her face. "You *are* an animal. Don't forget that. We're merely helping you regain your true form. It only makes sense. Once the magic has run out of this place, we'll need certain new economic principles in order to allow *people*, like us"—he waves his hand around his half of the room—"to maintain a privileged position. We're merely using the last of the City's magic, that which is contained in the bodies of the fairies themselves, to return us to a time when the beasts occupied a more appropriate position. Namely, as our labor. And as our food. An idyllic time when mindless wolves such as yourselves were hunted for sport."

"Yes," agrees Ludwig. "We merely wish to return to the natural order of things. *Permanently.*" With a flourish he pulls the sheet off the handcart, revealing the fairy skeleton underneath. The poor thing is curled in a ball, her back turned to us. The refined bone structure of her wings flares out from the spine like the spray of a fountain.

"All these years," I say, "you've been experimenting, trying to come up with the worst possible end for us all."

"Not *the worst*," says Karl, clearly insulted. "Merely the most sensible."

"Guys, guys," says Richard, cutting in. "I know what you're thinking. 'How did they get ol' Richie's keys?' Was he helping them, perhaps? Did he just pass them off to the first wolves he met? No! Of course not!" He points to me. "This guy here stole 'em!" As he says it, his voice crackles and he coughs to clear his throat. "And yes, I know I look—and maybe sound—a little funny right now. But trust me, it's just a temporary thing. At heart, let's face it. I live here. I work here. I'm an Edenite, through and through."

For a moment, Karl and Ludwig stand there gaping. It's hard to accept Richard's argument when you can see his face. Only Skinner, grumbling in the corner, seems unsurprised. He's probably used to hearing this kind of protest. He sits there with a small grin on his lips, gnawing calmly on his straw.

"Well then," says Ludwig at last, "there's a simple way to determine if indeed you're one of us."

Richard takes a step toward the rear of his cage. "Um, what do you mean?"

Instead of answering his question, Karl holds up a pair of something like garden shears. He applies them to the skeleton, cleaving a nugget out of the fairy's leg bone.

"What are you doing?"

Richard's question falls on deaf ears. None of us speak. We watch as Karl hands the chunk of bone to his brother, who opens the wooden flap on top of the radio-looking machine. He drops the chunk in and adjusts the dials carefully. Then he pulls a lever on the side. Lights flash, needles quiver, and there's a cool stirring of air all through the room, air that smells like a spring thaw—budding bushes and boggy soil.

The candles flutter out, and Ludwig's face seems to go rotten, valleyed in deep shadow. Then the air falls still. The candles reignite themselves. The earthen scent vanishes, quick as it appeared. From inside the wooden machine, there's a sound like soft, rancid almonds, crumbling in a nutcracker.

"There," says Ludwig. He opens a side flap and sweeps the contents into his palm. It's fairydust. No more than a thimbleful, pure and shimmering. Ludwig smiles. "Straight from the source."

He brings the dust over to Richard's cage. "You really believe you belong here, do you?"

Richard gapes at Ludwig's hand. "What is that stuff?"

"Weren't you watching? It's fairydust."

Ludwig blows gently and the dust wafts through the mesh of Richard's cage. It floats in slowly, filling the space with golden light. Richard holds his breath for a moment, but it's no use. He has to breathe. He inhales and the dust flows in as gently as I've ever seen.

Then he begins to change.

The skin all over his body shifts in color to match the sickly green around his bulging eye. His skin takes on a moist glow, oily and slick. His mouth widens even more, bisecting the whole of his face. And his eyes—they bulge and migrate upward, almost to the top of his head. Richard has become a frog.

This must be how he looked as a young man, before he was married, before he came up here to live as a hominid.

He turns away from us in shame. But then he shudders. The transformation isn't done with him yet.

Fiona covers her mouth. "What's happening to him?"

Richard's legs go even more rubbery than they already are—so rubbery he can't support himself. He folds down to the floor of the cage, his legs crossed behind him and his hands down in front. He's shrinking, getting smaller and smaller before our eyes. He could fit inside my palm. He turns his head to Fiona and me, regarding us with huge, sad eyes. He opens his mouth to speak, but all that comes out is a mournful croak.

Richard has become a frog, but not the usual sort—not the ones you see walking down the sidewalk, hurrying to work. This is something else entirely, something primitive, something millions of years old. This is a naked frog from one of Mrs. L's biology posters.

"So," says Ludwig, unlocking Richard's cage. "It would appear you're not an Edenite after all."

Richard flops mindlessly on the floor of his cage. But he's not entirely vacant. His primordial brain knows enough to frantically hop away when Ludwig reaches into the cage. But it's no use. The thaumaturgist scoops up Richard in one hand.

"*Yech!*" he says, squeezing the frog. "Slimy beast." He turns and tosses Richard at Skinner.

Startled, Skinner bumbles with Richard's tiny body until he finally catches him. "What am I supposed to do with this?"

"I don't know," says Ludwig. "Whatever you want."

Skinner shrugs. "Okay then," and a moment later, Richard has been turned to gold. "That oughta put him out of his misery." Skinner plunks the golden frog on a table beside his chair. "You can use him as a paperweight."

Karl and his brother come to stand in front of our cages.

I growl at them. "That's what you're gonna do to us, too, isn't it?"

"No," says Karl. "We have something a little more colorful planned for you."

Skinner slips out of his armchair and hobbles over. "Colorful, you say?" He points his twisted features at me and grins like a corpse, flesh pulling unnaturally away from his teeth.

"I've been looking forward to this part."

41
LIKE FATHER, LIKE SON

KARL TAKES A VIAL OF FAIRYDUST OUT OF HIS JACKET POCKET. IT'S NOT GOLD like the stuff they used on Richard. It's silver, tinged with blue. It squirms behind the glass like a scourge of insects.

"This," says Karl, waving the vial, "is one of our older blends. Experimental, you see. Before we perfected things."

Fiona points her chin at the "paperweight" on the side table across the room. "If you call that perfection," she says, "I'll happily take whatever's in your hand."

"Bold words," says Karl. "But I wouldn't be too hasty."

Skinner rubs his hands together. "I think I'll quite enjoy this."

I cower to the back of the cage, struggling to push myself through the mesh, but there's no escape. Both Skinner and Ludwig step forward.

Karl pours a thimbleful of dust into his palm. "As I said, everyone gets what's coming to them."

Instead of puffing the fairydust into my cage, he turns to Skinner, whose face curdles with shock.

"What're you—?"

That's all he gets out before Karl exhales. The dust leaps at Skinner's face. The little man waves his arms frantically, spitting and cackling, waving his gloved hands like a mad preacher. But it's all for nothing. As always, fairydust knows what it's for. It rushes in through his eyes and nose and every rutted fold of his face.

"*No!*" he screams. Skinner stamps on the floor, slapping and tearing at his eyes and cheeks until his face is streaked with blood. He throws his gloves off and points at Karl and his brother. "*You!*" he screams, blood and spit flying from his lips. "You can't do this!" His body curls into a dwarvish question mark, and he rips at his hair, tearing out chunks of scalp. "You'll see! You can't do this!"

Both brothers are unimpressed with Skinner's accelerating tantrum.

Ludwig frowns. "You allowed this wolf, barely more than a cub, to discern nearly every intricacy of our operation. You jeopardized everything." He shakes his head gravely. "You, my angry little friend, have failed us."

Skinner throws off his gloves and screams. He limps forward, shaking his head from side to side, trying to steady himself. He reaches for the handcart but the wheels spin it out of reach.

"I'll *kill* you!" he screams. On the word *kill* he stamps his good foot on the floor, ramming it so hard it bursts through the wood. He tries pulling it out again, but it's stuck. And for an instant, he peers down at his trapped leg and his anger vanishes.

"Not again," he whispers.

He looks back at the brothers and his rage returns. He reaches for them with his bared hand, gnashing his teeth together so fiercely I can hear them crack. "I'll kill you for this!"

Golden sparks pop from his fingertips as he lunges at the brothers. He strains and screams and then—something happens. There's a sound like thick, wet paper being ripped apart. Only it's not paper; it's flesh and muscle and bone. And then Skinner, number-one bagman to the nixies, tears himself in two.

"A bad destiny, indeed," says Ludwig. "Though I suppose now we know how he acquired that awful scar."

"Let's hope this time he doesn't put himself back together again," says Karl.

Ludwig gazes over the dwarf's steaming innards. "I should think not."

I'm swaying on my feet, as soft and lifeless as the guts all over the floor. It's because of the handcart. In his tantrum, Skinner spun it to face us. So now I can see the fairy skull from the front. I can see its screaming mouth, its hands held up to its face, both of them clenched in terrified fists. And on one of those fists—the left one—there are rings. A deep blue gem for every finger.

Faelynn.

Karl tips out another thimbleful of dust. "Now let's see what the fates have in store for you, my canine friend." He holds his hand up, palm wide open and glistening with pure fairydust. "I think you'll find that destinies are inherited. Like father, like son." He exhales and the dust spins around my head, blotting out the world. The last thing I see before blacking out is the table where Skinner was sitting.

There's nothing on it. The golden frog is gone.

The trees loom over me, lacing their branches together into dark, jagged bridges. The sky is tormented by fast clouds and a ghostly moon. I'm on all fours, padding through the forest. Every tree is electrified with wind. All I hear is a rage of leaves, urging me on, pushing me farther into the trees, my belly pressed low to the earth . . . only . . .

Only it's not earth.

It's pavement. The trees aren't trees. They're lampposts. They're buildings, crammed together like passengers on a train. I see clutches of steel. Glass cliffs. Canyons of cement. There's no cottage. No clearing. No door. I'm in the City. Can this be happening? It feels just like my dream, like I'm watching myself in a film.

There I am. Across the street. Below a window. Half-hidden. My huge, flat feet padding across the road. I stalk behind a defunct streetcar, dark and empty.

There I am. Shunning the puddles of light. Loping along the curb. Moving past a homeless, muttering mule.

There I am. Going into that alleyway. A recess between two redbrick buildings that—

Pine Street.

I watch myself saunter into the alley, all the way down to a plain wooden door at the deadest of ends. Number 1020. There's no buzzer. The door groans open when I push it. I climb the stairwell. Every one of them sighs, moist and rotting under my feet. Seven flights up, step by step, to 7B.

I've arrived at Siobhan's apartment, where she lives with Gram. Seeing myself from the outside, I can believe what folks say. I'm a beast. I'm a wolf at the door. Wet nostrils flaring, muscles on my back straining through torn clothes. Broomlike hair blossoming from my cuffs, doing nothing to conceal long, leathery fingers tipped with claws (or what's left of them, at least). Hot slaver foams between clenched teeth, dripping over my rubbery lips. I look like an animal.

There's a twitch inside me. I remember now: Eden. Fiona. Karl and Ludwig. Richard. Faelynn. Skinner—and what he did to himself.

What am *I* about to do? To Siobhan and Gram, a girl and her grandmother. Like father, like son.

The twitch is drowned out. There's nothing inside me but irrational anger. I've no control. I have to battle this. I inhale sharp, ragged breaths. I'm convulsing. My paw—cosmically huge in this elven place—reaches for the door. I tear the knob out of the wood, leaving a wound I can see through.

The scent of incense filters out. A dull smash of my shoulder and the door crumbles like bread.

Siobhan's lying asleep, swaddled in bloodred blankets. I'm on the verge of lunging. This can't be my fate. It can't be. I'm not a murderer.

I hear the click of loose joints, the creak of loose wood. It's Gram, crooked as a winter willow, wrapped in a black housecoat and elven slippers. She looks confused.

"Henry?"

Behind her is a window. The fire escape. There's another way. I can fix this.

The primitive bloodlust takes hold, and I lunge at her—but the moment my father described has come—the one moment I'm in control again. If I recognize it, I can use it.

Gram screams, and my brain sends a desperate message to my legs. I push sideways, veering into the glass, crashing through, spinning over the black metal, falling into the dark.

Motes of light hover like dust. They gather in wriggling caterpillars of light, crawling into shapes. A hand, a wing . . .

Faelynn floats down, humming her lullaby. She's real enough to touch. Her face is like a sun, brighter and brighter until she swallows me up in brilliant blue light.

This must be where they went. A distant land where winged creatures, luminous and divine, take care of everything.

I can only hope it's real.

42
ONCE IN A LIFETIME

THE LIGHT HURTS, SO I KEEP MY EYES SHUT. I SNIFF INSTEAD, BUT THERE'S only an empty scent. Wherever I am, it reeks of sterility. I try pricking up my ears.

"Henry?"

"See his ears? They twitched."

I recognize that voice.

"I think he's awake."

I recognize that one, too. Gravel and honey. My senses are returning. I can smell things again. I smell nutmeg. Old coal and applesauce. Peppermint and stale sweat. Cherry blossoms.

"Henry?"

It stings, but I open my eyes. All I see are hints of the real world. Everything is sideways. Because I'm lying down. In a strange bed. My big feet (as always) are hanging over the end.

"How do you feel?"

"Henry?"

"Why won't he say something?"

"Can you speak?"

"I think so," I tell them, but my throat's coarse and full of phlegm. I cough it up and spit sideways, over a silver railing.

"Gross!"

"Woah there, big guy, if you're gonna start puking, give us fair warning, huh?"

I *must* be dead. That sounds like—

"Jack?"

"I'm right here." I feel a little pink hand patting my forearm. "Guess you sorta saved my life. When Skinner kicked it, the spell was broken. Thanks for that." Jack's face comes into cloudy focus. Sly, boyish, full of mischief. "Welcome back to the land of the living," he says.

"I'm not dead?"

He grins at me. "You think heaven looks like the wolf ward at City General?"

"Who told you I was going to heaven?"

"You're *alive*—and thanks to you and your girl, so am I."

"Fiona?"

"She's right here."

Other faces emerge from the glare. They orbit me like planets. Siobhan, Mrs. L, Detective White, Fiona. "Glad to have you back," she says.

"What happened?"

"You've been unconscious for days now," Mrs. L tells me. "We've all been waiting."

Fiona places her paw over mine. "You're kind of a hero."

"I am?"

"Well, we both are, actually."

"I certainly don't feel like one."

White leans on my bed. "When we scraped you outta that alley, we found a roll of film in your pocket."

I look at Fiona. "The one you gave me."

White tosses a newspaper onto my chest. "Check it out. All thanks to you two." On the front page there's a photograph of me, taken in this room while I was still out. Fiona's standing beside me, holding my paw, gazing at my face (she's a hell of a lot more photogenic than I am). The headline says: WOLFISH YOUTHS UNCOVER CONSPIRACY. White taps the page with her finger.

"Nimbus Thaumaturgical," she says. "The whole company is under investigation. As we speak, the police are digging up the deadwood forest out east."

"What about the—" I'm not even sure what to call them. "The *animals*. The experiments. There was a fox called Jerry."

White shakes her head. "We found them, but it doesn't seem like there's anything we can do about it. Nimbus threw all their science at turning them into those things. It's doubtful there's enough magic left—in the ground, in the trees, *anywhere*—to change them back."

I remember how noble they looked, pacing in their cages. Pure and regal. Blood memories come to life. But it's hardly any comfort.

I turn to Siobhan. "I'm sorry about what happened."

She smiles. "You gave Gram a scare, but she claims she *enjoyed* it. Says it was like being the heroine of her very own fairytale."

I have to laugh at that. Like I said when I first met her, it's hard not to like that old woman. "And what about Roy?" I ask Fiona. "Is he okay?"

"I told you," she answers. "Guys like Roy always pull through." She leans in, nearly nuzzling my face. "Actually," she whispers, "he gave me express instructions. As soon as you come around, he wants to see you."

"I'm not sure," says Mrs. L, "it's such a good idea for Henry to be up and moving around right away."

Siobhan shrugs. "Don't worry. Jack can steal us a wheelchair."

Roy's lounging on his hospital bed like an emperor, limbs spilling over the railing on either side. There's a shunt taped into his arm, but otherwise he looks like his old self. Spread across his lap are two expansive trays, each covered with plastic bowls full of peas and carrots and an unidentifiable mash. Fiona parks me at the foot of his bed.

"Hank-man," he growls. "You came back to us."

"Hi, Roy." I wring my paws together in my lap. If I weren't sitting on my tail, it'd be dipping very low right about now.

"Relax," he says. "All I wanted to say is this: no hard feelings." He rips into a crusty dinner roll, nodding as he chews. "I mean it," he assures me, spraying a blizzard of crumbs all the way to his feet. "Bygones, right? Let 'em be."

"You mean that?" This is not the Roy I remember. Something's changed. I sort of imagined he summoned me here so he could pummel me back into a coma. I would've taken it, too. I deserve some kind of payback after what I did to him. And there's nothing Roy relishes more than a plate of icy revenge. But then I figure it out. "You don't remember what happened, do you?"

"'Course I do. You nearly killed me. But no big deal." He waves away any offense with a glass of orange juice. It spills a yellow glop on his propped-up pillows. "Turns out it was exactly what I needed."

"Excuse me?"

He looks to his sister. "Bring him around, Fifi."

"Fifi?"

Her eyes shoot daggers at me. "It's what *my mother* calls me," she says. "Roy gets special dispensation cuz he's my brother. *You,* one the other hand"—she pokes the back of my neck—"are *not* a relation."

"Hey," says Roy, "I was talking here?" As soon as I'm within reach, he snatches my wrist, squeezing until the bones creak. I assume this has all been a trick. He's been lulling me closer, calculating his revenge the whole time. But then I see his face isn't slung with its usual scowl. His eyes are wide and innocent.

"I wasn't out the whole time," he says. "Now and again, I

came around." He fills himself with a long breath. "This one night, I woke up and everything was dark. The only light was coming from way down the hall. Emergency lights, I figured. But they were weird colors, blue and green and gold." If he was trying to draw me in, he's succeeded. I prick up my ears. "The light was moving," he tells me. "Moving all over, spreading like a fire. It was getting brighter, too, coming down the hall. And I admit it, I was scared. The light came right up and then around the corner, right in through the doorway." He pulls me even closer. "Do you know what it was?"

I don't have to guess. I saw the very same thing.

"I don't know," I lie. "What was it?"

"A fairy, Hank-man, a *real* fairy. She was here. *Right here*—floating right over my bed. She came here to see me. *Me*—a big dumb wolf. Can you believe it?"

Fiona looms over my shoulder. "Tell him, Henry. It was all a crazy dream, right? I mean, you and me saw first-hand what really—"

"*No-no-no.*" Roy wags his head with a little of his old rage. "I know all about what you saw and what you found— Skinner and the nixies and the dust-makers and all that. And sure, maybe that's all true, but I know what I saw was real. It was no dream. And you know what that means? That means they never got rid of *all* of them." He looks up, searching the air around the room. "Me," he says softly. "She came to visit *me*—Roy Sarlat. And she's still out there, I guess. Lookin' out for me."

"Who knows? Maybe you're right."

Fiona flicks the back of my head. "Don't encourage him."

Roy's still lost in his memory. His eyes go glassy, and his grip on my wrist loosens a little, though he's not ready to let me go. "You know what she said to me? She said, 'What do you want?' That's all. 'What do you want?' And I thought, 'This is it—this is my once-in-a-lifetime chance.' So I thought about it real hard for a real long time, and in the end it was easy. I want things to get better, Hank-man. And that's what I told her. She turned to me and said, 'Then you know what you have to do.' So I said to her, 'Yeah, I think I do know.' I gotta treat folks better, stop throwing my weight around so much." He yanks me closer. His lips are flecked with crumbs. "And you know what I told her then? You know what I said to her?"

"What?"

"I said, 'I gotta be more like Henry.' That's what I told her. I even said your name. She smiled at me and she waved her wand, and *all this dust* came out. I mean, the real deal, the true pure stuff. And the next thing I knew the lights were back on and I was wide awake." He throws an apple into his mouth and chomps it whole.

Fiona sighs. "Who woulda thought my big lug of a brother was blessed with such a vivid imagination?"

Roy lets go of my wrist, patting it with the gentleness of a child. "I guess that's why I wanted to see you. If it wasn't for you landing me in this place, I never would've met my fairy godmother."

43
THE MOST BEAUTIFUL SPECIES

IF YOU LOOK AT IT FROM THE TOP OF SEAWAY HILL, THE DEADWOOD FOREST IS vast. Thousands of trees strain up from the earth, yearning toward Eden. Seeing them now—uprooted, lying prone on flatbed trucks, cordoned off by the garish yellow of police tape—it seems so obvious. All those trees are the final remnants of the old magic.

This morning, the newspapers reported that the assets of Nimbus Thaumaturgical have been frozen. It's unlikely their new slate of fairydust will ever leave the warehouse. There's even speculation that the company will file for bankruptcy in the coming weeks. They say it's only a question of time. So it seems things are really going to change. There's one thing, however, that's still the same.

I turn away from the deadwoods and face the prison. Loping up to the gates, I'm watched by the guards, who glare at me with leery eyes.

Dad comes out in chains. The same two globs I remember lock him to the chair on the far side of the glass.

"Hi, Dad."

He smiles. His face fissures into a million cracks. "I heard about what you did."

"I didn't do much."

"A lot of guys in here carry around hefty scores they'd like to settle with Skinner. Nearly all of them wanted him dead—I know *I* did. But none of us could figure out how to get it done." He taps the glass with one claw. "You made me a hero in here. I'm the pop of the kid who killed Skinner."

"Actually—"

"Don't spoil it for me, son. That dwarf was a cancer, and now he's gone. That's cuz of you."

"Maybe."

"Things're gonna change now. You'll see."

I press my palm to the glass. "They aren't changing the way I thought they would."

Dad doesn't say anything, but he knows what I mean. "They halved my sentence, at least."

"You told me they'd let you go. If it turned out you were telling the truth."

He gives me a watery, apologetic smile. "They have to be cautious. Like it or not, I'm still a wolf. We come with a reputation, one that goes way back."

"A blood memory."

He laughs through his snout. "That's a poetic way of putting it."

"So how long?" I ask him. "How long before they stop being cautious?"

"They're going to give me a retrial, in light of all the new evidence they're digging up. There's a good chance I'll be out of here in a couple years' time."

"A couple years?"

"Even if I wasn't in control that night, it was still these claws and these teeth that killed those folks."

I nod, and for a moment we both sit in silence.

"I know how it was now," I tell him. "There was nothing you could do, was there?"

He shakes his head and there's a long silence between us.

"You think they're really gone?" I ask him.

"I suppose they are. Then again, the fairies were always mysterious creatures. Magical. Beautiful. Maybe too beautiful for a city like this one. Maybe the old-time magic is too good for folks like us."

"Maybe."

Again, we're quiet.

"I'm sorry I never wrote back to you."

Dad shrugs. "Doc was trying to protect you."

"It doesn't matter. Even if he had given them to me, I wouldn't've written back. I was ashamed of you. I was afraid I was like you, a killer. And I almost was. Even before—and after—they gave me their dust, I did some awful things."

"As long as you know they're awful, and you try to make amends. That's what's important."

"I'll try."

Dad nods. "Then you *are* like me, son. Maybe that's not such a bad thing." He laughs. "Besides, up here"—he taps his temple—"and in here"—he taps his chest. "That's what counts, and all of that you got from your mother. Lemme tell you, if she were here right now, she'd be so, so proud."

Fiona and I stand at the railing that overlooks the reservoir. I was luckier than my father. For the most part, I was released, granted an honest reprieve from St. Remus. For that I owe much to Cindy and Mrs. L, and even to Detective White. Thanks to their vouching for me, I was transferred to a cushy, minimum-security halfway house for juveniles. It's way up north, and get this: There are no guards, no walls, no fences, and most of the guys inside aren't even wolves. It's mostly hominids and hedgehogs, locked up for a couple weeks for shoplifting. They give me a *very* wide berth. There are a couple of mules I can almost relate to, but much of the time I keep to myself. The place has its advantages. From dawn to dusk I pretty much get free rein, which explains why I'm out here in the middle of the morning with Fiona, standing on the southern edge of the city, watching the river drift out to sea.

"They're not letting him out, are they?" Fiona asks.

"Not right away."

Her gaze lifts from the ships and up to Eden. Just below it, the sun is blinding. "They really hate us, don't they?"

"Edenites?" I ask, though I know that's who she means. "Not all of them."

She thinks for a moment. "Maybe it's always gonna be like this."

"Like what?"

"None of us getting along, not really."

I know what she's talking about. Until the last couple of weeks, I never knew how serious it could be, how deep the divisions could run. It's shocking when you see it first-hand, the way we have.

"No," I tell her. "You have to believe it's going to change."

"I don't know. I used to think all of us getting along was a foregone conclusion. It'd happen eventually. That's what a lot of folks believe." She leans forward, pushing her elbows into the railing. "But then I met you and you dragged me through all this and now I'm not so sure." She stares into the sky, shielding her eyes with a paw. "Once you've been up there you get a different perspective on things. Everything looks different."

"What are you saying? You regret you ever met me?"

She shifts closer until our bodies are pressed together, side by side. "Don't be silly." She hooks her arm into mine. "Let's say for now that the pros outweigh the cons."

"I'll take that as a compliment."

She huddles closer. "I just never knew how much they could hate us. It's like the City's split in two." She shakes her head. "Think about what they wanted to do to us. What would it have been like? I can't even imagine."

The wind blows off the water, carrying with it a strong whiff of diesel and brine. There are fewer boats in the harbor now—now that Nimbus is out of business—but the fairydust trade still thrives. Already new companies are rising up, swelling to fill the gaps Nimbus left behind. I suppose folks will always crave their magic, even if it's cheap, synthetic, and fleeting. Folks will never shake free of it, never stop hoping for it.

Who can blame them? Is it any different from hoping the old-time magic will one day return? Is it any different from wishing the fairies were still here, still watching over us, still around to make our dreams come true?

"I can't imagine it either," I say. "I'm just glad we stopped them."

There's a smaller boat down in the reservoir, just now leaving the docks. The hull's barely visible from up here, but the yellow sail stands out against the dark of the water. It's unusual to see a pleasure boat down there among the tankers. Dockside has always been a commercial harbor, a hive of import, export, and industry. The tiny sail bobs between two tankers, a minnow among whales. It's headed outbound, upriver, toward the sea.

I turn to Fiona. "Do you ever wonder what's out there?"

She looks at me quizzically. "The ocean?"

"I know the ocean. But what comes after that?"

"The rest of the world?"

"Do you ever wonder what it's like? I mean, do you want to see it?"

She scratches her thumb-claw into the railing, etching away flakes of rust. "I've never really thought about it."

"What if there are more of them out there? More fairies." The yellow sail catches a gust and surges away. "One day," I tell her, "I'd like to find out."

Fiona lays her head on the bulk of my shoulder. "You'd have to take me with you, y'know."

I grin at her. "I'll consider it."

She nuzzles her face into me and kisses my cheek. "You better."

The sun is behind Eden now, blackening its mass into silhouette. The towers and palaces resemble something new. It's hard not to see them as headstones, monuments and cenotaphs to an extinct species. The most beautiful species of all.

Behind us, the pavement quakes as a streetcar rattles past. It's crowded inside. Elves, cats, ravens, humans, goblins, mules, nixies, dwarves, foxes, wolves—they're all pressed in tight, all knitted together, all making their way to someplace they need to be. It reminds me of Roy's wish. I really hope it comes true. I hope things get better.

Fiona tugs my arm and we turn back toward the City.

"C'mon," she says. "Walk me home."

NOTES AND ACKNOWLEDGEMENTS

Ideas for novels may occur in odd places. I discovered the first inklings of *Dust City* in a dentist's office. Lying among the waiting room's glossy magazines was an improbable copy of a book called *The Hard Facts of the Grimms' Fairy Tales* by Maria Tatar. It was a well-thumbed copy, and I imagined some unfortunate student from the local university had accidentally left it behind.

Tatar's book speculates on why children—or *anyone* for that matter—would be attracted to the terrible violence found in the stories collected by the famous Grimm brothers. After some thumbing of my own, I began to wonder: What would the modern world look like if it had evolved directly out of the magical folktales of medieval Europe? *Dust City*, I suppose, is one possible answer.

Novels, however, are rarely written in dentists' waiting rooms. As such, I'd like to acknowledge a debt of gratitude to all the people who helped along the way: my editor, Jessica Rothenberg, whose insightful feedback did wonders for shaping the story; Jennifer Notman, my editor here in Toronto, at Penguin Canada; my agent, Jackie Kaiser, her colleague, Natasha Daneman, and the wonderful folks at Westwood Creative Artists; Ben Schrank and the enthusiastic team at Razorbill/Penguin in New York; Natalie Sousa, whose cover designs are always beautiful and astonishing; my friends and family, who tolerate how often I vanish into meandering realms of reverie; and Mitch Kowalski, the earthquake aficionado who runs the Toronto Writers' Centre, without which I would almost certainly never bang out a single word!

Finally, my thanks to Ralph Manheim, translator of *Grimms' Tales for Young and Old: The Complete Stories*, which sat on my bookshelf as a reference text (and a source of inspiration) while I was writing. The Grimm Brothers' epigraph at the beginning of *Dust City* is taken from the 1983 edition.